The
Forbidden
Zone

The Forbidden Zone

JON GLIDDON

THE CHOIR PRESS

First published in the United Kingdom in 2020 by
The Choir Press

ISBN 978-1-78963-160-9

Contents

Part 2   123

To my wife Elaine, for her unfailing support.

Acknowledgements

Many people have been extremely generous with their time and expertise in reading various drafts and providing me with comments on the plot, pace and characters. I would like to thank Carol Du Toit, Mike Ricks, Mike Whateley, Ron Hall and Dave Worrall who reviewed the early drafts for me. Their input helped tighten the narrative.

My good friend, and author of *Fortune's Turmoil*, Dav Baulch, provided me with detailed technical and grammatical feedback which was invaluable. Special thanks goes to Marthe Bijman of Seven Circumstances (sevencircumstances.com), who shared her literary expertise and provided an in-depth critique.

Thanks also to Andy Davey, who provided advice on sourcing information on the history of diamond mining in Southern Africa and to Nick Roberts of Bright Design (www.bright-design.co.uk) who designed the artwork for the book cover and drafted the location sketch.

Last but not least my thanks go to Miles Bailey and his staff at The Choir Press (www.selfpublishingbooks.co.uk) for their friendly advice and support that has enabled me to self-publish my second novel.

Preface

Ishould make it clear from the outset that this book is a work of fiction. Some of the people, companies, organisations, place names and landmarks may sound familiar and have a ring of history about them, but in the context of this novel they are entirely fictitious.

'In the Beginning' provides an overview of the geological formation of diamonds and how there came to be such rich deposits on the beaches of South West Africa. This country was formerly German South West Africa and today is the Republic of Namibia. The original discoveries of the diamond fields and the subsequent changes in ownership provide the political backdrop to the plot. This information is sourced from publicly available documents that I believe reflect the current consensus of geologists and historians.

The plot is set around the build-up of military rearmament as Europe slipped inexorably towards World War 2. Nazi Germany blatantly and illegally expanded her military capability and other countries were forced to follow suit. Warships, submarines, fighter planes, bombers, tanks and large calibre armaments were manufactured on a vast scale. This required huge quantities of raw materials, including diamonds. In fine grain and powder form it was used to cut, grind and polish the high-performance, high-strength steel components. There was no substitute for this, the hardest naturally occurring mineral.

After the Wall Street crash of 1929, many of the diamond mines in Southern Africa were closed or put on care and maintenance. When the build-up in military production started in the mid-1930s, it came at a time when stockpiles were low. The scramble to secure industrial diamonds became cut-throat and political.

Because Germany was in breach of the Treaty of Versailles, direct diamond sales to the Third Reich ceased in 1937. They were forced to buy from whatever sources they could find. But political lobbying from Britain, and the eventual realisation of the imminent menace that Germany presented, resulted in all countries terminating their sales. This put the Nazis on the back foot and evermore desperate to access additional supplies.

This story imagines what they must surely have considered doing, to secure a large quantity of diamonds in support of the military ambitions of the Third Reich.

Sketch Map of South West Africa

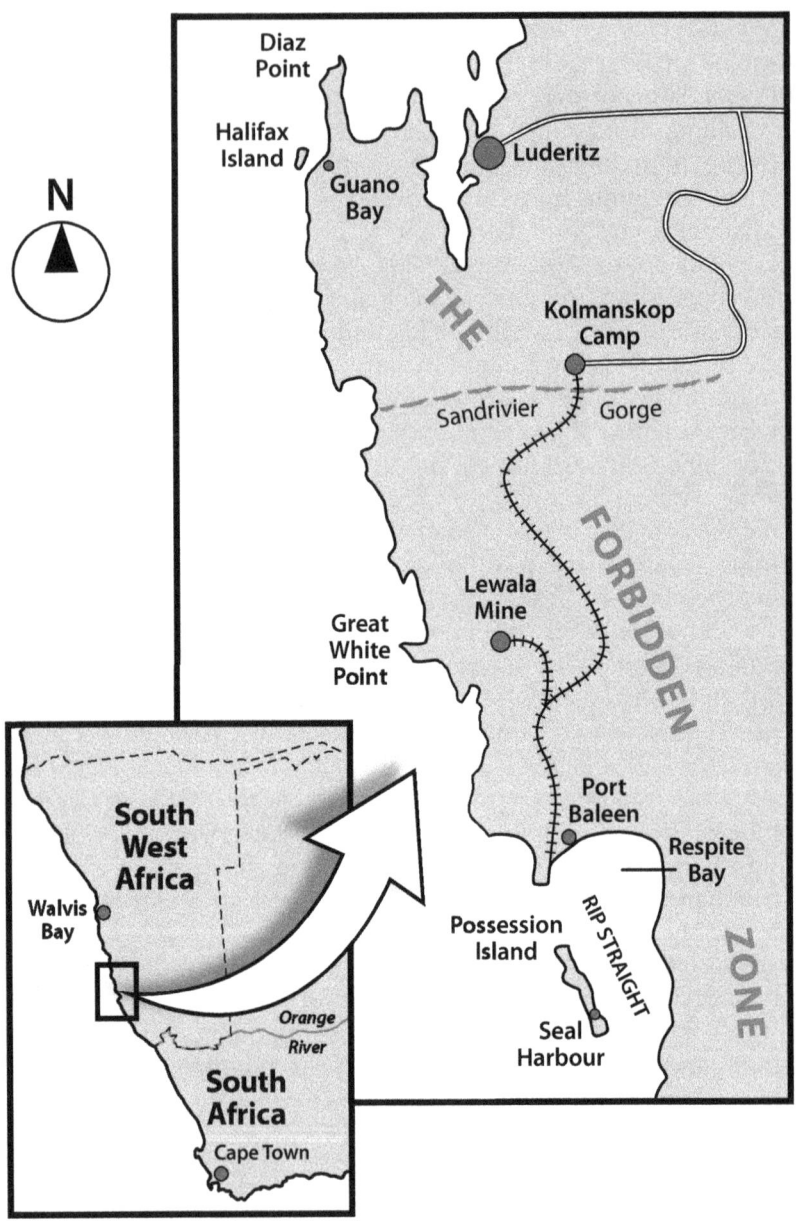

In the Beginning

The origins of this story go back a long, long way: one hundred million years, give or take. At that time, our planet was not the benign blue sphere it is today; it was undergoing tectonic change on a massive scale.

Deep beneath the region that today we call South Africa, molten rock was boiling and churning. Intense temperature and pressure caused natural carbon in the Earth's upper mantle to be compressed and re-crystallised into another form of carbon, diamond. From a depth of nearly one hundred miles, this gem-laden cocktail of liquid magma found weak spots in the Earth's crust and erupted explosively to the surface, forming dozens of volcanic pipes. This type of volcanic rock, subsequently named kimberlite after the South African town where it was first described, was the richest source of diamonds ever found.

Since their formation, the elements have eroded the land surface of that region by up to two thousand feet, in the process removing and transporting the tops of the kimberlite pipes. Slowly but surely each eroded rough diamond was conveyed downstream, being cleaned and polished as it went. The rivers that drained this region joined forces to form an ancient river, corresponding to the present-day Orange River. This flows a thousand miles west and empties into the South Atlantic Ocean.

The diamonds at the top of the kimberlite pipes started their journeys tens of millions of years earlier than those deeper down. They travelled the entire length of the river and were washed into the South Atlantic, then carried north by the mighty Benguela Current, that flows from the Antarctic up the west coast of Southern Africa.

These diamonds were washed onto the beaches of the Namib Desert, for up to two hundred miles from the mouth of the Orange River. The pounding waves smashed any flawed stones, depositing only the pure, hard, clean gems into the richest concentration of marine diamonds ever found. The persistent onshore wind transported large quantities of the smaller diamonds inland.

This one-hundred-million-year-old secret was discovered in 1867 on the Farm De Kalk near the small settlement of Hopetown in the Cape Colony. A farmer's son, fifteen-year-old Erasmus Jacobs, found a transparent shiny stone on the south bank of the Orange River. This found its way to a Dr Atherstone, the colony's foremost mineralogist, and he confirmed that it was a twenty-one-carat diamond, subsequently named the 'Eureka'. However, further exploration of this remote area was carried out with little success.

Then in March 1869, a Griqua shepherd boy found a superb eighty-three-carat alluvial diamond close to the confluence of the Orange River and its main tributary, the Vaal River. It was subsequently named the 'Star of South Africa'. News spread rapidly and prospectors flocked to the area and worked their way downstream to follow the alluvial diamonds and upstream to discover their source.

In 1871, the first diamonds were discovered in kimberlite on the Farm Jagersfontein and then, shortly after, sixty miles north on the Farms Dortsfontein and Vooruitzicht. On the latter, a rich pipe was discovered close to the farmhouse at Baxter's Gulley, later to become the De Beers Mine. A mile and a half west on the same farm, diamonds were found in abundance on a hill named Colesberg Kopje. This hill was the outcrop of one of the richest kimberlite pipes ever found and ultimately became the Kimberley Central Mine.

Through the 1870s, the seemingly endless supply of diamonds flooded the world market, and their value dropped. Thousands of claims were abandoned and illicit mining flourished. Amalgamation was the only way to bring order to the chaos. Many wealthy claim owners tried to achieve this, and eventually two men, Cecil John Rhodes and Barney Barnato, became the owners of almost all the claims in the area. They were bitter rivals, both striving for commercial pre-eminence.

Rhodes, who owned the De Beers Mine, devised a plan to get control of the Kimberley Central Mine, largely owned by Barnato. With backing from the financier N. M. Rothschild, Rhodes allowed production levels at the De Beers Mine to rise. In doing so, diamond prices dropped further, and his competition capitulated. In 1888, Rhodes wrote a cheque to Barnato for £5,338,650, at that time the largest cheque ever written. Rhodes created a single company that he named De Beers Consolidated Diamond Mines, after the brothers Diederick and Johannes de Beer, who had owned the Farm Vooruitzicht. He then proceeded to buy up the smaller mines in the region so that by 1890 he controlled more than ninety per cent of the world's diamond production.

But De Beers' pre-eminent position soon came under threat. In 1898, diamonds were discovered four hundred miles to the north east of Kimberley, near Pretoria in the Transvaal. The kimberlite pipe on the

Farm Elandsfontein proved to be particularly rich and in 1903 the Premier Mine started production. Its owner, Sir Thomas Cullinan, refused to join the De Beers cartel and instead sold the diamonds to an independent dealer named Ernest Oppenheimer. In 1905, the mine produced the famous 3,106-carat Cullinan Diamond, the largest and most valuable high-quality rough diamond ever discovered.

Then, in 1908, an even bigger threat to De Beers' pre-eminent position was discovered. Seven hundred miles west of Kimberley, the first marine diamonds, concentrated on the South Atlantic beaches north of the Orange River, were discovered in German South West Africa.

History has it that in April 1908, Zacharias Lewala found a shiny stone near Kolmanskop, inland from the small port of Luderitz. He showed it to his supervisor, August Stauch, who recognised it as a diamond. The area proved to be very rich and another diamond rush ensued.

When the Germans realised they could challenge the De Beers monopoly, the colonial authorities took control of the mining rights. They declared a large area along the coast the *Sperrgebiet*, the 'Forbidden Zone', a controlled area accessible only to government approved exploration and mining. The Imperial Government in Germany mandated that all diamonds had to be sold to the Diamant Regie in Berlin, in direct competition to De Beers.

That all changed when World War 1 was declared in August 1914. South Africa joined sides with the British against Germany. The following month General Jan Smuts' forces made a surprise seaborne attack on Luderitz and took control of the Forbidden Zone and, shortly afterwards, the entire country. In July 1915, a treaty was signed which handed over administration of the German colony to South Africa.

As it became evident that Germany would lose the war, the mine owners and investors were in a state of near panic, expecting their diamond claims to be expropriated. Ernest Oppenheimer, the dealer who had purchased diamonds from the Premier Mine, understood the huge opportunity that this presented. He came from a large German-Jewish family of diamond traders and had started his diamond career in London, becoming a British citizen. Before the war, he had personally assessed the German claims in the Forbidden Zone on behalf of the London Diamond Syndicate. He knew its value and the potential to compete with De Beers.

With the backing of the New York financier J. P. Morgan, he set up the Anglo-American Corporation, with a remit to acquire gold and diamond concessions across Southern Africa. Working through his network of cousins in Germany, he offered the main German diamond claim owners shares in the new company in exchange for their holdings in the Forbidden Zone. In 1920 he formed Consolidated Diamond Mines of South West Africa, and in 1923 negotiated the sole rights to mine in the Forbidden Zone.

With the potential to be a major competitor to De Beers, the canny Oppenheimer knew that to try and compete with them would be disastrous for both parties. Instead he sold them the diamond company, not for money but in exchange for De Beers company stock. With the two companies formally merged, the consolidation of the richest diamond-producing region in the world was complete.

Prologue
25 March 1939, Luderitz Bay, South West Africa

That Saturday had been a day of celebration, of sharing success with the people of Luderitz. The new Zach's Extension at the Lewala Diamond Mine had been commissioned and Harvey Tremayne, the Mine Manager, had invited the town folk and local dignitaries to the beach for a *braai*. It was one of those beautiful evenings when the wind blows off the desert, and it is hot and dry through the night. Draft Hansa beer flowed, an ox roasted slowly over a huge fire, and baskets of rock lobster were tipped onto red-hot grills fired by scavenged driftwood. Harvey watched Eleanor, as perfect a hostess as she was a wife, talking to the guests with charm and humour.

When the burgermeister had fallen down for the second time, it was clearly the moment to end the festivities. With the guests departed, or passed out on the sand, Harvey and Eleanor had walked back along the beach, arm in arm, to the Diaz Hotel. The Milky Way sparkled above them, millions and millions of stars and galaxies, seemingly so close you could reach up and touch them.

When they got to their room, they kissed and undressed, and he enjoyed her naked beauty and her smell, a heady mix of perfume and her body, warm and glistening from the hot evening. They collapsed on the bed, happy, slightly drunk and very much in love.

In the early hours, he was woken from a deep sleep by a piercing scream. 'He's got a gun!' Eleanor shrieked.

The last thing he remembered was an excruciating pain in his back, and then, like a shutter coming down, blackness.

August 1939

PART 1

Chapter 1

Café Paris, Place Petit Socco, Tangier, Morocco

In the Medina, the ancient trading centre of old Tangier, there is a square called Place Petit Socco. The area is dirty and rough around the edges, like the virus-ridden dogs and mangy cats that live in the labyrinth of alleyways surrounding it. But it has a strong heartbeat, bustling with an assortment of life. Cafes, bakeries, spice emporiums, tobacco and fabric shops surround the square.

On this day, the weekly market added colour and vibrancy. It looked like a paint palette that Van Gogh would have used. The reds, oranges and yellows of spices and fruit, green herbs and vegetables and the garish blues and purples of Indian fabric. Arms waved, headless chickens flapped, goats bleated and toothless hags sang of their wares in a cacophony of bartering. Snake charmers entertained, and resourceful pickpockets exploited the spellbound Europeans. The smell of cooking food permeated the square, ribbons of aromatic smoke swirled, trapped within its confines. To a visitor, this scene, which had been repeated for a thousand years, was inexplicably chaotic.

Café Paris was on the shady, north-facing side of the square. Unassuming and run-down like all the other buildings, no one could have imagined what lay behind the shabby facade. From his desk on the first floor, above the café, the owner looked out on those coming and going. He was secretive and mistrusting, a pair of binoculars always lying in wait on his desk.

Smoke from the charcoal grills in the square drifted up through the open window, making his eyes sting. Leaning forward, he pulled it closed.

Under sagging lids, his brown eyes watered. He pulled a stained rag from his pocket and wiped away the irritant. After years in the hot, dry, dusty Namib Desert of German South West Africa, his eyes were sensitive to such incursions.

Salamon Zaber was fifty years old and just a couple of inches over five feet tall. He had not weathered well on his journey through life. Spending each day at his desk and with a love of sugary Arab pastries and a penchant for sweet dates imported from Lebanon, he had cultivated a double chin and a triple belly. He was nearly as wide as he was tall.

Zaber pulled his chair forward and adjusted his gut to rest on top of the desk. He looked at the small pile of rough diamonds, top-quality crystals that originated from his friends in the *Adlerflagge Syndicate*, the Eagle Flag Syndicate, in South West Africa. But it was a fraction of the quantity he would have received eighteen months previously. Times had changed, and it worried him.

Diamonds were what he lived for and loved the most. Wearing thick magnifying spectacles and holding a pair of stainless steel tweezers in his fat, stubby fingers, he picked through the rough diamonds, talking to each one as if a new friend. Butterflies fluttered in his stomach at the pleasure.

Using the indirect, soft light coming through the north-facing window, he studied each diamond from every angle, looking for the 'four Cs': the combination of cut, clarity, colour and carat weight. He peered into the heart of the crystal to assess the size, cut and potential value of each diamond by understanding the flaws and irregularities. He placed each stone onto one of three piles, each destined for a different diamantaire. These Jewish cutters and polishers specialised in specific sizes and shapes of the final cut gem. His skill minimised wastage and realised the highest price to maximise his profit and that of his friends in the Adlerflagge Syndicate.

Zaber had learned his trade from a tender age. Born into a Jewish diamond-trading family in Frankfurt, Zaber & Company started trading in 1810 purchasing diamonds from India. From the 1880s, they sourced high-quality stones from South Africa and in 1910, from German South West Africa.

In 1912, the short, pudgy, twenty-three-year-old Salamon was dispatched to the German colony, to set up a purchasing office in Luderitz, the capital of the diamond mining region. The diamonds were amongst the finest in the world and there was a plentiful supply.

With the largest German-owned mining companies selling their diamonds to the Diamant Regie in Berlin, it was with the smaller operators that he did business. Many were of questionable legitimacy and all were mistrusting of their Imperial Government. Each night Zaber received a steady flow of high-quality stones at his lodging on Göring Strasse down near the harbour. If you were a diamond merchant in 1912, this was the place to be. He paid cash with no questions asked.

And life had been good. German beer, fresh seafood and local African girls provided him with the pleasures that he could not

3

otherwise enjoy. He particularly liked the Herero girls from the north of the country, with their ebony sheen, large pointed breasts and undulating hips.

But with the declaration of war in Europe in August 1914, Zaber's world came crashing down. The Union of South Africa sided with Britain and the following month, General Smuts' forces made a surprise seaborne attack on Luderitz, and Zaber found himself a prisoner. Being a German national, he was classified as an enemy alien and spent the first two years in a prison camp and after that under house arrest in Luderitz.

Initially, it felt like a death sentence, and he'd cursed himself for not leaving when he'd had the opportunity. But over time he became close friends with the colonial German diamond prospectors and miners who were incarcerated with him. He learned from them how to find the richest diamond deposits, how to mine them and, most importantly, how to smuggle them. In return, he showed them how to grade and value diamonds. While it was four years of misery and deprivation, it laid the foundation for his future enterprise.

In the post-World War 1 uncertainty surrounding the country's diamond claims, the now much leaner Zaber put his hard-earned knowledge and contacts to good use. He formed the Adlerflagge Syndicate with his embittered friends. For their part, they illegally mined high-grade pockets of diamonds in the Forbidden Zone. In return, Zaber sorted and sold them on their behalf.

But he was being watched by the South African authorities. It didn't take a genius to work out what he was up to. They knew of his diamond-trading background and his apparent lack of a real day job.

He needed to relocate to a place he could blend in. Somewhere that had no monetary controls, that was close to the Jewish cutters and polishers he used in Palestine and Lebanon. Somewhere that had a port frequented by shipping from the west coast of Africa. In 1920 he moved to the Tangier International Zone in Morocco.

Purchasing Café Paris as a cover, Zaber developed a network of shipping routes, north through Portuguese Angola and from there to Tangier. It was a risky business, and almost impossible to find a ship's captain that could be trusted. They thrived on black-market deals and any allegiance came at a high price.

He sorted and sold the high-quality diamonds, and in return supplied his colonial comrades with money after taking his commission. To cover the overheads, his cut was fifty per cent. Under the name of Indigo Trading Company, he channelled his substantial profits into his bank account in Frankfurt.

The butterflies in his stomach fluttered with delight as he peered into a near-flawless pure blue-white crystal of twenty-one carats, the most valuable stone he'd seen in over a year. He knew this hadn't been illegally mined. It had been stolen from the sorting plant at the Lewala Mine. This was the work of his old friend Scorpion, the leader of the Adlerflagge in Luderitz. He smiled with satisfaction.

The upright phone on his desk rang shrill, startling him. He put down the stone and lifted the earpiece.

'Yes.' He listened intently, his forehead creased. 'De Beers? What's his name? That's nonsense, he's dead.'

His face drained of colour and his voice faltered.

'When did he check in? What's his room number?'

In slow motion, he laid the earpiece back in its cradle, his stomach now visited by something sinister, something with claws and barbs. He felt as though he'd just been diagnosed with a terminal illness.

'It can't be,' he said, shaking his head. 'That's impossible!'

He wiped beads of sweat from the furrows on his forehead with his sleeve and took deep breaths to ease his thumping heart. Fat fingers picked a sweet date from a large glass jar on the desk.

He chewed thoughtfully, licking his fingers one by one, slowly, purposefully, noisily. His man in the Straits Hotel had to be mistaken. He couldn't have come back from the dead. One thing was for sure: before he shared this information, he needed proof of the man's identity.

He picked up the earpiece from the upright phone, dialled and waited.

'Fouad. I want you at the café immediately. I have a job for you and Ahmed.'

Chapter 2

The Forbidden Zone, South West Africa

The Namib Desert is hot, windy and dry. It stretches thirteen hundred miles along the South Atlantic Ocean but is narrow, mostly less than sixty miles wide. Hot does not do it justice; it is blisteringly hot. It straddles the Tropic of Capricorn and the sun is always overhead, brutalising the land like a blowtorch blisters ancient paint. The land is scorched to a thousand shades of ochre.

To add insult to misery, in the afternoon the south-west wind blows, steady and unrelenting. The sand from the seashore is whipped into dunes that march across the land like an invading army, burying everything in their path. Roads, railway lines and buildings are consumed with impunity by this sand-laden tempest. Where the wind has unlimited ammunition, it throws up dunes to nearly a thousand feet in height.

People and animals mostly avoid the Namib. The insects and reptiles that have chosen to remain are tenacious and cunning. Many are spiky or poisonous or both. They have been forced to adapt, spending the day deep under the sand or in rocky crevasses, only venturing out at night.

It is hard to imagine how anything survives because there is no permanent water. Those who know this land jest that there is ten inches of rain a year, and then laugh when they tell you that is the spacing between the raindrops.

It is a different story further inland. Here, torrential thunderstorms that develop once or twice in a lifetime form flash floods that cut through the drifts, the dry riverbeds of the Namib. It sends torrents of orange water to empty, wastefully, into the ocean. A few isolated trees live along the bank of these drifts, their deep roots tapping into the remains of the last, decades-old, storm.

The only hint of water in the desert, and it is no more than that, comes in the form of fog that regularly bedevils the coastal strip.

The mighty Benguela Current that runs along the desert coast has its origins deep in the Southern Ocean. It is frigid and does not willingly give up its moisture. But as it flows north into the heat of the tropics, moisture condenses over the cold sea to form the fog. For half the year, it can be dense and persistent, and over the centuries has been the cause of countless shipwrecks. In recognition of the fate of those vessels and unfortunate souls who fell prey to its grip, the shoreline in the northern part of the Namib Desert is named the Skeleton Coast. Those who celebrated making it safely to shore found no freshwater and had nowhere to go. The fog spends its day out at sea, wary of being blistered by the blowtorch. But when evening comes, and if the conditions are right, it takes courage and runs ashore and over the desert, sometimes for up to several miles. Those few insects and reptiles that have adapted to live along the fog belt survive on this miserly offering. The plants, too, have learned to absorb this moisture through their leaves.

But when the sun rises again, the fog slinks away to find refuge over the cold ocean. As it retreats, the blowtorch singes any indolent wisps and tendrils, hurrying them from its territory.

In the Namib Desert, the sun is lord and master and judge and jury.

On this August day, the intense midday sun was blistering the land, its light reflecting off the sand and rock and spiking the meagre shade of a gnarled camelthorn tree. Sitting at the base, a man waited. With his deep tan, rust-coloured and dust-covered clothes, he was visible only when he moved. A large, sweat-stained slouch hat gave some respite for his eyes. He licked his cinder-dry, cracked lips, shook his watch and put it to his ear. In this heat, even time seemed to stand still. A slight gust of air hinted at the arrival of the afternoon southwester.

He dug around in his rucksack and pulled out a stick of biltong and, with his sheath knife, cut a slice of the dried springbok meat. As he chewed, the salt and spice tingled in his mouth and he sucked greedily on the saliva.

Two sharp, beady eyes watched his every move.

'You want some, Falkie, hey? Just a small piece then, we don't want to spoil your appetite do we?' he said in a whisper.

The bird was tethered to a fallen branch. It had a slate-grey back and spotted and barred pale creamy breast. Its jet-black eyes were so piercing, it seemed they could look inside your head and mess with your mind.

They were in the *Sperrgebiet*, the Forbidden Zone, in the centre of the Namib Desert. Here the land is more rugged than further north. The shoreline is a mixture of cliffs and beaches, and in the interior, wind-fluted rocky hills compete with the sand dunes to see which is mightiest. Despite the brutal environment and extreme remoteness, the land was rich, holding treasures of untold wealth. Diamonds lay just beneath the surface of the beaches and in the flat, sandy valleys inland. Crystals sat like plump cherries in a cake, waiting to be plucked out. For those who were tough enough, those who were driven, it was irresistible.

Christoff Jager was one such man, a patriot, a 'South Wester', a resistance fighter, a smuggler, a man at one with his land, a man with a mission. He was forty-four years old and a native of Walvis Bay, his parents having emigrated from Germany. He'd had a hard and impoverished childhood in the early pioneering days of the colony. He left school at twelve and, being a tall muscular boy, went to work as a deckhand on cargo boats plying between Walvis Bay, Swakopmund and Cape Town. They often stopped at the small port of Luderitz, and that is where he fell for the allure of diamonds. Initially he worked for *Boegenfels Diamant Bergbau*, where he learned about the diamond deposits from the old-timers. Putting his skills to use, he started doing his own illegal exploration at the many isolated beaches along the Forbidden Zone. He and his friends were successful at finding rich pockets of diamonds and sold them to Salamon Zaber.

When Germany had lost control of the colony in 1915, he and his comrades fostered a burning resentment at having their homeland stolen. But now, more than twenty years on, there was a flicker of hope. With the resurgence of expansionist propaganda from the Third Reich, they looked to Adolph Hitler as their saviour. With his help, they would take back what was rightfully theirs. This had strengthened the resolve and determination of those in the Adlerflagge Syndicate.

But De Beers, the legal owner of the claims, was determined not to share these spoils. A special unit, the Diamond Security Police, diligently guarded the area. To be caught guaranteed a long and uncomfortable jail sentence, assuming, that is, the smuggler even made it to court. It was called the Forbidden Zone for good reason.

As security was progressively tightened through the 1930s, Jager and his friends were forced to adapt. It had been easy to find colonial sympathisers who worked on the mine, keen to share in the lucrative trade. But it was more than the money that motivated them. It was a matter of national pride and honour. They had created a network of trusted comrades who worked in key positions, including the Diamond Security Police. They now stole directly from the mine, from right under the noses of the fat, rich British Imperialists.

Jager threw a slice of biltong to the peregrine falcon, who caught it with ease in his blue hooked beak. Grabbing it with his yellow talons, he ripped and devoured it in seconds.

'Waaik, waaik', he screeched, bobbing his head from side to side.

'Shoosh, Falkie, you'll get your fill just now,' Jager said, stroking his bird's back to calm him.

He glanced at his watch.

'OK, come on Falkie, its nearly time.'

Putting on a long, thick leather glove he untied the strap holding the bird to the branch and Falkie flapped onto his arm. The anticipation of the hunt energised them both.

Jager moved from the narrow shade of the tree and cautiously peered over the top of the bank. The blistering sun made his flesh tingle and the blowtorched sand burned his knees and elbows. At one minute to the hour he scoured the desert for movement with his binoculars. Everything shimmered, making it difficult to focus, the sand and rocks seemingly ablaze with colourless flames. The falcon flapped impatiently.

'Shoosh, Falkie, not yet. Just wait, my boy,' Jager said, stroking his back. He searched the sky and caught movement.

'OK Falkie, go boy,' he said, and threw his arm in the air and launched the bird. With powerful wings, he gained height rapidly, eyes locked on to his distant quarry. With precision timing, Falkie folded his wings and plummeted at high speed, out of the sun, aimed at his doomed victim.

The carrier pigeon was oblivious of the attack until it was hit by eight scalpel-sharp talons travelling at fifty miles an hour. The falcon swooped lower in a wide arc and made a practised landing on Jager's raised arm. Falkie dispatched the bird, crushing its neck with his beak.

Jager slid back down the bank into the shade.

'Good boy, Falkie. Well done. You can feed just now.'

On the pigeon's back was a small cloth bag secured by two thin leather straps. Jager slipped the knife from his belt and cut the bag from the pigeon. He let Falkie jump back to the branch and tethered him.

The falcon started pulling feathers from the bird and ripped and devoured the flesh. Fine grey under-plumage drifted like snowflakes in the heat thermals and floated off in the breeze.

Jager opened the bag and poured the contents onto his palm. He whistled through his teeth. Fifteen top-quality rough diamonds glittered in a kaleidoscope of light beams.

'Wow Falkie, look at these. There must be nearly a hundred carats and the best of the best.'

Falkie took no notice. He was eating.

His comrade Karl had done well. It was illegal to keep homing pigeons in Luderitz, and there was a jail sentence for merely being in possession of one. They had to be brought in from Windhoek, the capital of South West Africa, where a resistance group specialised in breeding them. The birds were then hidden at a property on the outskirts of Luderitz, where their homing instincts were honed. And then they had to be smuggled on to the Lewala Mine, which was always fraught with danger. People and possessions were checked each time they entered and left the property. But with the resentment of the British, and with money crossing palms, some of the Security Police became short-sighted and forgetful. There was always a way.

'OK Falkie, we're finished here.'

Returning the stones to the bag he slipped it into his shirt pocket and buttoned down the flap.

He picked up his rucksack and crossbow, tied a small leather hood over the falcon's head, and let him jump onto his gloved arm.

'Come on, boy. Time to head home.'

'Waaik, waaik,' Falkie squawked.

Jager stood and listened and, once satisfied it was clear, headed down the drift. He kept to the hard, rocky areas, the heat seeping through the soles of his buckskin boots.

Minutes later he stopped dead. It was as if he'd been punched in the face. His sixth sense had kicked in. Something was not right. He looked either side for suitable cover, checked the wind direction and went to the north bank, jumping from rock to rock to avoid leaving tracks. He hid behind some large boulders under a half-dead quiver tree and dropped down on one knee. What was it that had alerted him? A noise? A smell? The Diamond Security Police were always on the lookout for suspicious activity, including unusual bird movement. Had they spotted Falkie? He tethered the bird to a fallen branch, pulled his crossbow from his back, and armed it with a steel bolt.

Ten minutes later, there was still no sound, no movement. Falkie was restless and Jager stroked his back to give reassurance. He was in two minds whether he should move off, but he knew to trust his instinct. He waited.

Then movement. Someone was approaching, one cautious step at a time. And a second! Rifles raised, heads down searching the ground. Jager's heart thumped. The khaki uniforms meant only one thing. He pulled his knife from its sheath, put it between his teeth and aimed the crossbow.

Falkie sensed the atmosphere and nodded from side to side. Jager touched him softly on the back.

10

The two stopped under the shade of the same quiver tree he was hiding behind. Too close for comfort. So close he could smell their sweat. He was on the downwind side of the drift so they would not smell him, nor catch the slightest noise from Falkie.

He aimed at the farthest policeman, thirty feet away, and put pressure on the trigger, but eased back after they rested their rifles against a rock.

'Come on, man. There's nothing here. If it was a hawk, it's long gone,' said the one with corporal's stripes.

'I definitely saw it. They must be here somewhere.'

'I need a smoke,' said the corporal.

Jager heard a match strike and the sulphurous billow wafted past him. He put one hand on Falkie – please be quiet, not a sound, not now. He could have killed the two policemen; it would have been quick – but they always patrolled in groups of four. The other two would be somewhere close by. He couldn't take the risk.

He listened to their idle chat and started to relax. They had lost interest in the search, but he still kept the crossbow aimed. After stubbing their cigarette butts in the sand, they picked up their rifles and walked on down the drift.

Jager waited for several minutes, planning his route back. He couldn't risk following them down the same drift and had no idea of the whereabouts of the other two policemen. He slung the crossbow on his back and picked up Falkie and walked north, parallel with the coast before turning west when he got to the next drift.

An hour later, the thundering of the ocean breakers and the cool salt-laden wind came as a welcome relief from the scorching desert heat.

'OK, Falkie, we're nearly there, my boy. We launch the boat and with this wind we'll be home in a couple of hours.'

Crawling up the last sand dune he lay down a few feet from the top and peered over. To his right, white-crested breakers crashed onto the seemingly endless silver sand beach, salt spray whipping off the heads of the waves like confetti. To his left, Great White Point, a rocky headland that jutted into the ocean and gave rise to the small protected bay. But straight ahead …!

'Shit,' he said. Falkie flapped his wings at the tone.

Less than fifty yards away, by a small rocky outcrop, two policemen were inspecting his eighteen-foot sailing boat. They were not the ones he'd encountered earlier. The taller of the two wore sergeant's stripes.

'Oh fuck, Falkie, we got a big fucking problem here, boy!' Jager said, glancing back into the desert, licking his cinder-dry, cracked lips.

Chapter 3

Straits Hotel, Rue de La Liberte, Tangier, Morocco

Harvey Tremayne lay on the large bed, lulled by the motion of the ceiling fan. It beat a hypnotic rhythm which made sleep difficult, yet without it the air would be hot and stale and sleep would be impossible. Flies buzzed behind the curtains, stirred by the first light on the eastern horizon.

A dry mouth and cigar breath were reminders of last night's session in Dean's Bar. After too many gins and too little food, he'd staggered back to the hotel through the narrow, winding alleys, trying to clear his head. Twice he thought he was being followed. When he'd backtracked, the shadows flickered and disappeared, like cheeky sprites playing hide-and-seek. It reminded him of keeping watch at night in the trenches, staring into no man's land, imagining that every object was the enemy moving forward. Sometimes it was.

When he'd walked into the foyer of the Straits Hotel shortly before midnight, the revolver still in hand, and just a little unsteady on his feet, there had been quite a commotion. The duty manager quickly and discreetly defused the situation and escorted Tremayne to his room.

At first, he had slept heavily, but in the early hours, screams echoed in his head. He sat bolt upright, reaching for his Webley revolver on the bedside table. He listened. Flicking his cigarette lighter, he walked across the room and cautiously unlocked the door and peered out. In the distance he caught movement at the top of the stairs. Or was it his imagination? He blinked hard, and when he looked again there was nothing.

He locked the door and switched on the light, making startled cockroaches scurry for cover like mice in a cat's dream. He walked cautiously in his bare feet. He hated that crunch. Falling back on the bed, with one arm behind his head, he stared at the picture on the bedside table. It was of a young woman laughing into the camera, her long blonde hair framed by Table Mountain in Cape Town. The picture brought Tremayne an ache in his belly. Sleep did not return, just fleeting naps.

Tremayne was forty years old, six feet tall with a slight but athletic build. His square-jawed craggy face was tanned, his short brown hair parted on the left, greying at the temples. His blue eyes were weary and troubled.

He came from a family of Cornish mine owners, once wealthy from the abundant tin and copper, but now farmers and landlords. At boarding school, he was academic and loved sports where he could rely on his own determination and stamina. He excelled at swimming and boxing and was the school cross-country champion two years in a row. That youthful idyll was cut short on his eighteenth birthday by military service. He was commissioned into the 6th Battalion, Dorsetshire Regiment for the last year of World War 1 and saw action in Northern France. Mentioned in dispatches during the attack on Y Ravine at Beaumont Hamel in June 1918, the Officer Commanding, Lieutenant-Colonel Shaw, had called it 'a victory by bomb, bayonet and bravery'.

After the war, he'd spent months on the family farm recovering his strength and exorcising the demons he'd brought back. In 1920 he'd followed in his father's footsteps and studied mining engineering at Camborne School of Mines. It was the most prestigious mining school in the world. Graduating in 1923, he joined De Beers Consolidated Diamond Mines in South Africa, working at the Kimberley Central Mine. Promotion came quickly and deservedly, and by 1933 he was Underground Manager.

One of the intractable problems faced by the company, across all its mines, was diamond theft. With a crystal the size of an acorn being potentially worth hundreds of pounds, it was a lucrative trade. Tremayne had masterminded a significant reduction in diamond theft, and this came to the attention of the company chairman, Sir Ernest Oppenheimer. At the age of thirty-seven he was transferred and promoted to Mine Manager of De Beers South West Africa, overseeing the development of the richest marine diamond fields in the world. Before his arrival, illicit diamond mining and smuggling had been rife. Within two years his success in reducing theft had Sir Ernest's gratitude but made him many enemies.

At that moment, his mind drifted back to those enemies and the revenge they had enacted on him. His life changed for ever. He tossed and turned, wondering if this bloody nightmare was ever going away. Every night it was the same. Every single bloody night since he'd woken up in that hospital in Cape Town. The worst moment of all was seeing Eleanor's father at his bedside. He had read it in the man's eyes. He didn't need to be told his wife was dead.

He reached for his cigarettes. Through tear-blurred vision, he watched the curls of cigarette smoke rise to the high ceiling only to be pulled into the fan and wiped out. Just like life, he mused.

As the sun neared the horizon, the buzzing in the window grew louder and ever more annoying. He swung his legs off the bed, rubbed his eyes and stretched. Although healed, the wound gave him a stabbing reminder. He pulled back the green velvet curtains and opened the window, the flies taking their freedom. A light breeze greeted him, followed by the noise of the city, then the smell. The day started early in Tangier, as it did right across North Africa, the call for sunrise prayers at the Grand Mosque echoing melodiously across the Medina. He closed his eyes and took in a deep breath.

Pouring brown-tinged water into a bowl, he shaved, watched by a long-legged spider peering over the top of the mirror. As he shaved, he examined the furrows on his forehead, the lines under the eyes and flecks of grey in the stubble. A year ago they hadn't been there.

Dressed in white flannel trousers, short-sleeved white shirt and brown leather brogues he strapped on the body holster and slipped on his cotton jacket. As he locked the door, he wedged a piece of paper low down against the frame and walked off along the bright marble-tiled corridor to the wide, elegant staircase. He didn't trust the lift, even if it was the best hotel in Tangier.

'Bonjour, Monsieur, have you taken breakfast with us before?' the waiter asked, with a sweeping bow.

Tremayne shook his head. He couldn't help but smile. The man had the quizzical look of a startled owl chick, with his crooked nose and oversized brown staring eyes. His red fez was set at a jaunty angle. Within a minute, he was back with a copy of the *Tangier Gazette*, coffee, fresh bread, goat cheese and honey.

Tremayne was engrossed in an article on the aftermath of the Spanish Civil War and the Franco regime's crackdown on the defeated Republicans. The journalist reported that the number of Spanish refugees fleeing to Morocco threatened unrest in the country. The news from Europe was dire. Talks in Moscow, between British Prime Minister Chamberlain's delegation and the Soviet Foreign Minister, Molotov, had broken down and any chance of an Anglo–Soviet pact was now lost. There were rumours of talks between the Nazis and the Soviets.

Tremayne was exasperated. 'Christ, we've just finished the war to end all wars,' he said. 'Put the bloody politicians in the trenches this time.'

Slipping the newspaper into his jacket pocket he went to the front desk and asked if there was any post. There was one letter from Cape Town. He gave the man some coins and thanked him. By the time he'd reached the stairs, the desk clerk was on the phone.

Tremayne took the steps two at a time and strode along the bright marble-floored corridor deep in thought. He barely noticed the thin Arab in a crumpled white suit pass in the opposite direction.

As he approached Room 249, he saw the piece of paper he had wedged against the frame lying on the floor. The door was shut. Perhaps it was the maid, come to clean the room? Standing to one side, he turned the handle. The door eased open. Pulling out his revolver he gave it a push and stepped inside, pausing to take in the scene. Every drawer had been pulled out, the lining of his suitcase slashed, the wardrobe emptied and the contents scattered over the bed.

Last night in town he'd been followed, and now his possessions had been searched. The person he'd come to Tangier to find must be worried.

'Indigo, you bastard, I know you're out there, and when I find you …' he said, his jaw clenched, and mouth set in a mulish line.

Chapter 4

The Forbidden Zone, South West Africa

Christoff Jager watched as the two Diamond Security policemen inspected his boat. His heart was thumping. It was his only means of escape. How the hell had they found it? Had he left tracks? He couldn't help a nervous glance over his shoulder. Where were the other two policemen he'd come across earlier?

He scrambled back down the dune, his mind racing. He looked at his watch. It was going to be dark in four hours. But without his boat, that was irrelevant. The alternative was a three-day walk across the parched desert, a walk that few could survive. He had barely enough water for three hours, let alone three days.

He took off his rucksack and tied Falkie to the strap. Arming his crossbow and gripping the sheath knife in his teeth, he worked his way around to the right of the rocky promontory. Peering over, he could see the two, fifty feet away, leaning against the boat, smoking.

'Smash a hole in the boat … I'm going for a piss,' the sergeant said.

The policeman climbed into the boat and picked up one of the oars raising it above his head, like a local woman about to pound corn. Jager's sole means of escape was about to be rendered useless. He had a split second to act. He aimed the crossbow and fired. The steel bolt sliced silently through the policeman's chest, exited his back and disappeared in the waves. Still holding the oar, he fell backwards out of the boat like a felled tree, and lay twitching on the sand. The sergeant glanced back but from his position he saw nothing.

Jager was over the rock in a flash and ran at the sergeant, knife in hand. The sergeant was in mid-flow but caught Jager's movement and fumbled for his revolver. The buttoned flap on the holster gave Jager the two seconds he needed. As the sergeant raised the gun, Jager grabbed it with his left hand and there was a loud crack and the bullet buzzed past his head. With his right hand he drove the knife into the sergeant's chest, and they tumbled back into the waves. The shock of the cold water seemed to revive the sergeant, and he hit Jager a glancing blow with the gun. Still holding the embedded knife, Jager twisted it, and the sergeant slumped back into the waves, motionless, eyes staring. Red ribbons drifted from his chest, colouring the water.

'Shit,' Jager said, trying to catch his breath, his left ear ringing from the revolver shot. He had to get out of there, and fast. The other two policemen must have heard that.

He cleaned his hands in the waves and dabbed the cut on his head with the cold water. He ran back to the boat and looked for any damage and breathed a sigh of relief. He'd acted just in time. Retrieving the water bag stashed in the boat, he drank deeply.

He picked up his crossbow, climbed back to the top of the dune and scanned the desert. He expected to see movement, but there was nothing.

A distant rifle shot rang out, followed by another.

'Kak-kak-kak-kak-kak,' Falkie screeched, giving his alarm call. The falcon flapped to escape his tether. Jager slid down the dune.

'Shoosh, boy. It's alright, shoosh,' he said, removing the leather hood and pouring water on him from the water bag. Falkie ran his wings over his head and stamped side to side as if treading grapes.

Two more rifle shots rang out. Jager judged they were about a mile to the south. It had to be the other two policemen responding to the sound of the revolver shot.

'Let's go, Falkie. We got to get the fuck out of here.'

Jager let Falkie hop onto his arm and picked up his bag and crossbow and hurried back to the boat. He put Falkie into the bamboo cage under the bow and draped a buckskin over the top. Falkie was not a good sailor.

It took him several minutes to get both bodies into the boat. He left no trace of them on the beach, recovering their rifles and cigarette butts and then he remembered the revolver. He couldn't leave that behind. The sergeant had been holding it when he fell back into the sea. He went down on his hands and knees in the waves and felt around. Minutes passed, and he became anxious. Then a loud rifle shot sounded followed by another, much closer this time. The other policemen could only be a few hundred yards away now. Adrenalin kicked in and Jager ran back to his boat.

The extra weight of the two dead bodies made it hard to move. He had to use an oar to lever the boat inch by inch into the sea, and after considerable effort it was afloat. He set the oars and heaved hard as they bucked through the breakers into the easier offshore swell. Stashing the oars, he slotted the small wooden mast into its mortise, slipped in the locking peg and pulled up the sail.

'Shit, Falkie, that was a close one, hey boy? Home in a couple of hours, and we get to feed the sharks on the way,' he said.

'Kak-kak-kak-kak-kak,' Falkie screeched, in alarm.

'Quiet, Falkie, we're safe now,' he said, looking across the bay for any sign of a dorsal fin and then at the shoreline, now disappearing in the haze of sea spray. News of two missing policemen was going to cause a big problem. He and his Adlerflagge comrades would have to lie low for a while.

'This is a fuck-up, Falkie, a big fuck-up,' he said, thinking about the unrecovered revolver. Without his hood, Falkie was also agitated.

Chapter 5

Luftwaffe Headquarters, Wilhelmstrasse, Berlin

In the back of a black Opel staff car, Kapitänleutnant Horst Nissen was speeding south along Wilhelmstrasse in Berlin. He looked out at the Reich Chancellery with its huge Nazi flags fluttering in the breeze and the well-dressed Berliners in their summer finery promenading along the wide, spotless pavements. Boys in brown shirts with swastika bands on the arms marched behind a banner, singing their allegiance to the Nazi Party. Nissen felt a shiver of pride at the new spirit and energy running through his country. Unified at last, twenty years after the humiliations of World War 1.

He wondered what the afternoon would bring. His commanding officer, Wilhelm Canaris, Chief of the *Abwehr*, the German Secret Service, had summoned him to an urgent meeting ordered by Generalfeldmarschall Hermann Göring, the Commander-in-Chief of the Luftwaffe. Nissen loathed the man. He thought him a dandy, with his jewel-encrusted baton and bespoke pale blue uniform. However, Göring was a dangerous and unpredictable man. Nissen rubbed his chin thoughtfully, his feeling of pride in the Reich replaced by a sense of apprehension.

Nissen was forty-six years old and the epitome of a modern German officer. His muscular face was broad, with penetrating grey eyes that were never still, always exploring and inquisitive. His full head of hair was cropped militarily short, rather greyer these days than brown. To his fellow officers he had a reputation for being pushy and arrogant, but his commanders saw drive and determination. He had the haughty air of a Nazi officer who was destined for higher calling.

Growing up on the North Sea coast, he had been extrovert and resourceful and loved the outdoor life. At the age of twelve, he had sailed single-handed from Cuxhaven around Heligoland and back, a journey of nearly one hundred miles. It had taken him three days, and he had slept in the boat, at sea. By the age of twenty, he had twice sailed around the Cape of Good Hope and into the Indian Ocean, crewing for Count Felix Von Luckner. On the second occasion, storm damage forced them into Walvis Bay in German South West Africa, for

19

emergency repairs. There they took on an additional crew member, Christoff Jager.

At the start of World War 1, Nissen was commissioned into the German Navy, one of six officers on the three-masted merchant raider SMS Seeadler. The captain of the vessel, Felix Von Luckner, had specifically requested him.

Their disguise as a merchant ship gave them the element of surprise and with camouflaged guns and powerful auxiliary engines they successfully raided Allied ships in the Pacific. This ended when a storm pushed them onto a reef of the uninhabited atoll of Mopelia in French Polynesia. With little fresh water and food, their situation was dire. In that remote part of the Pacific, they knew that if they were by chance rescued, it would be by a ship with Allied sympathies. That was unacceptable.

Von Luckner and Nissen rigged a longboat and sailed nearly fifteen hundred miles to the Fijian, Wakaya Island. There they planned to steal a ship and return to rescue their comrades. But on the second night, celebrating their successful arrival, they were overheard speaking German and taken prisoner. That was the end of Nissen's war.

With the rise of the Third Reich in the 1930s, the Nazis began rebuilding their military capability. With his daredevil reputation and sporting prowess, Nissen was hand-picked for training with the Brandenburger Special Forces. Top of his class, he quickly rose to head of the Southern Africa section at Abwehr II. Based in Hamburg, he was involved in directing covert contact and exploitation of discontented minority groups with German sympathies. With his connections in South West Africa he had found the ideal cohort.

Crossing Leipzigstrasse, the staff car pulled up outside the Luftwaffe headquarters, the heart of Göring's fiefdom. It was an imposing seven-storey building, clad with limestone blocks, in the style of National Socialist intimidation architecture, favoured by the Nazis. Göring had personally ordered its construction in 1933. With clean square lines, it had two huge eagles scrutinising all who entered.

Inside, a life-size bronze statue of Göring was front and centre in the voluminous entrance hall. Nissen's earlier feeling of disquiet returned with a vengeance. He presented himself at the desk with a crisp click of the heels and Nazi salute. He was relieved of his sidearm, searched and escorted to a meeting room on the second floor, where he was shown to a designated seat.

Sitting on the other side of the large mahogany table was a thin, grey-haired man in a suit that seemed at least two sizes too big for him. He had a noble face and a bone structure that suggested a once strong man of good pedigree, but now frail, with sunken, staring eyes. He rested his chin on steepled hands. Nissen nodded at him, but there was no acknowledgement. This didn't bode well, he thought.

He gazed around the ornate room with its crystal chandeliers and large oil paintings. One was of Göring himself, arrogantly posed in front of his Fokker fighter biplane in World War 1. A huge Nazi flag covered the end wall. Military headquarters were usually utilitarian, but this establishment was quite different.

The large mahogany doors opened noisily, jolting both men from their thoughts. Six soldiers in blue tunics with gold braid flashes entered and goose-stepped their way to the table, three either side. They were malignant, intimidating thugs, their machine guns held at the ready. Göring had personally selected them from the ranks of the Luftwaffe. Each wore an iron cross.

If Nissen hadn't been so taken aback, he would have laughed out loud at the theatre of it. But it was a sobering spectacle, just him and the old man, both unarmed, guarded by six soldiers with machine guns! Göring's paranoia was notorious even by Nazi standards. Nissen felt something squirm in his gut. The man opposite looked as though he was having a nervous breakdown.

Seconds later, the stout, double-jowled Göring entered, his metal-heeled boots clacking on the Italian marble floor. Two men followed him in. Nissen and the old man stood to attention and gave the Nazi salute. Göring ignored them and sat down at the head of the table. There was an unnerving silence as he ceremoniously removed his white Italian kidskin gloves, finger by finger.

'Be seated. This is Wilhelm Canaris, Chief of the Abwehr Military Intelligence Service, and Herr Fritz Todt the Minister of Armaments and War Production,' Göring said, introducing the two men who had entered with him. 'Over here is Kapitänleutnant Horst Nissen of Abwehr II and Heinrich Koppenberg, the managing director of the *Junkers Flugzeug-und Motorenwerke*.'

Nissen could not reconcile the ashen-faced old man opposite with the position of head of one of Germany's major military aircraft manufacturers. He looked more like a refugee. The alien in his gut squirmed again.

'Let me get straight to the point,' Göring said. 'Koppenberg, nine months ago I ordered you to accelerate the production of the Junkers 88A-1 fighter bombers. Our glorious Third Reich has ambitions that require military superiority. You assured me that within the year you'd be manufacturing three hundred aircraft a month. In retrospect, a very rash promise. Explain why you have failed your country.'

Koppenberg had trouble getting to his feet.

'Herr Generalfeld ...' his voice faltered to a cough. He tried to clear his throat.

'Herr Generalfeldmarschall, the A-1 is a larger and faster aircraft than its predecessors and requires more powerful and higher specification engines. To produce the numbers required, we need a regular supply of industrial diamond powder for the hard cutting, grinding and polishing tools necessary to make the high-precision parts. But for many months now' – he paused as if looking for the words – 'there has been a supply shortage.'

He stared straight ahead, looking at no one, his whole frame shaking.

'Has this shortage been communicated?' Göring said, in a passive voice. Always a bad omen.

'Yes, Herr Generalfeldmarschall,' Koppenberg said.

'What is happening here, Todt?' Göring snapped.

Nissen noted the relief that washed across the old man's face at someone else being asked a question.

'Herr Generalfeldmarschall, the build-up of military manufacturing across Europe, North America, Russia and Japan has resulted in a worldwide shortage of industrial diamonds. Until eighteen months ago, we purchased our diamonds from the biggest producer in the world, De Beers. However, Oppenheimer, the head of the company, banned direct sales to Germany, blaming it on a change of heart by the South African government. I spoke with President Herzog and he said that is a damnable lie. It was the British Government putting pressure on Deputy Prime Minister Smuts and on Oppenheimer. I told him we must have the diamonds, but his hold on power is weak, and he is unable to overturn the decision. Since then, we have been sourcing diamonds on the open market, including the purchase of surplus stock from America, Switzerland, Belgium and Holland. But De Beers has now stopped selling to those countries and is making it a condition of future sales that they will not sell on any of their diamond stock to Germany.'

The baton hit the table with a loud crack. Everyone in the room flinched in unison. Including the guards.

Göring was on his feet, and the baton hit the mahogany a second time.

'More dirty Jewish tricks, refusing to sell to the Third Reich. Who do these stinking animals think they are? They will reap their just reward for this. The Nazi Party will see to it, wherever they are in the world. And I promise that our revenge will be swift, merciless and final,' Göring ranted, globs of spit spattering the table.

Nissen watched the contortions of Göring's face and his staring glazed eyes as he wiped his mouth with a silk handkerchief and sat down again. His chest heaved as if he was having a heart attack. Rumours were circulating in the military that he was a drug addict. God help us all, he thought; the man is deranged.

'So, we must find an alternative to diamonds. We have the finest scientific and engineering minds,' Göring continued, having regained his composure.

Koppenberg looked at Todt, who was looking at him, each willing the other to answer.

The baton hit the table, 'Well?'

'Herr Generalfeldmarschall, there is no other material hard enough for the cutting and precision grinding of hardened steel. It has to be diamond,' Koppenberg said.

'Then, Todt, we have to get them from another source!'

There was a long silence, and Nissen wondered whether he should speak. Canaris nodded at him.

'Herr Generalfeldmarschall, we do have an option,' Nissen said. 'At least in the short term, to bridge the gap until we secure a long-term supply.'

Everyone in the room turned to look at him. They had learned to stay silent unless asked a question when Göring was in one of his black moods.

'This better be good, Nissen,' Göring said.

'Herr Generalfeldmarschall, there is a major source of diamonds in our former colony of German South West Africa. The Lewala Mine produces diamonds in large quantities, from large crystals down to the size of sand grains. Most of their production consists of diamonds below half of one carat in weight, not valuable as a gemstone but ideal for industrial use. As for the large stones, they can also be ground down to make the necessary abrasive powder. When they recently halted the sale of diamonds to America, Switzerland, Belgium and Holland, my sources tell me De Beers continued mining the Lewala Mine at the same rate and stockpiled these smaller stones. So, if they will not sell us these diamonds, we must get them by another means. I have loyal, trained commandos in South West Africa with weapons and munitions who are ready to follow orders … Their only expectation is that we help them raise the German flag once again over their homeland.'

They all glanced at Göring and, to make sure, glanced again. He was smiling.

'My father served as the Imperial Commissioner of German South West Africa in 1885. I have a personal interest in getting our colony back,' Göring said, the smile now a grin.

He ran his finger over the new dents in the mahogany table.

'Todt, Canaris, I want all the necessary resources assigned to Nissen to secure these diamonds. But be warned, Nissen – if you fail me, there will be serious consequences. What are we going to call this mission?'

Nissen thought for a moment. 'Could I suggest Operation Benguela, Herr Generalfeldmarschall?'

As Nissen walked to his waiting car, he paused to take stock of what had just happened. He was honoured to have a critical role in the Third Reich's rearmament programme, but there was also an alarm bell ringing in his head. Göring had been venomous about Oppenheimer specifically, and Jews in general. This was being borne out daily on the streets of Berlin and Hamburg, with ever-increasing Nazi attacks on Jewish businesses and synagogues. It was during Göring's outburst that he'd had a moment of dread. The man codenamed Indigo, who sold the high-end rough diamonds smuggled from the Forbidden Zone by Scorpion and his comrades, was Jewish. If this association was ever discovered, it would be the end of Nissen's military career, or worse.

With Indigo based in Morocco, he had turned a blind eye to his involvement, but that couldn't continue. It was now about delivering all diamonds to Germany for industrial use, regardless of size or quality. Well, perhaps one or two of the very best stones might be put aside to provide for future security. But they wouldn't need the diamonds valued anymore.

Indigo was now a liability and surplus to requirements. He needed to make a call to Moussa in Tangier. He also had to meet with Scorpion as soon as possible to initiate Operation Benguela. But he wouldn't mention what he had planned for the Jew.

Chapter 6

Café Paris, Place Petit Socco, Tangier

Salamon Zaber was in one of his black moods. The Jewish faith taught moderation in drinking alcohol, but he'd strayed from the teachings of the Torah years ago. When he was worried, whiskey helped him sleep, but too much resulted in a migraine. Last night he had finished the bottle.

When he was in this mood, the few people that knew him stayed well clear. His wicked temper, long hair and unkempt appearance had earned him the nickname Rasputin – although no one dared say that to his face. Even his trusted personal fixers, Fouad Sinai and Ahmed Allam, disliked him.

Over the years he had withdrawn from society, busying himself with his diamonds and listening to Mozart on his old Odeon horn gramophone. His surroundings mirrored this isolation and loneliness. His office was cluttered and dusty, papers and correspondence piled high on a barely visible old table, papers underneath the middle helping to support the weight. A large steel safe stood in one corner, also piled high with papers. The walls were bare apart from a single fading photo of his parents.

The bad start to his day had just got worse. His fixer, Fouad, had confirmed that the man in Room 249, checked in using the name Harvey Tremayne, with a billing address of De Beers Consolidated Diamond Mines, Kimberley, South Africa. Nothing had been found in the room to confirm his identity except a pair of gold cufflinks engraved with *HPT*. The man had put nothing in the hotel safe.

Zaber was sitting at his desk, thoughts churning in his throbbing head. Harvey Tremayne was supposed to be dead, for God's sake! His death had been confirmed by his old friend Scorpion.

But if it was him, that evil-spirited bastard had come back into his life a second time to cause him problems. The first time, nearly three years before, the flow of diamonds had begun to decrease shortly after Tremayne's arrival in South West Africa. He had built up the numbers of Diamond Security Police and they had cracked down on the illegal miners. In addition, the supervisors in key positions on the mine, who were being paid off, became fearful for their jobs. Many of his colonial friends and contacts had gone to jail and he had anonymously provided money to help defend them in court – not out of generosity, but to protect the syndicate. But it was to no avail. The diamond industry was all-powerful, and the outcome was always inevitable. And that was not the only problem that he had experienced.

When the Nazis had muscled in and effectively seized control of the Adlerflagge Syndicate, the number of high-quality stones that came to him was much diminished. The plentiful medium-sized stones that had provided most of his income over the years were no longer included.

To start with, when he'd picked up his monthly package of smuggled diamonds from the Santa Maria in the port of Tangier, a roll of dollar notes discreetly handed to Captain Ferreira had given him access to the diamonds destined for Hamburg that were stashed in the hold. This had worked well for over six months. Until, one day, he received a phone call from a man at the German Consulate.

He had met with him at the Borj al-Hajoui gardens. He was short and fat, with eyes that were set close together and hidden by small, round spectacles with bottle-glass lenses. He said he was looking after the interests of the German shipping agent that owned the Santa Maria. He'd been ordered to investigate the disappearance of diamonds that were destined for Germany. These had been stolen while the ship was docked in Tangier. The owners wanted to find and punish those involved.

Zaber had known immediately that the man was a Nazi agent. But the deliberate threat had worked. From that day on, he kept his head down and accepted only the diamonds he was offered.

The man from the consulate called himself Moussa.

For two years, Tremayne had remained the nemesis of everyone in the Adlerflagge. He had been unrelenting in his drive to eliminate smuggling. That's how he'd got his nickname, Tokolosh. In tribal folklore, this is an evil spirit called upon by wicked people to cause trouble for others – in this case, an evil spirit spawned by De Beers to render harm to Zaber and his fellow smugglers.

His murder had predictably backfired. It had been intended to send a message to De Beers that they could not plunder South West Africa with impunity. There was a price to pay. Had Zaber known of the plan he would have warned of the consequences.

All hell had broken loose. The Diamond Security Police cracked down on anyone who had the remotest link to diamonds. Mining was suspended, Luderitz was blockaded and all employees questioned.

Suspects spent weeks in jail being interrogated. Scorpion was forced to go into hiding at a remote bay, far to the west of Luderitz.

Killing Tremayne had been one thing, that got the anger of the government authorities and De Beers management. The murder of his wife had caused a national outrage. She had worked tirelessly to help the most impoverished people in the community and had set up evening classes so that people could better themselves. She'd volunteered at the local hospital and organised food deliveries to the destitute. She was admired, well liked, even loved. Scorpion had killed her as well. Zaber had been furious. He knew the Nazis were the instigators. In a fit of anger, he had phoned Moussa and told him, in no uncertain terms, what he thought about him and his fellow fascists. After that, Zaber received even fewer diamonds.

The Nazis now controlled the Adlerflagge, greedy for all the diamonds they could get, grinding all but the largest crystals into powder for industrial use. It was a travesty! For the first time in twenty years he was not sure what the future held.

And now, Tremayne had arrived in Tangier, apparently resurrected from the dead. Perhaps he was indeed the human manifestation of the African Tokolosh, an evil spirit sent to curse Zaber for eternity.

If it was him, he knew why he was in town. After Tremayne's shooting, the name Indigo had come up during the interrogations. This person was thought to be based in Tangier. He buried his head in his hands, rubbing his temples.

There was no way he was going to tell Moussa until he had incontrovertible proof of his identity. He needed Tremayne's passport. Fouad had confirmed he didn't keep it in his hotel room, and he had put nothing in the safe. So, he must carry it on his person.

He picked a sweet date out of the jar and licked his fingers one by one. A plan formed in his mind. He picked up the earpiece and dialled.

'Come on, come on,' he muttered, with impatience. 'Fouad, I need you to deliver a letter to the Straits Hotel. Tell our man there, Tremayne must get it immediately. It's an invitation to be at Café Taouz at 1 pm today, and I want you there at 12.30 in case he arrives early. Use Ahmed as a decoy to entice him away from the café and lead him down one of the alleys. Then rough him up and bring me everything he has on him, and I mean everything.' Zaber paused while Fouad queried something. 'No, not yet, I want him alive until I know for sure.'

Zaber slammed the earpiece back in the cradle.

As well as getting his passport for confirmation, he needed to know what he looked like in person, just in case Tremayne found him first.

They had never met. From his office he had a good view of Café Taouz across the square. He picked up his binoculars and carefully cleaned the lenses and set the focus wheel to get a clear view of the clientele sitting outside. He returned the binoculars to the desk, checked his watch, picked another sweet date from the jar, and started writing the invitation.

Chapter 7

Straits Hotel, Rue de La Liberte, Tangier

Harvey Tremayne was talking with the hotel manager and Captain Meurant of the Tangier gendarmerie. A theft from an international guest in Tangier's finest hotel had prompted the senior duty officer to attend. However, the captain was dismissive, calling it an opportunistic theft probably involving a member of staff. Entry to the room would have been impossible without collusion. The hotel manager objected and waved his arms in displeasure at such accusations. But Tremayne knew he was being deliberately targeted. He'd been in Tangier for just over twenty-four hours, and the people he was looking for had shown their hand.

'Morning, Tremayne. What happened here?' a man said in a posh English accent. He was tall and portly, dressed in a smart, but slightly crumpled, grey suit.

Tremayne looked up. 'Do I know you?'

'The name's Cartwright, from the British Consulate,' he said.

'How the hell did you get here so quickly?' Tremayne asked, shaking Cartwright's hand.

'Nothing happens in this town without me hearing about it. This is a bit of a mess. What's missing?' he said, smiling as he walked around the room.

Tremayne hesitated, sizing up the visitor. 'Oh, some clothes, but they're replaceable.'

'Monsieur Tremayne, will you please provide us with a list of the things stolen? The hotel manager will make sure it is delivered to me,' Captain Meurant said.

The hotel manager suppressed a comment and nodded reluctantly.

'Come and have tea, Tremayne. We need to talk. In private,' Cartwright said.

Meurant glared at Cartwright. Clearly there was no love lost between them.

'Well actually, I'm rather busy at the moment, if it's all the same with you,' Tremayne said.

'You can be busy another time. We need to talk,' he said.

Downstairs in the hotel café, Cartwright chose a quiet table in the garden and ordered a pot of mint tea and two glasses.

'I just want to tell you to be careful in the Tangier International Zone. It's a joint French and Spanish protectorate, and both have their own agendas and do not take kindly to outsiders. There are as many vagabonds and brigands here as there are grains of sand in the Sahara,' he said, smiling. 'And now there's you.'

'What the hell does that mean, Cartwright? The consulate has been kept fully informed of my visit by De Beers.'

Tremayne was in no mood for smart-arse comments. He was feeling fractious after the four-day flight from Cape Town and the gin dinner he'd had the previous night.

'Well, Tremayne, as I see it, you have no jurisdiction here, no powers of arrest. You're just a businessman. If you get into trouble, the British Consulate has limited powers to assist.'

'I'm only here to fact-find. Is that a problem?'

'Tremayne, let's be clear. You're armed and looking for some dangerous people. We don't want trouble, particularly from a British businessman.'

'I'm here to investigate those responsible for smuggling diamonds through Tangier from South West Africa.'

Cartwright studied him while he finished his tea. 'And when you find them?'

Tremayne said nothing but held eye contact.

'Here's my card. Call me if you get into any bother and I'll try and help you. Remember, trust nothing and no one in Tangier,' he said, giving him a stale grin.

'There is one thing actually. Do you have a contact in the customs police at the port?'

Cartwright retrieved his card and wrote on the back.

'He's not high-ranking but he's a good man. I'll call him to say you'll be in touch. Keep out of trouble, Tremayne. You do not want to end up in a Moroccan jail, trust me on that,' he said, smiling but not offering his hand. He leaned over and whispered in Tremayne's ear, 'Remember, I'm watching you.'

Tremayne finished his tea, wondering what to make of the man. His card said he was Philip Cartwright, Liaison Officer, British Consulate, Tangier International Zone, Morocco. That's a likely story, he thought.

'Excuse, Monsieur.'

Tremayne looked up to see the concierge, who bowed politely, holding out an envelope. He smelled of cheap tobacco, his grey moustache stained orange with nicotine.

'Excuse, you are Monsieur Tremayne, in Room 249?'

Tremayne nodded.

'Then this letter is for you, Monsieur.'

Taking the envelope, he slit it open with a knife and pulled out the single sheet of paper. The neat handwriting read: *Tokolosh, meet me at Café Taouz 1 pm today.* It felt as though one of hotel cockroaches had just crawled down his back. He squirmed uncomfortably against the chair.

He checked the back of the letter and the envelope but there was no indication of the sender. But the name Tokolosh. That was the bombshell. It was the nickname given to him by the miners in Africa, because of his crackdown on smugglers.

He smiled to himself. This was an early breakthrough. It meant that Indigo, the very person he had come to Tangier to find and hold to account, must know he was here. Only someone involved in diamond smuggling would know that nickname. He went to the concierge's desk.

'Who delivered this?' he said, holding up the letter.

'Monsieur, it was a man.'

'Does he have a name?'

'I do not know him, Monsieur.'

'What does he look like?'

'A thin man in a white suit.'

'A local?'

'Yes, Monsieur. He's Arab.'

'Where is Café Taouz?'

'It is on Place Petit Socco, Monsieur.'

'Thank you,' Tremayne said, handing him a few coins.

As he returned to his room, he thought about Cartwright and decided he would keep him out of the loop, at least for the time being. He needed answers of his own, and at this time he was not sure who he could trust. He'd learned two things this morning: Whoever sent him the invitation knew his identity, knew the South West Africa mining connection. And, it seemed, he was being watched by the British Secret Intelligence Service.

Chapter 8

Office of the Foreign Secretary, Whitehall, London

Winston Churchill walked doggedly down a long corridor in the heart of the Foreign Office. He puffed on a half-finished Cuban cigar, his hands clasped tightly behind his back. He had a newspaper tucked under his arm. At the end of the corridor a door opened, and a young man appeared.

'Michaels, I have an appointment to see the Foreign Secretary,' he growled.

'Good morning, Mr Churchill. Pease take a seat. I'll tell Lord Halifax you're here.'

But Churchill was in no mood to be kept waiting. As the young man knocked on the large mahogany door and entered, he was one step behind him.

'The Right Honourable Winston ...,' Michaels started to say, as Churchill pushed past him.

'Morning, Halifax. I suppose you've seen these headlines?' he said, slapping a copy of *The Times* on his desk. 'Germany and Russia are about to sign a Non-Aggression Pact. More like the Nazi–Soviet Pact of Aggression,' he said, ignoring the other two men in the room.

Lord Halifax got up and walked around the large polished-oak desk and shook hands.

'Hello, Winston. Thank you for coming over,' he said in a conciliatory manner, not looking forward to engaging with his old adversary.

'Would you care for Michaels to take your hat and coat, and what about a cup of tea or coffee? A bit early for a cognac, I'm afraid,' he added, raising his eyebrows.

'Coffee thank you, Halifax. Unlike you Whitehall types I don't touch liquor until the sun's gone down ... over Delhi,' he said, checking his watch and doing the calculation.

Halifax smiled. There was something roguish about Churchill that he almost admired. He nodded at Michaels.

'Winston, I think you know Sir Alistair Wilson, Head of MI6, and Sir Richard Williams, my Principal Private Secretary.'

'Yes indeed. Gentlemen,' Churchill said, nodding.

'In answer to your question, Winston, we are aware of and deeply concerned about the alliance.'

'Halifax, I warned this government that we faced a choice between "war and shame", and that having chosen shame we would later get war on less favourable terms.' He leaned forward conspiratorially. 'And Halifax, that moment is nigh. Germany is poised to attack and catapult the whole of Europe into war.'

'Winston, I understand the argument, but you surely realise that just twenty years ago we lost a million men fighting a war with Germany. The Prime Minister believes we owe it to our nation to do everything possible to avoid another. And as a matter of record, I agree with him.'

'Don't patronise me, Halifax. I commanded a battalion in that war. What beggars belief is that despite the overwhelming evidence of massive military build-up, in contravention of the Versailles Treaty, you and your handwringing, spineless cabinet have done nothing to stop it. Did those million brave soldiers you talk of die in vain because of this government's incompetence? It is astounding how indecisive and ineffectual democracies make it so easy for fascists like Hitler to prosper.'

Churchill glared at Halifax. There was an uneasy silence, broken by a knock on the door. Michaels entered with a tray and put it on the desk. A wave of Halifax's hand saw him quickly depart.

'Winston, I've called you here because we need your help. Indeed, the country needs your help.'

Churchill sat up straight and looked at Halifax. He reached into his pocket, pulled out a lighter and relit his cigar.

'And how may the Right Honourable Member for Epping be of service to you, Foreign Secretary?' he said, with a crooked smile.

'Sir Alistair, why don't you set the scene?' Halifax said.

'Mr Churchill,' Sir Alistair began, 'for some time, our intelligence has shown that the Nazis are rebuilding their military capability, but more important information has recently come to light.'

'For Christ's sake, Wilson, you don't have to tell me this—'

'Winston, please,' Halifax said, interrupting. He raised is hands as if in surrender.

Sir Alistair continued, 'What you might not know, Mr Churchill, is that the Germans have a problem, an Achilles heel. They are running short of industrial diamonds and this is affecting their military build-up. Finely ground diamond is used as a hard coating for cutting, machining and polishing high-precision steel parts.'

'Well, here at least is some good news. So, what are you doing to exploit this?' Churchill asked.

'Well, De Beers has not directly supplied Germany for nearly eighteen months. Sir Ernest Oppenheimer, the chairman, is Jewish, born in Germany. He is deeply disturbed by the Nazis' military build-up and the treatment of his fellow Jews in Germany, and now Austria and Czechoslovakia. With the De Beers supply cut off, Germany has to source diamonds from wherever they can.'

'Bravo,' Churchill said, waving his cigar in the air. 'So there is someone in this world prepared to take a stand against the Nazis. Perhaps you should follow his example, Halifax?' he added sarcastically.

'Please continue, Sir Alistair,' Halifax said, surveying the ceiling.

'Mr Churchill, the problem is the Nazis have been forced into sourcing diamonds from the few countries still prepared to sell to them. When those avenues dry up, they will have to resort to desperate measures to replenish their stocks. They have been buying smuggled diamonds from South West Africa for years, and because of their colonial history they know the people and the country. We need you to discuss with General Smuts how we jointly protect the diamond fields from Nazi interference. We know he was a colleague of yours in World War 1, and as Deputy Prime Minister of South Africa, he is an influential figure.'

'And what intelligence do we have that gives you this concern?' Churchill said.

'In the last few months, our naval base at Walvis Bay has picked up an increase in Morse code messages along the South Atlantic coast. The concern is that because the messages are in code, they must be of military origin, and the few decipherable words are in German!'

Churchill puffed on his cigar, ash falling unnoticed onto his waistcoat.

'This is indeed ominous. That fascist Hitler will stop at nothing to control Europe and send his malignant tentacles around the world. We must stop him in his tracks, Halifax.'

Churchill sat back, puffing on his cigar, contemplating the ramifications.

'And what has our Punch-and-Judy Prime Minister done to address this? Anything?' Churchill said.

Halifax looked apologetically at Churchill and said nothing.

'What an utter bloody mess this government has got us into,' Churchill said, shaking his head. He got up and paced across the room and pushed through the large mahogany door.

'Michaels,' he yelled, 'get my car around the front immediately. I have to save this country from its bloody government.' He slammed the door after him.

The three men looked at one another.

'I think that went quite well, considering!' Halifax said.

Chapter 9

Kolmanskop Camp, Forbidden Zone, South West Africa

Captain Niels Kruger of the Special Investigations Unit had received a call from Commander Nico Steenkamp of the Diamond Security Police. Two members of a four-man unit on a routine patrol north-west of the Lewala Mine were missing. A two-day search had found no sign of them. They suspected foul play and Kruger was being asked to take over the investigation. It was the sort of work he loved: eliminating the spurious, examining the ambiguous and identifying the possible, then the excitement of the chase and finally, justice. That's what made him tick.

He was ideally suited to the role. Even as a child in Kimberley, the centre of diamond mining in South Africa, he'd had a sixth sense for people up to no good. His father included. One Saturday, Kruger had seen him next door talking with a neighbour, their heads close together in hushed conversation. And then a package changed hands. Watching from his hideout, high in the marula tree in his back yard, he'd seen the neighbour bury the parcel in his vegetable patch. Intrigued by this subterfuge, the following Sunday, when the family were at church, he'd dug up the parcel and had taken it to his hide. The oiled linen cloth held four beautiful diamond crystals, each the size of one of his small marbles. Not wanting to risk being caught putting them back, he'd hidden them in the tree.

He observed the same thing a few weeks later and added a further six small diamonds to his hoard. Days later, his father asked if he'd seen anyone snooping around next door. He'd said there were thieves about, and if he and his neighbour caught them, there'd be trouble. That evening his father was angry and stormed out of the house. Kruger was woken in the night when his father returned drunk and abusive. He'd heard his mother sobbing.

This worried the young Niels because he knew that drunks, wife beaters and people who smuggled diamonds ended up in prison. Plucking up courage, the next Saturday, he took the oiled cloth containing the ten diamonds to the police station and said he'd found it hidden in a wall. He was bundled into the sidecar of a motorcycle combination and off they went. He'd enjoyed the journey, the sense of doing the right thing, the sense of justice. He told them they'd find nothing because he had already searched the wall. But the police combed the area anyway.

On the way back, and despite young Kruger's protests, the sergeant dropped him off at home and insisted on telling his parents what a fine and honest son they had. His father looked him in the eye and went ash-white. He knew the truth. But it was too shameful, too embarrassing, and was never mentioned again.

That episode in his early life was the catalyst for his career in the police. At the age of eighteen, in 1921, he'd first followed in his father's footsteps working for De Beers at the Kimberley Central Mine. The work was physical and lacked the intellectual challenge he needed. Going underground at dawn and returning to surface at dusk was not for him, and in 1923 he had joined the Diamond Security Police.

His energy, dedication and ability to get into the minds of smugglers led to promotion. He had worked with the then Underground Manager, Harvey Tremayne, to develop the random checking of workers going off-shift. They also instigated spot checks based on covert intelligence. He had undercover police working in the local bars and even had one at the Kimberley Club, the exclusive domain of mine officials.

After sixteen years in Kimberley, he accepted a promotion to Captain of the Special Investigations Unit, based in Luderitz, a section of the Diamond Security Police. He and his small team sought out known and suspected smugglers and dealers and followed up on all known thefts. This was his first assignment to investigate missing persons.

At first light the following morning, Kruger left Luderitz and drove south to the Diamond Security Police headquarters at Kolmanskop Camp. Accompanying him was Sergeant Samuel Ndakolo and Constable Isaak Japie, his two most trusted trackers.

The forty-mile drive through the inhospitable, dry desert was on brutally rough dirt roads, often covered by drifts of windblown sand, and sometimes sharp, loose rocks when traversing the steep, lifeless hills. Telegraph poles lined the roadside, stretching from horizon to horizon, inducing a fatigue in the mind of the unwary driver that could lead to serious injury or death.

By 8 am it was blistering hot. The land shimmered, and the desert mirage promised a lake of water that remained elusive. All the windows of the Ford Model A Fordor were wound down, allowing for some breeze, but the air that entered was hot and dusty, affording little relief.

Then they got a puncture. As a matter of survival, they carried three spare tyres, of which one was already flat. Kruger cursed himself for not checking more thoroughly. In the Namib, such an oversight could cost lives.

His destination, Kolmanskop Camp, was the site of the first diamond mine, started by August Stauch in 1908. Although fabulously rich in its day, after twenty years of production the diamond-rich gravel beds were worked out. Mining was now concentrated seventeen miles further south at the Lewala Mine, named after Zacharias Lewala, who had discovered the first diamond in German South West Africa.

The old mine buildings had been put to good use. Stripped of their original equipment, they now accommodated the Diamond Security Police. They provided both the desert patrols of the northern sector of the Forbidden Zone, and the security for the mine, plant and port. It was a dangerous area to police. There were no roads, no radio communications and no rules. Each team patrolled the Forbidden Zone for up to three days at a time. For longer-range patrols they used horses, but within ten miles of the mine, patrols were on foot. There was also a dedicated camel team that delivered fresh water to stashes at strategic points across the desert.

The smugglers they were up against were well-armed and expert marksmen. The last few years had seen an increase in the use of the latest high-calibre German hunting rifles. If a smuggler was spotted at a distance, a carefully aimed rifle shot was preferable to the risk of getting too close and being ambushed or shot by a marksman. The police had the advantage of the freshwater stashes in the desert and as a result were able to pursue smugglers for days. If found alive, those captured were immediately arrested and taken to jail.

Kruger and his team arrived just after midday and they were met by Kruger's old friend, Nico Steenkamp, the police commander of the northern sector. They had both joined the Diamond Police in Kimberley in 1923, but Steenkamp had moved to the newly formed Diamond Security Police unit in South West Africa three years later.

They entered a large room with six ceiling fans struggling to move the air around, all wobbling and clanking. On a table, in the centre, was a detailed map of the northern sector of the Forbidden Zone. Steenkamp introduced Corporal Gam Maasdorp and Constable Jurie Norseb, both dressed smartly in crisp khakis, saluting with exaggerated precision. Gam had his left foot bandaged.

The corporal reported that, four days ago, they had spotted a bird they thought was a hawk north-west of the Lewala Mine. They quickly picked up some fresh tracks in a drift but lost them again in a rocky area. They had separated from the other two members of the four-man team, Sergeant Jan Gamab and Constable Hendrik Tseib, in order to cover more ground. Gam and Jurie worked their way down the drift to the coast and that was when they heard a single revolver shot. It was the standard alarm signal in the desert. Gam had fired his rifle twice in reply, but there was no response. He fired further shots, but to no avail. They had searched the area until nightfall, camped overnight and planned to resume their search the following day.

During the night, while putting driftwood on the fire, Corporal Gam was stung on the foot by a flat-tailed scorpion. After a painful and sleepless night, it was clear that he was not going to be able to walk unaided on the badly swollen foot. Supported by Constable Jurie, they had hobbled to the nearest freshwater stash, where they spent a further night. At first light, leaving Gam at the stash, Jurie had walked to the Lewala Mine and raised the alarm.

'Show me on the map where you saw the hawk,' Kruger said.

The two policemen studied the map with embarrassment. Kruger despaired at the men's inability to read maps. They were the very best bush trackers. They could follow a snake for miles across the desert and tell you when it last defecated. They took their lead from nature's fingerprints, from shapes and shadows, from things not as they should be, not from lines on a flat piece of paper. That was how the European found his way around. Following a line on a map to a destination, not reading the land. He knew this, but it was still frustrating.

'So, where did you split up from Sergeant Jan and Constable Hendrik?'

'At the top of Riet Drift, Captain.'

'Right, that's up here. What direction did you go in after that?'

'Sergeant Jan and Constable Hendrik went to search Jakkals Drift to the north and me and Constable Jurie continued down Riet Drift. We went about three miles and picked up some tracks, but lost them in a rocky area,' Gam said.

'And where did you lose the tracks?' Kruger asked.

'Where is the bend in Riet Drift, sir?' Gam asked.

'Well, there are several. Which direction was the bend?'

'It was sharp, to the left, looking downstream,' Gam said.

'Well, it must have been this one,' Kruger said, reassured there was progress. 'And where were you when you heard the shot?'

'Much further down, not far from the beach. The shot was to the north, less than a mile.'

'And you're sure it was a revolver shot, not a rifle?' Kruger asked.

'Yes, sir, it was a Webley Mark IV, police issue,' Gam said, with confidence. He'd heard one hundreds of times.

'So, Sergeant Jan must have fired the shot, because he was the only one with a revolver.'

'If Jan and Hendrik were moving down Jakkals Drift, here, and you were coming down Riet Drift, that puts you about a mile apart at the coast! That fits with your estimate of the distance the shot was fired,' Kruger said.

Gam smiled and nodded. 'Yes, sir.'

'So why would Sergeant Jan fire just one shot? Was it a warning, or was he shooting at something?' Kruger said.

'Sir, it couldn't be a warning shot. Otherwise he or Hendrik would have replied to Isaak's two shots,' Sergeant Samuel said.

'That's a good point. So what did he fire a single shot at? And where was Constable Hendrik with his rifle? They must have been in some kind of trouble.'

Gam and Jurie nodded their heads in unison and stared at the floor.

'Well, assuming they came in by sea, the only safe landing place near Jakkals Drift is here, just north of Great White Point,' Kruger said, pointing at the map. 'It's a sheltered sandy bay, ideal to beach a small boat. That's where we'll start. The three of us will leave at first light tomorrow and land in the bay, search the beach and then work inland.'

'Harvey, you can take Constable Jurie with you if that would help? He knows the area,' Steenkamp said.

Jurie looked at Gam with unblinking eyes, like a goldfish in a bowl. The thought of a boat journey to Great White Point, the home of the dead-eyed monsters, was going to give him nightmares. Corporal Gam was thinking how lucky he was to have been stung by a flat-tailed scorpion.

'Thanks, but I want to bring a fresh set of eyes to the search. Besides, the launch can only take three, plus provisions.'

'Oh, thank you, sir,' Constable Jurie blurted out, and everyone turned and stared at him.

Chapter 10

Abwehr II Headquarters, Knochenhauerstrasse, Hamburg

When Kapitänleutnant Horst Nissen took over as head of the Southern Africa Section of Abwehr II, he had found an ideal cohort in the discontented German colonials of former German South West Africa.

Humiliation burned in them after the overthrow of their country in 1915. Anger pumped through their veins as they watched the wealth of their land being robbed by the British and South Africans. Revenge simmered in their hearts.

On Nissen's first visit, he'd spent time assigned to the German Consulate in the capital, Windhoek. He was able to travel the country with ease. He met with dissidents in the key mining areas of Tsumeb, Abenab, Uis and Luderitz and they, in turn, introduced him to their friends of similar disposition. They all had the same burning desire. What they lacked was organisation and resources.

Within a year, Nissen had formed six commando units across the country, each consisting of about ten men and designated by a colour. He arranged for Abwehr operatives to train the resistance fighters in disruption techniques, sabotage and clandestine radio communication.

His most important group was Red Commando, based in the Luderitz area. This unit was headed up by his old sailing friend, Christoff 'Christo' Jager. He and his colleagues illegally mined diamonds throughout the Forbidden Zone, selling them to a trader codenamed Indigo, based in Tangier. He was the original brains behind the Adlerflagge Syndicate. He sorted them and sold them to independent diamond cutters at premium prices.

Nissen knew that Indigo was good at his job, but there was a problem: He was Jewish. He had turned a blind eye to his ongoing involvement, but to be sure he was not pocketing more than his fair share, he had asked Moussa, one of the Abwehr's North African operatives in Tangier, to watch him.

When he formed Red Commando, using the members of the Adlerflagge Syndicate, Nissen had immediately seen the opportunity to increase the flow of diamonds. The Nazis had an aggressive rearmament programme that needed diamonds of any quality and from any source. In addition to illegally mining the high-quality stones, he had them also mine the smallest diamonds, something they hadn't done before.

The first task he tackled was to organise a more efficient smuggling route through to Germany. Nissen leased two vessels, an old South African fishing boat named Octopus to carry the diamonds from Luderitz to Swakopmund and a Portuguese-registered sailing ship named Santa Maria to carry general cargo from Swakopmund.

The Octopus, which Nissen codenamed Neptune, was a registered fishing boat and regularly offloaded her catch in Swakopmund. She had been armed and fitted with a powerful radio transceiver, but as far as the authorities were concerned she was a local trawler.

The Santa Maria carried an assortment of legal cargo from South West Africa to Germany. Vanadium mined at Abenab was used in the manufacture of low weight, high-strength steels. Copper from Tsumeb was used to produce the wire for use in electric motors and tin from Uis was used in the making of bronze metal, for bearings and shell casings. The industrial diamonds were easy to hide within the voluminous cargo hold. With Hamburg her final destination, she stopped in Tangier, where Indigo collected the high-quality diamonds. The small and low-quality diamonds remained on board, destined for Hamburg.

On the return leg, her cargo included arms and ammunition, radio transceivers and German liquor and tinned foods.

Initially, the flow of gem diamonds had increased. Radio transmission allowed the leaders to coordinate their efforts, powerful binoculars enabled them to spot the Security Police at a greater distance and the latest sniper rifles kept the patrols further away.

But this more aggressive approach by the smugglers was soon matched by larger numbers of Diamond Security Police, and the supply of smuggled diamonds had again declined.

Nissen passed on messages to his old friend Christo Jager, codenamed Scorpion, that it was essential the Third Reich receive an increasing flow of diamonds and that Red Commando should do whatever was necessary to achieve this.

He'd heard about the killing of Harvey Tremayne from Moussa. Indigo had telephoned Moussa at the German Consulate, something he was forbidden to do, and had called him and his fellow Nazis 'fucking idiots'. Nissen had agreed with Moussa that Indigo could no longer be trusted and would have to be eliminated. After the anti-Jewish outburst by Göring at the first meeting, the time was now, and he had given Moussa the order.

Horst Nissen marched up the steps to the imposing Abwehr II headquarters on Knochenhauerstrasse in Hamburg, his shiny black boots clacking a rhythm on the stone slabs. In true National Socialist style, the building was large and austere, and draped with large Nazi flags. Nissen relished it.

As he entered the office, the two men at the table stood and saluted. Admiral Werner Windisch of Atlantic Command gave his crisp Nazi salute, Commander Felix Von Luckner of U-boat Deployment gave the old school military salute, raising his right hand to the eyebrow. Nissen did the same and walked across to Von Luckner and they embraced, as long-lost friends do. Windisch watched without comment.

'So, Horst, I hear Generalfeldmarschall Göring has set you a bold task in South West Africa. Tell us how we can help,' Von Luckner said.

'Admiral, Commander,' Nissen said, acknowledging them both. 'I have been tasked with securing a large quantity of diamonds to support our military rearmament programme. The codename for this is Operation Benguela.

'Our target is the diamond safe at the Lewala Mine, known as the Kaiser's Closet. It is the richest diamond mine in the world and they hold all their production there before shipping it to Cape Town once a quarter.

'The mine is connected to Port Baleen on Respite Bay by a narrow-gauge railway. We will use the jetty there to offload our men, rock drills, air compressors and explosives and use a train to take us up to the mine.'

He pointed out the location on the map.

'Commander, you will remember Walvis Bay here, Luderitz here and Respite Bay about forty miles further south. From the port, it is ten miles by rail to the spur and then a further two miles to the Lewala Mine,' Nissen said.

'Tell me, Kapitänleutnant, if it's the richest diamond mine in the world, the South African and British military will surely have it well protected?' Windisch said.

'Admiral, you are correct. There is a substantial contingent of Diamond Security Police that patrol the Forbidden Zone, but because of the vast area they are spread very thinly. Their main base is at Kolmanskop Camp, a further fifteen miles north from the Lewala spur, but the key thing is, we can isolate that camp by blowing up the access bridge across the Sandrivier Gorge at Mile 23. The Security Police on duty at the mine and port are the only ones we'll have to deal with. And we'll have one big advantage: the element of surprise. They will not be expecting an attack from the sea.'

'That is how General Smuts did it in 1914, Horst,' Von Luckner said. 'Surely they will be wise to this and have naval patrols to prevent such an attempt?'

'Our intelligence suggests that marine patrols are practically non-existent. The closest South African naval base is nearly three hundred miles north at Walvis Bay, where they have a trawler converted to a radio direction finder, plus two old motor torpedo boats. I have men monitoring their comings and goings. They spend more time on the slipway than in the water.'

'So, how do they export the diamonds if there's no protection offshore?' Windisch said.

'De Beers has an old World War 1 minesweeper, named the Eureka, that steams up from Cape Town four times a year to Respite Bay to pick up that quarter's production,' Nissen said.

'So, why don't we go after the diamonds when they're at sea? Board the Eureka, transfer the diamonds and sink her?' Von Luckner said.

'Well, she's armed and in theory could put up a fight. Plus, we have to anticipate that she would send an SOS message and blow our cover. I have received orders from Generalfeldmarschall Göring that under no circumstances can Germany be seen to act against South Africa, which is a self-governing British Dominion. Any Kriegsmarine vessels found within their territorial waters can be legally detained, so this must be clandestine.'

'If there are no naval patrols along that coast, why do you need a U-boat at all? On the way south it will have to refuel at Lobito Bay in Portuguese Angola, and the British will have their spies out. They'll immediately know we're in the area. It's risky,' Windisch said.

'Admiral, as soon as the mine is attacked, the South Africans and the British will throw everything they have at us, and there's no way of knowing what naval ships and submarines might unexpectedly be in the area. They have a base at Saldanha Bay, four hundred and eighty miles south, and of course at Simonstown. A U-boat will provide us with the discreet military capability in case of the unexpected.'

'I still think it's risky. The British have Catalina flying boats at Saldanha Bay, and they have the range to patrol the coast, right up to Walvis Bay,' Windisch added.

Nissen's bright grey eyes stared at the Admiral for several seconds. 'Admiral, this is undoubtedly a challenging and dangerous task that Generalfeldmarschall Göring has set. But the rearmament programme is our overriding consideration. A U-boat can afford us protection against the unexpected, but more importantly, I want to use her to provide safe passage for the diamonds. When we have attacked the mine, the South African military will be on full alert and challenge every ship in the ocean for hundreds of miles. A U-boat can by-pass Luderitz and Walvis Bay submerged and out of sight and deliver the diamonds, to Lobito Bay in two days. There, we can transfer the cargo to the Santa Maria for shipment to Hamburg.'

There was an awkward silence.

Von Luckner said, 'Horst, you have planned this well, but I still have one question. How will you load two tons of diamonds onto a U-boat in the South Atlantic?'

'We will rendezvous with the U-boat in the lee of Pomona Island, where it is sheltered from the prevailing wind and ocean swells. Possession Island, which is further north, has a better harbour, but it's too close to Port Baleen. I want to get as far away as possible after the attack.'

Admiral Windisch sat back in his chair and stroked his chin.

'What is your timing for this, Kapitänleutnant?'

'We will attack the mine on Sunday 27th August, four days before the Eureka arrives from Cape Town on 1st September. That will give us the maximum quantity of diamonds on-site.'

'What U-boat do we have available now, Commander?' Windisch said.

'As it happens Admiral, U-46 is carrying out reconnaissance of the Portuguese Azores under Kapitänleutnant Herbert Sohler.'

'Have her redirected to Lobito Bay, top priority and refuelled and ready for immediate deployment,' Windisch said.

'What will her codename be, Horst?' Von Luckner said.

'She will be call-sign Moby. I will meet her in Lobito Bay, in five days,' Nissen said, with a broad grin.

Chapter 11

Café Taouz, Place Petit Socco, Tangier

Harvey Tremayne left his hotel at 11.30 am. After walking for ten minutes, he found a shady seat and lit a cigarette. He looked around, hoping to see that someone was following him. Walking back from Dean's Bar on the first night, he'd been followed, his room had been ransacked, and now he had been invited to a meeting at Café Taouz by a nameless person. This was all being orchestrated.

During the interrogations that followed his shooting, the name Indigo had been mentioned several times. A seemingly mysterious person, he was revered as the brains behind the smuggling ring. But no one had ever met him or knew anything about him, except that he was rumoured to be based in Tangier. Was this Indigo's doing? It had to be. What he needed was a face, a name, a person, to put to the codename.

Dozens of people passed by, but none seemed to be taking any interest in him. He finished his cigarette, stubbed it out on the pavement and, having taken one last look around, moved on.

Turning down Rue Bramel, he made his way through the jumble of narrow shabby streets with their peeling paint and splashes of black mould. Occasional pots of flowers and small palms struggled to brighten the alleys. Washing hung on lines stretched from roof to roof and the smell of fresh coffee competed with the sickly odour of the drains. In Place Taqaddum, toothless old women were selling fresh fruit and vegetables.

'Hey! Monsieur, Monsieur, viens ici. Come look at these lovely peaches.'

When he ignored them, they dismissed him with a curse and a wave of the hand.

Reaching the far side of the square, he turned down Rue Ouezzane, a wealthier area with inhabitants of Spanish origin. *Viva Franco* was splashed over the walls and a Spanish radio channel chattered away in one of the upstairs rooms. Five minutes later he was at his destination: Place Petit Socco.

He saw the sign for Café Taouz on the sunny side of the square and chose an outside table. He wasn't taking any chances and sat with his back to a wall. Ordering coffee, he pulled out his *Tangier Gazette*.

He looked around, familiarising himself with his surroundings. The square was surrounded by shops: a bakery, spice shop, tabac and one selling cloth, with its rolls of brightly coloured material leaning against the window in the sunshine. There was one other café, at the end of the square, Café Paris.

The waiter brought his order and gave him a friendly nod and a smile. Was this his contact? But he walked off, making no attempt to communicate. Tremayne glanced at his watch: it was twelve forty-five. Reaching under his jacket, he unclipped the flap on the holster. He sipped the thick black coffee.

By five past one, the café was busy. But no one had made contact. He pulled the note from his pocket: *Tokolosh, meet me at Café Taouz 1 pm today.* If no one came, could it mean he was being watched? There was one man, an Arab in a shabby pale suit, who sat three tables away, a cigarette lodged in the corner of his mouth.

Sipping the remainder of his coffee, he watched as the Arab beckoned to a man dressed in a dark brown djellaba robe standing across the square. He walked over to Café Taouz and spoke with the Arab, nodded and quickly departed. Tremayne watched him go. He knew instinctively that this was about him.

Moving his chair to get a better view, Tremayne saw him enter Café Paris. A few minutes later he came out and signalled to the Arab at Café Taouz.

Tremayne beckoned the waiter over. 'Who owns that café?' he said, pointing towards Café Paris.

'Monsieur, please, I keep to myself,' the waiter said, nervously.

Tremayne pulled out a twenty-franc note and waved it at the waiter.

His head nodded to one side, glanced around and said, 'He is not a good man, Monsieur. I do not want trouble. He has people everywhere.'

'What's his name?' Tremayne demanded in a loud voice.

'I don't know, some people call him Rasputin—' The waiter stopped in mid-sentence catching the eye of the Arab three tables over.

That split-second glance was all Tremayne needed. He dropped the note on the table and in four strides was beside the man in the shabby suit. He looked up in alarm and tried to get to his feet, but Tremayne pushed him back.

'My name is Tokolosh. What's yours?' he hissed in his ear.

The man stared at him with fierce brown eyes. He had a hook nose and there was a scar running across his right ear and cheek. His upper lip curled in a sneer, black-stained teeth showing, his breath stinking of aromatic tobacco. This was a born fighter if ever he'd seen one.

'Why are you watching me? Who sent you?'

The man reached inside his jacket but Tremayne dug his thumb and forefingers deep into the flesh either side of his collarbone. The man was paralysed with pain, mouth open as if to scream but no sound came out.

'I said, why are you watching me? Who do you work for?'

Tremayne dug his fingers in as hard as he could.

'I want answers, you lowlife,' Tremayne shouted.

The clientele of Café Taouz went silent and stared at them.

'Monsieur, please, no trouble,' the waiter said, behind him.

In that split second, the Arab jabbed his elbow in Tremayne's face and was off. Tremayne followed, just yards behind, but the man was agile and knew the dark alleyways intimately. He weaved left and right, through doors that led to another alley, and soon Tremayne was twenty yards behind him, then thirty yards and then the man was gone. He listened for footsteps or doors slamming or people shouting, but there was nothing. He had disappeared.

Cursing, he turned to retrace his steps and stopped dead. There at the top end of the alley was the man wearing the dark brown djellaba. He walked purposefully towards him, a knife in his right hand.

Tremayne knew immediately he'd been led into a trap.

Chapter 12

Search at Great White Point, South West Africa

At first light, Captain Niels Kruger and his two trackers Sergeant Samuel Ndakolo and Constable Isaak Japie started their twenty-five-mile journey from Kolmanskop Camp to Port Baleen at Respite Bay.

They were on the narrow-gauge railway that was constructed to transport heavy equipment from the port to the original Kolmanskop Mine. It now provided transportation of men and supplies between the port, the Lewala Mine and the camp. The Diamond Security Police headquarters, police barracks and the stables for the Forbidden Zone patrols were located in the larger buildings.

Riding in the comfortable visitor's coach and being pulled by an old German-built Swartzkopff diesel-electric loco, they departed Kolmanskop in unfamiliar luxury. Two miles south of the camp, they passed a board that read *Mile 23* and rumbled over the steel arch bridge across the Sandrivier Gorge. Kruger stared down into its dark shadows and steep vertical walls.

He watched the distance boards go by, counting down the miles to Port Baleen. Twenty-five minutes later they passed the Mile 10 board and the spur to the Lewala Mine. Fifteen minutes later they passed through the Port Baleen security gate and arrived at their destination, the jetty on Respite Bay. To the west, a ridge curved around the tranquil bay, and to the east the power generating plant providing electricity to the mine and camp throbbed a low bass note. The maintenance workshop clanged and banged even at that early hour. Tied up at the jetty was a small ship from Walvis Bay, delivering the weekly refill of drinking water to the potable tank.

They clambered down the ladder into the waiting security launch, double-checked the fuel and loaded their provisions. They motored out of Respite Bay, sheltered from the South Atlantic swells by Possession Island to the south west. The morning fog was patchy; one minute pale blue sky showed overhead, the next it was lost from sight.

As they travelled north the fog thickened, and at times Kruger was as good as blind. The rise and fall of the boat in the deep swell was disorienting. His two passengers, wide eyes showing beneath their slouch hats, gripped the gunwales as if trying to steady the boat.

The launch was not built for use in the open ocean. Its purpose was

49

to meet incoming ships and security-check them and then pilot them into the jetty. With her diesel engine amidships, she sat low in the water and the steeper waves splashed over her bow, soaking all on board. Isaak pushed and pulled the handle on the manual bilge pump.

After nearly an hour, Kruger knew they must be close to Great White Point. He cautiously edged east towards the shore, occasionally cutting the engine, listening to the sound made by the breaking waves. Sections of this coast were flanked by cliffs, often fronted by reefs. Striking those meant certain death.

Turning the boat north, he hugged the shoreline. Reducing the throttle, he listened for the softer tumble of waves on sand. He felt the boat being tugged by the current and he was sure that they were in the rip created by Great White Point. Deciding not to risk getting any closer, he turned the boat out to sea and waited.

The sun slowly but surely burned off the fog and blue sky appeared overhead, and then a few hundred yards east, the shore came into view. Kruger identified Great White Point to the south.

The passengers stared nervously across the water. The local legend of the 'dead-eyed monster' was ingrained in their psyche, and not without reason. The cold nutrient-rich Benguela Current was teeming with marine life and the great white sharks, for which the point was named, grew to an enormous size by feasting on the abundant seals and dolphins. The legend was heightened by their apparent aggressive behaviour. They deliberately bumped against small boats, testing whether they were prey, but the legend construed this as an attack. What added credence was that on occasion, a fisherman would be caught off-guard and off-balance when the shark bumped, and would topple into the water, meeting with a grisly end.

This was not lost on Kruger either; he too kept an eye out. He had been bumped on one occasion and found it an unnerving experience. After the impact, the shark's head had emerged from the sea, grinning with its tangle of teeth, its eye assessing the boat. And him. Its long, fat body scraped down the side, like coarse sandpaper. No one ever forgot an encounter like that.

But this time, he saw only one triangular fin, and that was some distance away. He soon had the boat beached on the fine silver sand. The two policemen couldn't get out of the boat fast enough.

Kruger and Samuel refuelled the boat from cans for the return journey and Isaak went off to collect driftwood along the tideline. Kruger knew his men could not function when cold and wet. They were desert people; their blood was thin, and their bodies craved heat. They lit a fire and toasted black bread, heated fat, rich *boerewors* spiced sausage, and brewed rooibos tea with lots of sugar. They sat close to the roaring fire, driving off the last vestiges of the cold and damp that had chilled their bones.

'We've got to start back in four hours, so let's get moving,' Kruger said. 'We'll walk north, ten yards apart. Samuel, you take the highwater line, Isaak, you walk inland and I'll be in between. The smugglers will have landed here somewhere, so we go slowly and check carefully.'

By the time they started out, the sun was beating down out of a cloudless sky, any evidence of the cold fog burned to a memory. The men, now in their element, zigzagged along their prescribed route, occasionally bending down for closer investigation. After more than an hour they turned back, searching the same area, this time with the sun at a different angle, seeing the same beach differently, as if for the first time. When they were almost back at their starting point Samuel called, and Isaak joined him. They sat on their haunches, studying something, chatting and pointing.

Samuel waved, and said, 'Captain, here's part of a feather.'

Kruger studied the object. It was white and had been cut at an angle on three sides.

'It looks like a flight from an arrow, but why on earth would someone bring a bow and arrow here?'

The two shook their heads. Smugglers used hunting rifles in the Forbidden Zone, not bows and arrows.

'Samuel, check this area. Isaak, you work inland from here.'

Minutes later Isaak shouted and waved. 'Someone was here, a few days ago.'

'Could it have been Jan or Hendrik?' Kruger asked.

'It's nearly blown away. It's difficult to be sure,' Isaak said.

The two spread out and searched the area.

'And there was something dragged on the ground here,' Samuel said, pointing.

'Right, I want this area thoroughly checked. If our smuggler was here he'll have left in a hurry. There might be something else between here and the beach.'

The three slowly and painstakingly worked their way back inch by inch. Samuel stopped at the base of the dune and knelt down. After a few seconds he started to brush away the sand.

'Captain,' he said with great excitement, holding up something.

It was a tiny leather bag with two straps. He blew on it to remove the sand.

51

'It's a hood! The sort falconers use when transporting their birds. Well done, Samuel.'

Kruger looked around, trying to imagine what might have happened. He climbed up the dune and looked over. From here the smuggler would have been able to check the entire beach.

'Perhaps when he looked over, he saw Jan and Hendrik,' Kruger said. 'But did Jan fire at him? If so, why a single shot?'

The sun suddenly dulled, obscured by a wisp of fog, and the temperature instantly dropped. Kruger looked at his watch.

'Shit, the fog's coming in early,' he said.

He climbed up on the promontory and inspected the scene. His heart sank. The fog bank was sitting there, like a chained dog, guarding their route back to Respite Bay.

'It's not safe to take the boat back tonight,' Kruger said.

Both policemen looked relieved. They would rather sleep in the desert than return by boat in fog, particularly in this bay.

'Samuel, catch us some fish, and Isaak, get plenty of driftwood stockpiled. I'll unload the supplies.'

With the setting sun, the fog plucked up courage and left the safety of the ocean and crept onto the land, enveloping all it touched. The crackling fire did its best to fight it off, and the smell of cooking fish raised their spirits.

'Sir, if Jan fired that shot, the smuggler would have been hit. He never missed,' Isaak said.

Kruger mulled over the comment. 'They must have been on to something. Jan was the only one with a revolver so he must have fired the shot. Did the smuggler have a bow and arrow? Did he shoot Hendrik and then Jan shot him? Three people and a boat vanished, and a single revolver shot. It doesn't make sense.'

They all sat in silence, the flames hypnotic, the wood crackling and spitting, sending bright embers up into the gloom.

'Perhaps they shot the smuggler and wounded him and decided to leave using his boat?' Samuel suggested.

Isaak shook his head sagely. 'Jan had a brush with a dead-eyed monster once. After that he was terrified of the sea. You would have to kill him to get him in a boat.'

They sat staring into the flames, listening to the waves crashing on the beach and the mournful howl of a scavenging hyena in the distance. There was only one inescapable conclusion. And with that realisation, the cold fog wrapped around them, taking advantage of their despair.

Chapter 13

Kasbah Quarter, Tangier

Harvey Tremayne pulled out his revolver and, keeping his back to the wall, walked crab-like to the end of the alley. Glancing around the corner he could see the Arab in the djellaba robe in front. As he approached him, the man would slip down a side alley or into a building. Each corner he turned, the man in front disappeared and the man in the white suit behind him reappeared.

Taking stock of his predicament, Tremayne thought back to the trench raids in France, the cat-and-mouse night stalking. Hiding in plain sight. The enemy suspecting you were there, but not knowing exactly where.

He backed into a doorway and flattened himself against the wall. He counted to thirty, stepped out into the alley and there was the man in the robe, like a rabbit caught in headlights. He had not expected Tremayne to start stalking him. Tremayne pointed his revolver and the man ducked and gathered up his robe and ran. Tremayne gave chase, vaulting down some steep steps to a busy road, just thirty yards behind. The man ran straight across the flow of traffic, seemingly oblivious to the danger, tyres screeching and horns blowing. He bounced off the front of one car with his hand and by some miracle avoided being hit. Tremayne hesitated momentarily but took advantage of the stopped traffic and followed. The man disappeared down an alley and into a maze of small market stalls. He shouted something, and immediately the crowd passively but deliberately obstructed Tremayne's progress. He barged through them roughly, knocking several over. Two gendarmes, who had been smoking in a doorway, shouted and gave chase.

At the bottom of the hill the alley split into three. Two young boys stood at the junction, looking inquisitively down the street to the left. Tremayne turned and ran in that direction and slowed to a halt, catching his breath.

It was dark and dingy with many doors and passageways leading off. The lowlife could have gone anywhere. As he turned, the man jumped from the shadows, knife in hand. Tremayne blocked his arm and kneed him in the groin. As his opponent fell to the ground, he kicked him hard in the ribs and then the stomach. He bent over, grabbed him and, looking into the fierce staring eyes, punched him hard in the face.

'Who sent you?' Tremayne snarled, punching him in the face a second time. He fell back, unresponsive. Tremayne searched the two long pockets in the robe and found a packet of aromatic cigarettes and a piece of paper with writing scribbled on it. Standing up, he read it: *sanmar w5 23*. He didn't get to think further. A crack on the back of his head resounded like an explosion in his ears, his mind went into freefall, and then darkness.

When Harvey Tremayne started to drift back from unconsciousness, something was slapping his face, persistent and annoying like a mosquito buzzing in your ear during restless sleep. He waved his arm to get rid of it; he just wanted to drift back into darkness, but it wouldn't go away. Echoing in the distance was a voice that slowly became louder.

'Monsieur, Monsieur, comment allez vous? Are you alright?'

As he started to focus, the face of a gendarme materialised. 'Are you hurt, Monsieur?' he said, helping Tremayne to his feet. He would not have managed to get up on his own.

'I'm alright, I think.'

This was the last thing he needed. The bloody police.

'Have you been robbed, Monsieur?'

'Uh, no, I don't think so. I wasn't carrying anything valuable,' he said, attempting a smile.

'As long as nothing is missing, Monsieur. In future you should keep to the tourist areas.'

'Yes, thank you,' he said, exploring the painful lump growing on the back of his head. 'I'll be fine.'

After the gendarmes had gone, he felt his pockets. His wallet and passport were gone, and his holster was empty.

Tremayne took a circuitous route back to the hotel, contemplating his predicament. It was clear at least two Arabs were working for Indigo, Thug One in the light-coloured suit and Thug Two in the dark brown robe. Come to think of it, Thug One had probably ransacked his hotel room; he vaguely remembered seeing him.

The good news was that he could now recognise them both. The bad news was he'd lost his passport and gun, and more important his wallet and the precious photo. He'd have to contact Cartwright when he got back to the hotel. He'd be in danger without his gun, unable to pay his way without cash and stuck in Tangier without his passport. What a fuck-up!

Halfway to the hotel, he found a shady bench by a fountain. He washed some of the pain from his head with the crystal-clear, cool water and sat there for nearly an hour, partly dazed, part dozing. His mind drifted from the moment to another time, somewhere between memory and nightmare, and the last time his head had hurt this badly.

He was lying in a shell hole in a valley called Y Ravine, near Beaumont Hamel in the north of France in June 1918. His Company had led the attack on the German stronghold. They had gone over the top from Beaumont Trench and marched across no man's land under cover of a moving barrage of Royal Artillery shells. When they'd exploded just a hundred feet in front of his leading platoon, the noise was deafening and the flashes in the pitch-black night left bright blind spots in the eyes. As they approached the enemy stronghold, the shelling moved further ahead and the Germans, taking advantage of the lull, were scurrying out of their bunkers in swarms, like rats from a sinking ship.

Fighting was hand-to-hand, bayonet to bayonet, with grenades being traded by both sides. A mortar bomb landed just feet behind Tremayne and the concussion knocked him senseless, the dirt and soil thrown up, partially burying him. When he came to, the world was silent, and he wondered if he'd entered the afterlife. Then his ears started ringing, and something trapped in his skull was banging to get out. He was alive.

And then, the noise of the battle returned: screams, shouts, guns, grenades and shells. The sound reached a crescendo, the individual contributors indistinguishable from each other. Tremayne moved his head and some of the dirt fell away. In front, in the light of a falling magnesium flare fired high above the battle, he saw a slow-motion duel. Private Dixon, a soldier from his platoon and a German sergeant, hand-to-hand in a dance of death. When the flare died, everything went pitch-black. Another whooshed into the sky and burst into life, illuminating the sergeant standing over the body, wiping his knife. Tremayne stirred with the outrage of it. He wanted to scream but made no sound. He rose from his tomb and lunged towards the German. Realising he was still holding his revolver, he fired at point-blank range and the man fell back. Tremayne pulled the trigger again and again but the gun just clicked; he was out of ammunition. The man clutched his chest and Tremayne flung himself forward and landed with his knees in the sergeant's stomach, grabbed the arm holding the knife and swung at him with his revolver. The sergeant raised his arm in defence. He was a powerful man and even though dazed and wounded he pushed back, but he lacked the Herculean strength that blind rage brings. Tremayne lifted himself and with all his might brought his pistol down on the sergeant's head. Then again. And again. He screamed at the prostrate man, at the inhumanity, at the terror, and even louder to extol the revenge he had enacted.

He woke with a jolt and stared. He saw no German sergeant, no mutilated body, just pedestrians standing in the sunshine staring at him. He stood up, took a deep, gulping drink from the fountain, splashed his face and walked away.

When he arrived at the Straits Hotel, he picked up his key but instead of heading to his room he turned into Caid's Bar. His nerves were jagged and needed steadying.

'Tanqueray and tonic, please, Abdul. Make it a double. And a pack of ice, if you would.'

A tall, plump man in a crumpled grey suit, sitting in the corner, folded his newspaper and came over and sat beside him.

'Hello, Tremayne. I hear you had a spot of bother this afternoon.'

Tremayne turned to the voice.

'Oh, hello, Cartwright. A bit early to find you in the bar … even for a civil servant,' he said, not looking him in the eye.

'Now, now, don't be like that. I got a call to say a British businessman had been involved in a fight down in the Kasbah Quarter, and I thought, what idiot would be stupid enough to do that? And then I thought of you.'

'Fuck you, Cartwright.'

'Well, how are you? You don't look so good.'

'Apart from being bashed on the head, and robbed of my wallet, passport and revolver, everything's just fine, thanks.'

'I warned you about this, but you didn't listen, did you? You're bloody lucky there were gendarmes in the area, or you'd now be in the morgue.'

'Why are you here, Cartwright? To gloat and give me a lecture?'

'No, to tell you to be at the Diplomatic Country Club tonight for 7 pm. Richardson wants to see you. The car will pick you up at 6.30 pm, sharp.'

When Cartwright had gone, Tremayne thought about the call Cartwright had received. Who the hell would that have been? And who was Richardson? His head throbbed and it was too hard to think.

'Same again please, Abdul.'

Chapter 14

Office of the Foreign Secretary, Whitehall, London

Winston Churchill marched down the long corridor in the heart of the Foreign Office, a trail of smoke curling from the cigar gripped in his teeth. Without missing a step, he pushed open the mahogany door into the outer office of the British Foreign Secretary.

'Evening, Michaels. Don't get up – I'm expected,' he said, raising a hand. Before Michaels could stand, Churchill had barged into the minister's office.

Lord Halifax looked up and frowned.

'Sorry, sir, just a moment please,' he said, covering the mouthpiece of the phone with his hand. 'I haven't quite finished this call, Churchill. Would you mind waiting outside for a few minutes?'

'My dear Halifax, what could be more important than thwarting the Nazi threat against Britain and her allies?'

Churchill took off his coat and sat down in front of the large oak desk. He was going nowhere.

'Can I call you back, Prime Minister? Something has come up. Yes, thank you sir,' Halifax said.

Michaels was standing at the door, looking apologetic.

'Would you like Michaels to take your hat and coat, and what about a tea or coffee?'

'I'll have a cognac thank you. The sun's down in Delhi.'

Halifax nodded at Michaels. 'Make that two.' He had a feeling he was going to need it.

'I have spoken twice with Deputy Prime Minister Smuts, and this afternoon with Sir Ernest Oppenheimer.' Churchill sat back, grasping the lapels of his jacket.

Halifax guessed what was coming. 'And how did that go?' he asked.

'Halifax, you have a problem. It seems that Sir Ernest has an unresolved grievance that you failed to mention to me,' Churchill said, leaning forward in an accusative manner.

'And what might that be?' Halifax said, repositioning himself further back in the chair.

'He feels he has been treated contemptuously by your apologist government, and by your Prime Minister in particular,' Churchill said.

'And why might that be?' Halifax ventured.

'Being of German birth and the Jewish faith, he has friends and family that have experienced first-hand the appalling treatment of his fellow Jews. He has seen the ominous build-up of the Nazi war machine. He is concerned that in the last six months some of the diamonds sold by us to the United States have been sold on to Germany,' Churchill said, banging his hand on the table. 'Can you imagine such crass bloody stupidity? Oppenheimer has communicated this to Prime Minister Chamberlain, but he hasn't even been given the courtesy of a bloody reply.'

'But Churchill, we're not selling diamonds to Germany.'

'For Christ's sake, Halifax, wake up. Sir Alistair Wilson from MI6 sat in this very chair and told us of the Nazis' Achilles heel, and all the time we're indirectly selling diamonds to them. You haven't told me the whole truth, have you? It turns out that's exactly what's happening. We're an accessory to this heinous crime. Has Chamberlain done nothing to voice British displeasure to the Americans and stop this immoral business? Knowingly selling diamonds to the Nazis, to the enemy! What utter bloody madness! It's akin to a condemned man making the hangman's rope for him. He is now questioning the morality of selling diamonds to us!'

'Are you saying he's going to blackmail the British Government by refusing to sell diamonds to us?' Halifax said.

'Could you blame him? Perhaps, Halifax, we should have brought Oppenheimer into His Majesty's Government as the minister of common bloody sense. God knows we could do with at least one!' Churchill shouted, his face red.

In the silence that followed, Michaels laid a tray on the desk and poured two glasses of cognac.

'Christ, Michaels, is this stuff rationed? More …' Churchill said, holding out his glass.

Michaels filled the glass nearly to the top. Halifax declined the offer.

'So, what do you suggest is the way forward?' Halifax asked calmly, sipping his cognac.

Churchill took a large swig and relit his cigar.

'Many of the De Beers diamond mines have been closed since the Wall Street crash. The only significant production is coming from their low-cost, high-grade operations in South West Africa. While they produce gem-quality diamonds, a high percentage of their production is stones under half a carat in weight. Oppenheimer has agreed to increase production and sell us all the additional small-sized diamonds we need for industrial purposes.'

Churchill sat back and took a puff of his cigar.

'Now do tell me, Winston, for this he wants what?'

'That Britain will sell to the Americans all the diamonds they need under an international condition of sale that ensures the diamonds will not be sold on to any third-party country. That can't be too hard, now can it? That way the Americans are guaranteed all the diamonds they want.'

'Winston, that's blackmail!' Halifax said.

'It's called common sense, Halifax. Something this government sorely lacks.'

Churchill sat poker-faced, puffing on his cigar. Halifax poured himself some more cognac.

'And what about protecting the South West Africa coast, as we originally discussed?' Halifax asked.

'Smuts and Oppenheimer have requested our assistance with patrolling the diamond coast. The problem is that black-market industrial diamond prices have soared because of the demand for military manufacture. Illicit mining and theft from the operating mines has increased dramatically. It seems that most of the diamonds are smuggled to Germany.'

Churchill sat back and took another large swig of cognac, then relit his cigar.

'And?' Halifax said, knowing there was more to come.

'Well, I've agreed that His Majesty's Royal Navy will immediately send three motor torpedo boats from Simonstown naval base on the Cape Peninsula to Luderitz to help patrol the diamond coast. Oh yes, and I've agreed that we will relocate some of our senior naval intelligence staff from Cape Town to Luderitz.'

'You agreed that with him?'

'Yes, I gave him my word that you would approve it.'

Halifax snorted and shook his head, his brow furrowed. 'Are you serious, Churchill? You're in no position to agree to such a thing!'

'No, but you are, Halifax!'

Churchill stared at Halifax as a matador does a bull.

'There is one more thing,' he added.

Halifax looked at the ceiling, as if pleading to a higher authority.

'Oppenheimer has his key diamond security man in Tangier trying to infiltrate the smuggling pipeline through to Germany. Apparently, he's on to something but is not getting any help from the local consulate. He needs diplomatic and MI6 support. I told Sir Alistair Wilson that you had agreed he should provide him the necessary government support. His name is Harvey Tremayne.'

Churchill stared at Halifax, but he did not meet his eyes. The matador had delivered the sword to the bull's neck. The deed was done.

Chapter 15

Diplomatic Country Club, Rif Foothills, Tangier

The black Bentley arrived at the Straits Hotel promptly at 6.30 pm. The driver introduced himself to Tremayne as Mark Timpson and opened the back door for his passenger. Tremayne couldn't miss the gun holster on his driver's right hip.

After the minimum of pleasantries, he settled down in the back seat and looked at the terraces of square, squat, white and brown houses, tumbling down the hillside like children's play blocks. Leaving the city, the road to the Diplomatic Country Club twisted and turned as it gained height through the foothills of the Rif Mountains and up into the treeline. The city was laid out below, tinged purple, the Bay of Tangier shimmering in the last of the evening light. Tremayne had just dozed off when the car pulled up. He breathed in the cool air, laced with the scent of cedar, a welcome respite from the oppressive city heat. It was like a tonic and he felt his head clearing.

He was shown to a small alcove on one side of the member's lounge, furnished with plush brown leather chairs and a low mahogany table. Lighting a cigarette, he poured some iced water and took in the surroundings. The room had a high ornate ceiling with dark wood panelling on the walls. Smoke-stained oil paintings of once-famous racehorses hung ceremoniously on the walls. The large stone-dressed fireplace was full of dried flowers, and on a shelf to one side lay a stack of newspapers. Tremayne picked up the most recent copy of *The Times*; it was a week old. He read about the acrimonious debate between the different factions in the House of Commons, concerning the country's preparedness for war. It reported that Winston Churchill had given a rousing speech to the house, about the irrefutable evidence of the German arms build-up and the woeful lack of preparedness of the British Government. He claimed Chamberlain was trying to negotiate with Hitler, using an apologist Plan B. A group under Churchill was trying to bring to Parliament's attention the necessity for a more assertive Plan A.

Tremayne shook his head at the thought of yet another war.

'Hello, you must be Harvey Tremayne.'

'Uh, yes,' he said, getting to his feet, surprised at the female voice.

'My name is Charlotte Richardson,' she said, offering her hand. 'How's your head? I heard from Cartwright that you'd met with some trouble?'

'The butt of a pistol, if I'm not mistaken,' he said.

Tremayne studied her. Forty-ish, beautifully dressed, chestnut-coloured shoulder-length hair and a radiant complexion. An English rose if ever he'd seen one. He felt awkward, almost embarrassed, at the unexpected pleasure. He had become unused to attractive female company.

'Can I get you a drink, Miss Richardson? Monsieur?' a waiter asked.

'I'll have my usual, please,' she said.

'Tanqueray and tonic please – make it a double,' he said and sat back, absorbing her presence. 'Well, Miss Richardson, this *is* a surprise.'

'Why is that, Mr Tremayne? Were you expecting a man?'

He felt his cheeks tingle.

'I decided I wanted to meet you in person. After all, you are getting quite a reputation. You're giving Cartwright quite the runaround.'

'I expect he's here somewhere, spying on me.'

She looked at him with raised eyebrows and sat back and smiled. 'No. I've given him the night off.'

Tremayne looked her in the eye, searching for any hint of mockery, but there was none.

'We know all about you, Mr Tremayne. Mining engineer with De Beers and now an expert in diamond security and a trusted advisor to Sir Ernest Oppenheimer. How is your chest wound, by the way?'

Tremayne was trying to get to grips with the unexpected nature of the conversation. He rubbed the scar without thinking. Did the Secret Intelligence Service have a file on him? He felt defensive.

'So why did you invite me?' he asked, curtly.

'We'll come to that later. Tell me about yourself, what you did before joining De Beers.'

Tremayne looked at her. He was about to ask what this was all about, but on reflection he had nothing to lose. He had a drink in his hand, there was promise of a good meal and the company was pleasant.

'I was born in St Agnes in Cornwall and went to boarding school in Sherborne and before going on to study at Camborne School of Mines I was in the army for a year, in France. That was a bloodbath. We lost nearly half our battalion, I came close to catching one on several occasions, but somehow, I survived,' he said, his voice faltering.

He cleared his throat and sat up straight, avoiding the emotional precipice that had just opened up in his mind. He cursed himself. He knew better than to talk about his war with people who had no idea of the horrors.

He glanced up at her and felt as though Charlotte Richardson was assessing him, searching for his weaknesses. Well, she's certainly found that one, he thought.

Changing the subject, Tremayne said, 'This is a nice place. How do you become a member?'

'Oh, Mr Tremayne we're very selective here, I'm afraid,' she said with a dismissive smile and a slight wave of the hand.

Despite the put-down he felt comfortable. There was something about her. He liked her demeanour and her understated beauty. The pearls she wore over her blue blouse emphasised her shapely figure.

'Tell me about the work you do.'

Tremayne lit a cigarette and sat back.

'I joined De Beers in 1923 and worked at the Kimberley Central Mine. The kimberlite pipe that contains the diamonds was discovered in 1871 and thousands of miners dug a huge open-cut mine with picks and shovels. But it soon became too deep and dangerous to continue mining from the surface. They sank shafts to be able to mine more safely from underground, but the mining methods weren't very productive. My job was to develop a new mining system. That was fortuitous because by the time the financial crash came in 1929, it was one of the few De Beers underground mines still operating at a profit.

'And that created a big problem with diamond smuggling. Theft has been endemic since the day diamonds were first discovered. Being the only big operating mine, the smugglers became very brazen and inventive. The mine had a double perimeter security fence, with guards and dogs patrolling in between. The smugglers developed all kinds of ploys: using catapults to shoot small bags of diamonds over the fence, carrier pigeons to do the same, hiding diamonds in false compartments in their lunch boxes – you name it, they tried it. We clamped down on all of that and then they started hiding diamonds about their person. Sometimes they swallowed them or simply inserted them … well, you can imagine where they hid them,' he said, looking up apologetically.

She held his gaze, fascinated to hear of the dark underbelly of the otherwise glamourous diamond business.

'I developed a system of random checks so that no one knew when they were going to be searched. With a lengthy jail sentence for theft, only the very hardened individuals continued, and they were invariably caught.

'In 1936, I was transferred to South West Africa to expand mine production. During the great depression nearly all of them were closed, and illicit diamond mining had become commonplace. It was carried out by the colonial Germans who were taking what they felt was rightfully theirs.

'For a while we had a former World War 1 French pilot take aerial pictures as they had done on the front line, and it was amazing to see the number of trial pits they had dug. By taking regular photos we could spot the new excavations and it was very effective until, one day, he crashed his plane. But by then we had increased Security Diamond Police patrols.

'In the early days, there were diamonds everywhere. They had been washed onto the beaches and, being heavier than the sand, became concentrated in gullies and channels. When you know the land, and what to look for, you can find them just a few feet below surface. Some of those diamond-rich pockets had to be seen to be believed. Literally a sparkling diamond gravel.

'But give them their due, they knew how to find the very best pockets. We always made a point of mining the whole area after locating an illegal digging. It was invariably a rich spot.

'Once illegal mining was curtailed, they resorted to theft from the Lewala Mine. That's where the central processing plant is located. We mined high-grade diamondiferous gravel beds in many heavily guarded locations across the Forbidden Zone and took the material there to be processed. They tried the same tactics as they had at Kimberley, but I was wise to that and we reduced theft to a trickle. But someone wasn't happy about that. Earlier this year my wife and I were attacked in Luderitz. I was shot in the back and left for dead ... and Eleanor was ... well, not so lucky.'

Tremayne rubbed his chest, taking a swig of his drink. 'I've been convalescing in Cape Town for most of the last six months. By rights I shouldn't be here.'

'I'm really very sorry,' Richardson said.

Again, he looked her in the eye, but he could not read her expression.

'We know colonial resistance fighters were behind it. It was a revenge attack,' he said, clearing his throat. 'For all the smugglers I put in jail.'

'So, tell me, have any of the men who did this been caught?' she asked.

Tremayne shook his head. 'No, not yet. During interrogation of suspects after the shooting, one name came up several times, a man in Tangier who handled the diamonds. He is known as Indigo. If I can find him and make him talk, I can get to the leader of the smuggling ring back in Luderitz and find out who killed Eleanor. That's why I'm here, Miss Richardson. I'm on a mission. I have a personal score to settle with this Indigo … and his murderous friends.'

'Well, so far, Mr Tremayne, you haven't been very successful, have you? A complaint of assault on a citizen at Café Taouz, and now you've been robbed of your passport, wallet and revolver.'

Tremayne pursed his lips; he felt as if he'd been slapped. He stirred from the cosiness of the pleasant company and the drink. He lit a cigarette and leaned forward, peering at her through the smoke.

'Listen, Miss Richardson' – he almost spat out the words – 'I've been robbed twice and beaten up, and quite frankly I don't seem to be getting any help from the British Consulate. Sir Ernest was told by the Consul General that I would receive the necessary support. I have communicated with him that I have not. If Cartwright has been given that job then I'd rather work alone.'

There was a silence. Tremayne could see indecision in her eyes.

'With or without your help I will find Indigo. He's going to regret ever crossing De Beers, and me in particular.'

She sat back, turning her empty glass in her hands.

Leaning forward she said, 'Well, Mr Tremayne, perhaps we can work together. I need your help, and in return I have something to offer you.'

'Miss Richardson, what do you have that I could possibly want?'

He couldn't help himself. He deliberately looked her up and down, taking in the curves of her body. He knew it was wrong.

Charlotte Richardson's cheeks flushed. She put her empty glass to her lips.

In the silence that followed he wondered why he'd done such a bloody stupid thing! But he knew. He was on the back foot and she had the upper hand. It was like the kick from a spiteful child. But she did have something he wanted, and that feeling, having been dormant for months, came as a surprise.

He knocked back the last of his drink and looked at her and said, 'I'm listening.'

'I need you to feed me your information, Mr Tremayne. The British Government is concerned about the supply of diamonds from South West Africa to German industry. Their military build-up relies on a regular source of diamonds. We're after the same people but for different reasons.'

'I work for De Beers. Why doesn't the government do its own dirty work?'

She went to sip her drink and realised again that it was empty. She beckoned to the waiter.

'Mr Tremayne, you're obviously a man of the world. The British Government cannot be seen to be actively working against a sovereign nation. We get other people to do that for us.'

There was a long pause as Tremayne thought about it.

'So, what would I get in return?' he said.

'A word in the ear of the chief of police for a start. And what about a passport, money and gun? You won't settle any scores without them, will you? I should point out that getting a replacement British passport in Tangier through the normal channels can take a damnably long time.'

Chapter 16

Café Paris, Place Petit Socco, Tangier

Salamon Zaber was seated at his desk, staring out the window, the small element of doubt that he'd held on to now vanquished. Three items lay in front of him: a British passport, a calfskin wallet and a Webley Mk IV.38 calibre revolver. From inside the wallet he pulled out a wad of francs, a gun permit for the Tangier International Zone, and a letter of introduction signed by Sir Ernest Oppenheimer.

Also in the wallet was a head-and-shoulders photograph of an attractive young blonde woman. If that was who he thought it was, losing that was really going to anger Tremayne. He wondered if he should anonymously return it to the hotel.

The passport belonged to Harvey Petroc Tremayne, the De Beers General Manager who had been assassinated but was now resurrected from the dead. Had Jager shot the wrong man? Or perhaps Tremayne really was a Tokolosh, an evil spirit that could not be killed?

The consequences churned in his mind. He should inform Moussa, but he was trying to avoid that. There was no telling how that little German weasel might react.

Scorpion would also have to be informed. He'd fired the shots that had killed Tremayne, and the woman. That was the fuck-up. Where it had all gone wrong. He had claimed she saw his face and would have been able to identify him. Zaber suspected he might have enjoyed doing what he did and used that as an excuse. There were rumours that she had been sexually assaulted.

Now Tremayne was very much alive and looking to find those responsible. He had to be stopped, but how to do that in Tangier? Perhaps arrange a meeting up in the Rif Mountains and dump him into one of the many inaccessible ravines? Or get him down to the port at night on some pretext and have Ahmed slit his throat?

He would have to think through the options. There would only be one chance, and it would need to be soon.

Chapter 17

Guano Bay, Diaz Peninsula, South West Africa

Far to the west of Luderitz stands the desolate Diaz Point, named for Bartholomew Diaz, the Portuguese explorer and the first European to visit the spot in 1488. It is the northern tip of a rocky, mean peninsula that thrusts arrogantly out into the ocean. The South Atlantic breakers test this arrogance by continually probing the reefs and cliffs. Huge waves rise up with malign intent, only to be knocked back time and again in thundering, chaotic, foaming fury.

To the south west of the peninsula lies Guano Bay, an isolated and more sheltered location. Lying offshore, Halifax Island protects it from the worst of the ocean's anger. The sea is a beautiful clear turquoise blue when the sun shines and a slick steel grey under the fog. It is protected from the worst of the south-west winds by the high, rocky Black Ridge that sits like a scar across the base.

The bay is named for the deposits of bird and seal excrement that had accumulated over the millennia. The lack of rainfall and the blowtorch heat of the sun dried and hardened the deposits into what was often referred to as 'white gold'. Discovered in the mid-nineteenth century, guano was used as a valuable source of agricultural fertiliser in Europe and North America. Fortunes were made, but within a few years the deposits were exhausted, and the area was abandoned.

Gannets, cormorants, gulls and oystercatchers still nest noisily on the cliffs and ridges, thousands of them squabbling with their neighbours and trampling their chicks underfoot. They are attracted by the plentiful fish and crustacea that thrive in the nutrient-rich Benguela Current. Cape Fur seals breed here in large numbers, filling the beach at the north end of the bay with a cacophony of barking and bad-tempered bullying. Even when you can't see them, you can hear them, and when you can't hear them you can still smell them. Jackass penguins share the same sandy beach, like drunken old men in dinner jackets, running the gauntlet through the blubbery bickering.

Pods of dolphins and porpoises are regular visitors. Humpback, baleen and southern right whales often calve in the shelter of the bay and, always, the great white sharks patrol, searching for an opportunistic meal, their black dorsal fins often seen cutting the surface. Onshore, jackals and hyenas do the same, patrolling the beaches for the dead and dying.

There are few signs of human activity, just five near-derelict cottages, set back above the silver-white beach in the lee of Black Ridge. They are sometimes used during the season by local Nama fisherman, people of small stature, wizened by the harsh, unrelenting climate, but the toughest and most resilient of people.

Originally painted white, the small huddle of buildings is now grimy grey, the once thatched roofs replaced with rusty sheets of galvanised iron, streaked white with bird droppings. There are no roads to the settlement at Guano Bay. If you want to get there, and there is no reason on earth to do so, you go by sea. No reason, that is, except perhaps to hide. It afforded Christoff Jager the kind of seclusion that he needed, his only neighbour a Nama woman and her two daughters.

As the blistering heat of day waned over the desert, the wind dropped and the grey Benguela fog inched towards shore. The setting sun was extinguished in the fog bank, leaving an eerie orange light across the horizon. Within an hour it had enveloped Jager's cottage and he lit two oil lamps and shut the windows and door. It consisted of a single spartan room with a compacted dirt floor and a cast-iron stove in the middle of the long wall perched on some stone slabs hewn from Black Ridge. In this often foggy, salt-laden climate, everything made of iron corroded in an instant, and the stove was streaked and bubbled with rust. Opposite was a wooden-framed bed and at the far end a table and three chairs. His meagre wardrobe of clothes hung from hooks behind the stove to keep them dry and stop them going mouldy. A crossbow was set on the wall above the bed. To one side, a wooden ladder led up to a small open loft in the roof space, used only for storage and occasional visitors. The heat from the stove made the loft warm, but the wisps of smoke that regularly escaped resulted in a smog in the roof space that could be cut with a knife. Jager slept downstairs.

He stoked the leaky stove with sun-bleached driftwood, giving the pot on top a stir. He tasted the contents and added more salt. Falkie watched intently from his perch by the door.

'You won't like this, Falkie. It's stew.'

Above the stove hung strips of dried salted fish and game meat. Jager reached up and cut off a slice of springbok biltong.

'Here you go, boy. You like that, don't you?' Falkie grabbed the piece, holding it in his yellow talons, and ripped it to shreds, swallowing it in large pieces.

After his meal of fish stew and black bread, Jager cleared the table and went through his nightly ritual. He lifted one of the black stone slabs under the stove to expose a small cubby lined with driftwood planks. It was the hiding place for his prized possessions: diamonds, money and his Luger pistol – and its silencer. Reaching in, he retrieved two leather bags. He carefully tipped the contents on to the table, the diamonds tinkling as they rolled. Even in the dull yellow of the oil lamps, pinpoints of light radiated into the darkest recesses of the room. Falkie watched with interest, bobbing his head from side to side.

Jager chuckled. 'Not for you, Falkie. These are for our friend Horst. He says one day we'll get our land back and we'll be rich, and you can have all the fresh meat and lady falcons you want. We'll have a big house in town up on the hill by the church on Diamantbergstrasse.'

Falkie bobbed his head as if in approval.

Jager worked through the pile of diamonds, judging the quality of each stone. He then totalled the number of carats. He already knew the figures. It was just a ritual, a reminder of his and his comrades' contribution to getting their beloved homeland back.

Jager was the leader of the local Red Commando, set up by his old friend Horst Nissen of Abwehr II. It was formed from the local members of the Adlerflagge Syndicate. In return for the industrial and small and medium-sized diamonds, Nissen, codenamed Sidewinder, provided them with Morse transceivers, guns, ammunition and explosives – plus a selection of German hard liquor and tinned food. Nissen looked after his friends in Red Commando.

Jager's two lieutenants in the commando force were Karl Bosman and Siegfried 'Siggie' Moritz, who both worked on the mine. Jager was responsible for the collection and delivery of the smuggled stones. He would rendezvous monthly with a trawler, codenamed Neptune, transfer the diamonds and receive cash, weapons and provisions in return. The large gem diamonds were valued and sold by his old friend in Tangier, Salamon Zaber, codename Indigo. They had been imprisoned together during World War 1 and had struck up a close bond in those tough years and had plotted and schemed about getting their revenge on the British and their South African lackeys.

The most valuable diamonds were stolen by Siggie Moritz, who worked in the sorting plant at the Lewala Mine. Here they recovered the largest and highest quality stones by a process of washing and screening, then passing the cleaned coarse sand and gravel over stainless steel tables covered in grease. By some miracle of nature, diamonds stuck to the grease and the valueless sand and gravel did not. It was then a simple matter of scraping off the diamond-laden grease, heating the mixture to separate them, and then reusing the grease.

The carrier pigeons were smuggled into the mine by Karl Bosman. He attached a small bag containing the stolen diamonds and released the pigeon at a designated time on an agreed date. Jager caught the pigeons using Falkie. It worked like clockwork, or at least it had done until the last time.

Now he had recurring nightmares about his journey, escaping from the Forbidden Zone and sailing back to Guano Bay. In the dream, his boat had a huge hole in the bottom, and he had to bail for all he was worth. And then the police sergeant would appear up through the hole with his arms outstretched. At that point he'd always wake with a start, sometimes with Falkie screeching in alarm.

He rubbed his face and checked his watch, then repacked the diamonds and returned them to their hiding place. He removed the Luger and put it under his pillow.

'Got to be careful, Falkie. There are diamond thieves about,' he said, with a chuckle.

Fifteen minutes before the scheduled transmission, Jager poured a large glass of fine Bavarian *kirschwasser*, cherry schnapps, and took a swig. His eyes involuntarily squeezed shut at the pleasure, and as the warmth permeated his body, he took a second swig.

From under the bed, he pulled out a well-worn canvas-covered box and placed it on the table. It was the latest model of portable Morse transceiver, used by Abwehr operatives and agents. Often disguised inside a suitcase, this one was fitted inside a military-grade waterproof metal box. The moist salt-laden air would otherwise have rendered it inoperable within days.

The case had four compartments. There was a receiver for picking up messages and a transmitter for sending them. To one side was the battery and charging unit and in the other, spare diodes, headphones and a Morse key.

He connected the wire aerial that ran up a tall wooden pole fixed to the end of his cottage. Fitting a small crank-handle into the slot on the charging unit, he wound it for a minute to charge the battery, then switched it on to warm up the diodes.

Taking another swig of schnapps, he put on the headphones and consulted a small book that contained the codenames used to scramble the messages. At the allotted time, he started to tap out his message using the Morse key.

Scorpion to Neptune.
He waited.
Neptune receiving.
Parcel ready for transfer.
Scorpion rendezvous Moby one mile west of Halifax as scheduled.
Jager wondered if he'd heard that correctly? That didn't sound right.
Repeat rendezvous Moby.
Confirm rendezvous Moby
Understood, Scorpion out.
Good luck. Neptune out.
Jager sat back and took a large swig.

'Well, well, Falkie,' he said, scratching his stubble. 'There's a turn-up for the books. The rendezvous is not with the fishing boat. This time they're sending a U-boat. I wonder what that's about.'

As he packed away the radio there was a knock on the door.

'Me, Baas,' a voice said.

'Wait,' he shouted, making sure the box was properly hidden.

He opened the door. It was the Nama woman who lived three cottages along the beach with her two daughters. Almost destitute, she scraped a meagre living out of catching crayfish and washing Jager's clothes; and selling her daughters' favours. She grinned at him, exposing black and missing teeth, her breath stinking of liquor.

'You want Joaba tonight?'

Joaba was about fifteen or sixteen years old with pale brown skin, a slightly angular pretty face, and fair curly hair that gave away her mixed parentage. Jager guessed she'd been fathered by one of the many Scandinavian whalers that visited Luderitz each year. The dress she was wearing was just a collection of patches.

'She washed, she clean, I seen to her,' the woman said. Jager gave the woman a coin, beckoned the girl in and bolted the door.

'Joaba you do what Baas say,' her mother shouted from outside.

The girl cowered by the bed with her arms tight to her chest, staring at the floor. She knew what was coming. Jager walked over to the falcon and put a leather hood over his head and tied the straps.

'Now, Falkie, we don't want to upset you with all the goings-on, do we, hey? Best you sleep now.'

Chapter 18

Medina Quarter, Tangier

Harvey Tremayne arrived early at the British Consulate. He had his photograph taken and filled in a passport application. In a small office on the first floor he signed more paperwork and received an envelope full of cash, billed to De Beers in Kimberley. He wrote a report to Sir Ernest Oppenheimer on his investigations, taking advantage of the diplomatic bag via London to Cape Town. As Cartwright had said, 'trust nothing and no one in Tangier.'

He had been given a new Enfield snub-nose revolver, smaller than the Webley he'd had stolen but it still fitted his shoulder holster. All markings had been removed so it could not be traced. It was only accurate over short distances, but it was better than nothing.

As he was escorted from office to office, he wondered if he would meet Charlotte Richardson. He had enjoyed her company at the Diplomatic Country Club and thought it would be nice to have dinner with her again. But he knew he was kidding himself. She hadn't shown the slightest bit of interest; in fact, just the opposite.

As Tremayne waited for the final documents he thought about his next move. His only lead was the two thugs who had been targeting him. It was more than a coincidence that they happened to be at Café Taouz at the very time of his meeting. They had to be working for Indigo.

He had an appointment with Cartwright's contact in the Tangier Customs Police at noon and decided to leave early and go via Place Petit Socco and Café Taouz. He had a feeling the waiter there knew more than he was letting on. Perhaps he might even be lucky enough to meet the thugs again and get his revenge.

When the waiter saw him sitting at the same seat at Café Taouz, he stopped in his tracks, as if he'd walked into an invisible wall. He nervously looked around and went back inside. Tremayne followed.

'Monsieur, please, you should not be here. It is not safe,' the waiter said, in a state of near panic.

'Tell me about this man you call Rasputin,' Tremayne said, pulling out a wad of five-franc notes.

'Monsieur, it is more than my life is worth,' he said, almost in tears. 'They said they would kill me if I talk to you.'

'Tell me, and this is yours and I'm gone,' Tremayne said, waving the notes in the man's face.

The waiter eyed the money and looked around furtively. 'I have heard him spoken of as Salamon Zaber.'

'Why is this Salamon Zaber such a bad man? What does he do?'

'I don't know, Monsieur. He deals in the black market, I think.'

'Does the name Indigo mean anything to you?'

'No, Monsieur,' he said, shaking his head, looking Tremayne in the eye.

'And the Arab in the white suit, with the cut ear, who was here yesterday?'

'He works for Monsieur Zaber,' he said. 'He is the one who threatened me.'

'His name?'

'I don't know, Monsieur. Please, he will kill me.'

'Do you want me to go over to Café Paris and tell Monsieur Zaber you and I just had a nice chat?' Tremayne snarled.

The waiter's eyes rolled back in their sockets and his legs buckled. Tremayne caught him and leaned him against a table for support and slapped him across the cheek.

'His name, damn you,' Tremayne said, shaking him.

The waiter shook his head and started to focus.

'He is known as Fouad.'

'And the other one in the brown robe?' Tremayne said.

'I don't know.'

'The name?' Tremayne said, slapping him again.

'Ahmed, I think, I do not know him.'

'Where can I find them?'

The waiter stared, eyes like saucers, tears running down his cheeks. Tremayne raised his hand again.

'Rue Khatami, red house, top floor,' the waiter gabbled, before the hand could strike him.

Tremayne tucked the wad of notes in the waiter's shirt pocket and left.

As he walked to his noon rendezvous, Tremayne took stock of this new information. He could now recognise the two lowlifes who robbed him. Thug One in the white suit was called Fouad and Thug Two in the brown robe was Ahmed. They worked for the owner of Café Paris, who was called Salamon Zaber. Well, after two days, he was finally making progress. Now he needed to prove that Indigo and Zaber were one and the same person.

He arrived at the gardens of Borj al-Hajoui a few minutes early. Situated on the steep hillside overlooking the harbour, he found the meeting place on one of the cultivated terraces under the shade of a large argan tree. Sitting on the cool stone seat, he took in the sparkling waters of the Bay of Tangier laid out before him.

'Monsieur Tremayne?' a man said. 'I am Sergeant Youssoufi.'

Sergeant Mustafa Youssoufi worked for the Tangier Customs Police. He was in his early fifties, tall and lean, with slightly stooped shoulders. His sun-wrinkled face was topped by a red fez and he wore a newly laundered white suit and leather sandals.

'Thank you for coming at such short notice, Sergeant Youssoufi. Philip Cartwright from the consulate recommended you. I need some information please.'

'I will help if I can, Monsieur,' he said, bowing his head.

'I'm investigating the smuggling of stolen diamonds. They probably come into Tangier by ship from South West Africa. Are you perhaps aware of any consignments of diamonds arriving from there?'

Tremayne looked at Youssoufi, who was studying the ground, rolling a stone around with his foot.

'If a boat brings in stolen diamonds, they will not be on the ship's manifest. They'll be hidden amongst the cargo,' Youssoufi said. 'It would be like finding a flea on a camel.'

Tremayne eyed the sergeant, who still rolled the stone.

'Yes, but every boat has to declare its port of departure on the ship's log, doesn't it?' Tremayne added.

'Monsieur, the ports and ships in West Africa are a law unto themselves,' Youssoufi said, spreading his hands dismissively.

'Can you get me a list of the ships that have docked in Tangier who record Walvis Bay or Swakopmund as their port of embarkation?'

'I do not have such information, Monsieur, but I can find out,' Youssoufi said.

'Thank you, Sergeant. This information is very important. The money made selling these diamonds goes to buy arms for the colonial resistance fighters. Innocent people have been killed, and the trader based here is complicit in this. I intend to find him and, if he cooperates, bring him to justice.'

'And if he doesn't cooperate?'

Tremayne stared unblinking at Youssoufi.

'Can I count on your help?' Tremayne asked.

Youssoufi nodded. 'As long as you stay within the law, Monsieur.'

'By the way, if you do find a diamond manifest with the name of Indigo on it, I would very much appreciate a copy.'

Tremayne caught the slightest tic of recognition in the corner of Youssoufi's eye.

'If I find a document with that name on it, I will make a copy.'

'Well thank you, Sergeant Youssoufi. I look forward to seeing some documentation. You can leave a message at the Straits Hotel and I will call you,' Tremayne said, holding out a roll of twenty-franc notes. Then he paused. 'Oh yes, one last thing. Have you heard of a black-market dealer called Salamon Zaber, who owns Café Paris on Place Petit Socco?'

Youssoufi looked up, opened his mouth to speak, but stopped. Tremayne could see his mind racing, trying to recover his composure.

'It is not a name I have heard,' Youssoufi replied, shaking his head. But his expression said it all.

You wouldn't make a good poker player, Tremayne thought.

Youssoufi bowed and took the money.

Tremayne sat down again on the stone bench and lit a cigarette. Why would Youssoufi, the man recommended by Cartwright, lie to him? How was he involved in all this? He knew a hell of a lot more than he was letting on. Perhaps Cartwright had warned him to be careful of the De Beers man, or was there more to it?

Chapter 19

West of Halifax Island, South West Africa

For days, the fog bank had waited out to sea, only changing form and colour as the sun rose and set. Today the wind direction had shifted, just a degree or two but discernible to the experienced sailor. This was the trigger for it to roll onshore and smother the desert coast.

Jager glanced at his watch. Still another thirty minutes before his rendezvous with Moby, and for that he had to have good visibility. Overhead an albatross checked him out, swooping over the boat, heading south at speed, wings motionless.

From Guano Bay, Jager had sailed south-west, between Halifax Island and the mainland, manoeuvring between jagged reefs that cut through the narrow channel. This was only possible in good visibility and calm sea. He took one last back-bearing on the fading Diaz Point lighthouse, the land disappearing and reappearing as the swell carried the boat. Satisfied he was in the right area, he lowered the sail and waited.

As the sun touched the horizon, the fog bank, now a little closer, glowed like an orange wall. Jager had experienced this dramatic spectacle many times before, but why again today? Why now? He'd have to make the rendezvous as short as possible or he'd be fogbound on the return journey.

He buttoned up his jacket, pulled his black woollen hat down over his ears and put on his gloves. It was going to be a cold wait. A swig of cherry schnapps from his hipflask put some fire in his belly and gave a warm glow.

At the allotted time, he flashed a signal with his torch, waited a minute and did the same again. He repeated this a few minutes later and waited as he was lulled by the swell, the boat lifting and falling, up and down.

On his port side the water rippled. He watched nervously, checking for a telltale dorsal fin, and rowed away a few strokes to keep his distance. The ripple turned into a torrent and slowly the visitor took form. Masts, a conning tower, deck mounted gun, then the massive hull. As the U-boat surfaced, water cascaded off in all directions, its decal, U-46, large and bold. It looked ominous, a huge grey fighting whale, just like its namesake. But this was no nemesis; these were Jager's kindred folk, his German comrades, coming to champion his fight to reclaim a stolen land.

Figures appeared on the conning tower and shouts were exchanged. Jager rowed closer and was thrown a rope. Friendly hands helped him on board. He climbed up the conning tower and dropped down through the hatch into the bowels of the submarine. After the pure, fresh South Atlantic air, the stench of confined living was like raw sewage, and it caught in his throat. He held his fist to his mouth and swallowed hard, eyes closed.

'You must be Scorpion? I am Kapitänleutnant Sohler,' a man said, as they shook hands.

'Good to meet you, sir,' Jager said.

'Come, I have a special visitor who joined us in Lobito Bay. Let's go and talk business,' Sohler said.

Stooping, they walked down a narrow corridor to a small cubicle. Sohler pushed aside the curtain and Jager entered. The interior was spartan, with just a bunk, drop-down desktop and a chair.

'Ah, my God, Horst, what the hell are you doing here?' Jager said, and they embraced with much back-slapping. 'Are you fucking lost again? You never could navigate!' They laughed raucously.

'It is good to see you, Christo. It's been more than a year,' Nissen said.

Sohler banged three glasses on the table and poured schnapps.

'So, Horst, what brings you down here? This is a surprise,' Jager said.

'I have orders for you. This is the big one, my friend.'

Jager was intrigued.

'Christo, the Third Reich needs diamonds, lots of diamonds.'

'Well, since you asked,' Jager said with a smile, reaching in his rucksack and pulling out one large and two small bags.

'Close to five thousand carats of top-quality stones, and nearly twice that amount of industrial,' he said with a grin.

Sohler let one of the small bags tumble open on the table and whistled. Beams of light radiated around the cabin.

'Hell, these are beautiful … Very nice,' Nissen said. 'I'll have them in Lobito Bay in two days and they'll be on their way to Tangier next week.'

He did not mention to Jager that his friend Salamon Zaber was no longer going to receive the largest stones. There was too much riding on this raid. It was better left unsaid.

He handed a leather wallet to Jager, who opened it and fingered through the thick wad of South African pounds. He gave the two men a broad grin.

'Christo, we need a lot more diamonds than this,' Nissen said.

'What sort of quantity?' Jager asked, swigging his schnapps.

'About two tons!' Nissen said, holding his gaze.

Jager tried to speak, but the last trickle of schnapps caught in his throat and no words came out. He pushed the glass forward for a refill, coughing.

When he'd recovered, he said, 'Two tons is nearly six months' production at the Lewala Mine. How the hell do you propose we smuggle that quantity?'

'We're not going to smuggle them. We're going to steal them.'

Jager stared, his schnapps glass stopped halfway to its destination.

'You have written orders,' Nissen said, with a grin.

He handed over a small cream-coloured envelope sealed in three places with bright red wax. Jager couldn't make out the stamp imprinted on the seal.

'I have to make sure you read this in my presence and then we destroy it.'

Jager downed the schnapps, opened the envelope and pulled out a single piece of paper.

Operation Benguela

Agent Scorpion,

The Third Reich is about to create a new world order that will restore the honour and glory of the German people, wherever in the world they may live. The Fatherland calls upon the brave patriots of German South West Africa to deliver two tons of diamonds to Hamburg within four weeks. You will take orders from Agent Sidewinder. In return, and in due course, the Fatherland will show its gratitude.

Heil Hitler
Orders of Generalfeldmarschall Hermann Göring.

'Christ, this comes from Göring himself,' Jager exclaimed.

He finished his schnapps and looked at Nissen, realising that the signature on the letter made it a command.

'But two tons, Horst. That's a hell of an ask!'

'Well there you are, Christo. This is the big one for you and Red Commando.'

While the pair worked through the plan of attack, the crew loaded munitions and provisions into Jager's boat. Jager was delighted that his friend Horst would be with them for the attack. On the 24th, Neptune was to dock in Swakopmund and that night would load the men of Blue and Green Commando. At first light on the 25th they were to rendezvous with U-46 two miles offshore and Nissen would transfer to the trawler. They would meet with Jager and Bosman at Seal Harbour on Possession Island that evening. There they would plan the final details of the raid and the commandos would use the deserted island to practise the attack on the 26th.

U-46 would remain offshore from Possession Island to provide military backup, but only in case of an emergency. Nissen stressed that the Third Reich must not be seen to be involved. This had to be an internal South West Africa operation.

A rating knocked and looked in through the curtain to say that the fog was getting thicker and the visitor needed to depart.

'I can't emphasise how important this is, Christo. We must succeed. I think you know the consequences if we fail, for both of us! We even have a modified set of codes for Operation Benguela, for both radio and Morse. Take my book and memorise and destroy,' Nissen said.

Jager glanced at the small book, its maroon cover stamped on the front with the Nazi black eagle.

'I'll message Cobra to come over to Guano Bay with Siggie Moritz so we can plan the details of the raid,' he said. 'We have a lot to work out. We'll brief you and the other commandos on Neptune at Seal Harbour on the 25th.'

Bidding Nissen and the crew *auf Wiedersehen*, he climbed back in the boat. After the stuffy confines of the submarine, the cold, damp, clean air bit into his lungs and he shivered. Under a spotlight on the conning tower he fixed his oars and pulled away. Within seconds the submarine was gone, just a swirl of white water left in its place, and that in turn quickly disappeared. It was as if the rendezvous had never happened. Wisps of fog drifted around him, like octopus tentacles searching for prey, and he felt a tinge of panic. No stars, no light, just his torch, and all the time, the mighty Benguela Current was pushing him north past Halifax Island.

Without any reference points to navigate by, he initially resolved to spend a cold, miserable night at sea, waiting for daylight. But then over his left shoulder he heard a familiar distant booming. The Diaz Point foghorn was sending out its warning to those mariners foolish enough to be at sea. It was like a siren song leading him to home and safety.

There was no way he could set his sail, so he started to row towards the sound. But the boat disobeyed his pull on the oars. There was a bump and the boat swung alarmingly. He pulled out his torch and shone it over the inky water. Something cut the surface and disappeared into the blackness just yards away. Then there was a second, much harder bump. His heart thumped, his breathing shallow. He pulled hard on the oars, but the loaded boat was heavy and slow. Another bump and the heat drained from his body. He shone the torch. There was movement right beside the boat. Then a dead eye reflected back, cold, menacing and searching. From deep in his chest, panic erupted into a shout. He pulled out his Luger and fired blindly at the intruder. Seconds later and he was alone again, his nightmare disappeared into the blackness. But it was still there somewhere.

He rowed hard for another ten minutes, keeping the booming foghorn off his right shoulder, his lungs burning, his arms fighting through the pain. When he heard waves crashing on rocks, he rowed further south and caught the stench of the seal colony. Ten minutes later with the smell gone and the softer sound of waves breaking on the beach, he knew he was near home. He could make out the phosphorescence of the breaking waves and a few yards from shore he jumped over the side into the icy water, holding on to the bow rope. The shock of the cold took his breath away, and the boat bucked like a wild horse. He could barely hold on and was about to let go when a large wave dumped them both on the beach. He fell face down, gasping for breath, his hands digging in and grasping at the sand. The image of that cold, dead, staring eye etched in his mind.

Chapter 20

British Consulate, Rue Amerique du Sud, Tangier

Charlotte Richardson put the phone down and contemplated the discussion she'd just had with Sir Alistair Wilson. He had briefed her on the latest British intelligence that indicated the Germans were now critically short of diamonds, something His Majesty's Government wished to exploit. MI6 had been put on the highest response level to do whatever was necessary to ensure their supply chains were cut or at least compromised. The Foreign Secretary, Lord Halifax, had made it clear that the British Consulate in Tangier was to offer the De Beers man Harvey Tremayne their full support. He had to find out who was involved in the German smuggling ring – names, locations and the ships they used. As much information as possible.

To help achieve this, Tremayne must be provided with diplomatic immunity and given access to the military resources of the British Government. A letter of engagement from Sir Alistair would arrive for her in tomorrow's diplomatic bag. He was to be seconded to Section D of MI6. She had to make sure that he signed it immediately, whatever it took. His current employer, Sir Ernest Oppenheimer, fully supported this assignment.

She was to see to it that he was given every assistance. His investigation in Tangier had to be brought to a swift and successful conclusion. He was urgently needed in South West Africa.

Naval Intelligence had picked up coded messages along the coast of the Forbidden Zone that were of military origin. The little they had deciphered was in German. The Nazis were up to something and it had to involve diamonds.

The consulate was to arrange the flights to get him to Luderitz. There he was to report to Commander Mike Crosson, Head of Naval Intelligence. Sir Alistair was not going to commit this to paper. She had to memorise this and pass it on verbally.

When she put the phone down, Charlotte Richardson felt a strange sense of disappointment. She barely knew Tremayne, yet she would miss him. Something had happened when they'd met. There had been a connection. It had been a long time since she'd felt such an affinity with someone. For years she'd had an empty space in her life. The label of old maid seemed ever more fitting. One of these days, she half expected to see that designation on her office nameplate.

Harvey Tremayne was different. Despite his tough persona she sensed he was a kind, self-effacing man. He'd shown his emotions openly. She liked that. But her mind kept going back to their earlier discussion. When he'd asked her what she had that he could possibly want, she'd seen it in his eyes. He had looked at her with desire, but there was also a sense of respect. She couldn't quite put her finger on it. But in the cold light of day, it was just something imagined after too much wine.

If she could get him to sign the appointment, she was going to work directly with him, if only for a short time. That would dictate how she must behave. There was nothing for it. The label of old maid would remain firmly attached.

Chapter 21

Robert Harbour, Luderitz, South West Africa

Commander Mike Crosson was seated in his makeshift office on Robert Harbour, distracted by the view. The turquoise blue of Luderitz Bay shimmered in the heat of the day. It was a sight to behold. A flock of pelicans skimmed effortlessly over the water, banking in unison. In the distant shallows, flamingos gave the bay a pink shimmering edge.

The moment was spoiled by an old fan that clanked and rattled in the corner of his hastily converted office. Until recently this poorly insulated galvanised iron shed had been a fishing net store. Evidence of its former occupants still hung heavy in the air, and with the heat it was playing havoc with his constitution.

Commander Mike Crosson of British Naval Intelligence had been posted to Cape Town six months earlier, a move he relished. At forty-eight years of age he was a thirty-year veteran of the Royal Navy. In World War 1 he was a petty officer on HMS King George V during the Battle of Jutland and saw active service throughout the North and South Atlantic. After the war, he had served on many different vessels and three years ago had been made Commander of the naval base at Scapa Flow in Scotland. The base having been largely abandoned after the Great War, his responsibility was to rebuild the submarine detection and defence systems for the largest naval anchorage in the British Isles.

His recent transfer to the other end of the world had come unexpectedly. The British Government was concerned that in the event of war, Germany, and its Axis partner Italy, would blockade the Suez Canal, forcing vital supplies from the East to be diverted around the Cape of Good Hope. The Germans had ex-colonies and friendly ports in both East and West Africa and could present a serious threat by disrupting this remaining trade route.

Crosson's role was to assess and commission the required coastal defences around the South African coast. It was three thousand miles from St Lucia on the Portuguese East Africa border, around to the Kunene River, the northernmost point of South West Africa and the border with Portuguese Angola. So, when he was transferred from the cold, wet and windy Orkney Islands to Cape Town, it was like arriving in a tropical paradise. The magnificent harbour was framed by the city and crowned by the iconic Table Mountain. His wife had accompanied him and had loved it from the moment they landed.

But just days ago, he had received new orders from the Admiralty in London giving him a top-priority assignment. His brief was to introduce intelligence gathering and marine defences along the diamond-rich coast of the Forbidden Zone. Leaving his wife in Cape Town, he flew the six hundred miles north to Luderitz via Saldanha Bay. He'd barely had time to pack a bag.

Upon arrival, he found that the naval capability of the area was almost non-existent. Based at Walvis Bay, three hundred miles to the north, there were two armed motor torpedo boats and a converted whaling boat, fitted with radio direction finding equipment. The whaler had been converted in Simonstown dockyard and renamed HMSAS Table Bay but was affectionately known as 'The Stinker'. Thirty years of whaling in the Southern Ocean had left an indelible mark.

Crosson needed radio direction finding capability and had quickly relocated HMSAS Table Bay to Luderitz. She was at least armed. The two motor torpedo boats had to remain, to provide at least some armed protection for the largest port in South West Africa. He had commandeered three motor torpedo boats plus mechanics and supplies from the naval base at Simonstown to be stationed at Luderitz. The facilities at Robert Harbour were basic and he had expropriated the slipway and harbour buildings, which included his new office.

Crosson was still staring out to sea, deep in thought, when there was a knock at the door.

'Commander, I thought you'd want to see this. The Stinker picked up another of those messages last night. The transmission lasted less than thirty seconds and it's coded.'

'So, do we know where it was transmitted from?'

'Stinker was two hundred miles south of Luderitz when they picked it up. Judging by the strength of the signal, the radio operator reckons the source was probably two hundred miles to the north, so it was right here in the Luderitz area. The radio direction finder here at Luderitz couldn't pinpoint the source of the signal because the message was too short, sir.'

'Well let's send it down to Cape Town and see if Military Intelligence can shed any light on it.'

As the door closed Crosson frowned. He scratched his short grey hair and chewed on the end of his pencil. There was something going on.

The frequency of coded transmissions was increasing and the one yesterday was the third in four days.

The problem was that they were not able to pinpoint the source of the short-duration radio signals. The Stinker was fitted with the latest high-frequency radio direction finding system, known as an RDF. This could determine the bearing of the signal with good accuracy in seconds. The radio direction finding system installed in Luderitz was of the old type. Although it could hear the message it took over thirty seconds for an experienced operator to determine the bearing of the signal.

Crosson needed The Stinker and at least two dispersed shore stations fitted with the latest RDF systems to be able to triangulate the source of short duration radio signals. If three stations heard the same message, they could determine the location from the intersection of the three bearings to an accuracy of less than a mile. He had ordered two RDFs from Cape Town and arranged to have them flown up to Luderitz by an RAF Singapore flying boat. Until he received them, locating the source of any messages was little better than guesswork.

Whoever was communicating sent short messages to avoid being located and went to the trouble of coding them. Given the location along the Forbidden Zone, it had to involve diamonds.

He picked up the black phone on his desk and wound the handle.

'Get me Captain Kruger of the Diamond Security Police.'

Chapter 22

The Borj al-Hajoui Garden, Tangier

Sergeant Youssoufi of the Tangier Customs Police walked in long stilt-like strides through the gardens of Borj al-Hajoui towards the seat under the argan tree. The man he was to meet was short, fat and had eyes that were too close together, masked by little round spectacles with bottle-glass lenses.

Youssoufi had met him on many occasions and each time he hoped it would be the last. There was something unnerving about his weasel eyes and the strong German pronunciation of his broken English.

The man, who introduced himself as Moussa, had first contacted Youssoufi two years ago as a representative from the German trade delegation. His business card had no name, just a telephone number at the German Consulate in Tangier. He had an interest in the arrival dates and cargo manifests for all the ships arriving from South West Africa, particularly the Santa Maria. He said he was doing this on behalf of the owner.

Youssoufi had put two and two together. Here was someone from the German Consulate, taking an interest in a ship that sailed from former German South West Africa, with packages intercepted by Salamon Zaber. It all led to one inescapable conclusion: illegal diamonds.

Youssoufi was very hesitant about dealing with the weasel-eyed German. He was a loyal and dedicated member of the customs police, priding himself in his honesty. Time and again over the years, he'd seen kickbacks and hush-money change hands between the unscrupulous and the disloyal. Those who had been disloyal bought houses and farms. It was rumoured that one of the senior officers in the customs police owned an apartment in Paris. And what did he have? Except a clear conscience and personal pride?

But Moussa had produced a very large wad of notes and, like iron filings to a magnet, his hand had gone out, and he was trapped. He cursed himself for his stupidity. From then on he was pressed for more and more information, always with the subtle threat of exposure. What he passed on was well rewarded, and inside a year Youssoufi had bought a goat farm in the Oued Ouerrha Valley in the Atlas Mountains, something he could never have afforded on his salary.

So, when he'd met with Harvey Tremayne from De Beers who was asking informed questions about Salamon Zaber and diamond shipments from South West Africa, Youssoufi thought Moussa would like to know. And Moussa was indeed delighted with the information and rewarded him generously.

He had looked astonished to learn that Harvey Tremayne was in Tangier and fired a number of questions at Youssoufi, clarifying the detail. The initial look of disbelief turned to deep thought, then consternation and finally a sneer creased his mouth.

The instructions that he passed on surprised Youssoufi. Moussa needed to get Zaber and Tremayne to the Santa Maria on the night she docked. He was to let them both know when she was due in port. Just the date, time and wharf number, nothing else. They would both have their different reasons for accepting the invitation.

As Youssoufi got up to leave, Moussa looked at him and grinned. 'Like unsuspecting flies to a spider's web,' he said.

Chapter 23

Medina Quarter, Tangier

'Ah, Monsieur Tremayne, there is a telegram for you,' the concierge said. It was addressed to *Mr Harvey Tremayne, Esq, Straits Hotel*.

Ordering his usual Tanqueray and tonic in Caid's Bar, he ripped it open and pulled out the message:

Harvey.
Join them with my blessing but drive a hard bargain. Remember I
need you back soon.
Yours.
Sir Ernest.

What the hell did the old codger mean by that? As he savoured the drink, his mind drifted back to those memorable days in Africa. The sun, the people, the friends. And then, he remembered why he was in Tangier.

Tremayne left the hotel in the late afternoon and walked towards the Medina. On this occasion he didn't want to be followed and walked quickly, taking the dark, dingy alleyways and backtracking several times. He was on a mission to find and interrogate Zaber's thugs.

He made his way to Rue Khatami, confident that he hadn't been followed. The waiter had said they lived on the top floor of a red house, but in the long shadows of the late afternoon it was difficult to find. Having discreetly walked up and down he finally located it. Access was through a large ancient wooden door, with a small door set within it. Tremayne checked around, pulled out his revolver and stepped through. He crouched and listened. He was in a courtyard and the smell of spiced food filled his nostrils. In the centre was a palm in a large Alibaba pot, behind which a fountain gurgled.

He climbed the stairs to the top floor and listened at the door. There was no sound. Tremayne carefully turned the door handle and pushed. It was unlocked. Was this another trap? He double-checked his revolver, raised it in front of him and inch by inch he pushed the door open.

He found himself in a kitchen. To the left, there were two open doors, and ahead a seating area. Beyond that, a glass door led to the outdoor terrace. He quietly closed the door behind him and slid the bolt.

On the small kitchen table, the ashtray was full of brown paper cigarette butts. He picked one up and sniffed. It had the same aromatic smell as the thug's breath.

There was a sound coming from one of the rooms. The first was a bedroom, but the noise was coming from the other. He pushed the door and glanced into the washroom. He caught his breath at the smell of the Turkish toilet. Water was trickling from a rusty tap into the sink, but the room was empty.

Tremayne swung the gun around and held his breath. He was back on a trench raid. The enemy knows you're there, but not what you have planned. He stepped back into the kitchen. He could see no obvious hiding place in the living room, the kitchen was empty and he'd checked the toilet. That left just one room.

He pushed the door and winced as its dry hinges objected. He checked behind the door. Nothing. Then he got down on one knee and looked under the bed. Again nothing. As he stood up, an arm grabbed him around the neck and a knife was pressed to his back.

'Drop the gun,' a man said in accented English, pushing Tremayne into the kitchen. 'What are you doing here?'

'Meeting with Monsieur Zaber,' Tremayne said. It just came into his head.

Not expecting that answer, the man lessened the pressure on the knife. Taking the opportunity, Tremayne grasped the arm around his neck and flipped him over his shoulder onto the concrete floor. He immediately recognised the swollen eye and bruised cheek that he'd given him.

'Well, if it's not my old friend Thug Two, AKA Ahmed,' Tremayne said, kicking him hard in his stomach.

Ahmed groaned and retched and Tremayne kicked him again, this time in the kneecap. He screeched with pain.

'Right, lowlife, do you work for Zaber?'

Ahmed spat at him. Tremayne looked at the glob on his trousers and kicked the Arab's face. Blood ran from his nose. He reached for his collarbone and squeezed his thumb and forefinger either side. Ahmed was paralysed.

'I will ask you again, do you work for Zaber?'

Ahmed nodded, unable to speak. Tremayne released his grip.

'Zaber will kill you for this,' Ahmed sneered.

'Listen, I don't want threats. I want answers.'

Tremayne resumed his grip on his collarbone and squeezed even harder.

'Who is Sanmar? Is that who Zaber get his diamonds from?'

'Fuck you,' he said, in a screamed whisper.

Ahmed raised his head and stared. Tremayne followed his gaze. Someone was trying the kitchen door handle.

A loud voice outside shouted and there was banging on the door. In that momentary distraction, Ahmed kicked Tremayne's legs from under him and was up in a flash, and with an obvious limp he ran out through the open door onto the roof terrace.

'Oh no you don't,' Tremayne said, picking up his revolver and following.

Ahmed jumped over the low walls that separated each house terrace. At the last one he tried the door to the building, but to no avail. He jumped onto the front wall but within a few paces, it ended. He hesitated and looked back. The next building was the other side of an alley, the gap was wide, but the terrace opposite was one storey lower.

'Who is Sanmar? Tell me,' Tremayne yelled.

Ahmed laughed and walked slowly towards him. 'You are going to die, Tokolosh. Zaber will kill you,' he said, pointing his finger and spitting at him again.

Tremayne looked down into the blackness of the street forty feet below. This was no place for a fight, but he couldn't let the thug escape. He'd have to shoot to wound. But if he did that the police were sure to be called.

'Tell me about Sanmar and I'm gone,' Tremayne said, in a more measured manner.

Ahmed turned away and ran along the wall and leaped for the terrace across the alley. As he launched himself, his knee seemed to give out. With his arms and legs flaying in the air, his upper body hit the top of the wall opposite with a crunch, his feet scrambling for grip on the smooth white plaster. Tremayne watched the struggle. With one final effort, he got his foot onto the wall, and Tremayne aimed to take a shot. As he was pulling himself up, the top brick dislodged, and he plunged head-first out of sight. The terrible scream was cut short with a sickening thud.

There were shouts from the alley below. Tremayne knew he had to get out of there immediately. The police would be called. He walked quickly, retracing his steps. Returning to the roof terrace of Ahmed's flat, he was about to enter when he saw the kitchen door wide open, the frame splintered.

Fouad appeared from the bedroom and in one fluid motion he raised his gun and fired, and the bullet whizzed past Tremayne's ear. He leaped back over the wall to the next property. Fouad followed him onto the roof terrace. Tremayne searched around. There was an access door just behind him. Tremayne fired a shot and grabbed at the handle. The door opened, and he dived in. The top pane of glass in the door exploded into a million pieces as a bullet hit.

A flight of stairs ran down into the darkness and Tremayne leaped down, taking several steps at a time. Another shot and a bullet ricocheted off the wall behind him as he turned the corner. The stairs carried on down and two flights later he turned a corner and there was light at the bottom. The large wooden main door was locked. Tremayne fired back up the stairs, unlocked the door and pulled the key. As he stepped out into the courtyard, he fired twice at his assailant, slammed the door shut, locked it and made his escape.

Chapter 24

Café Paris, Place Petit Socco, Tangier

Salamon Zaber stared out of his first-floor window across Place Petit Socco. It was a thousand-yard stare. With a shaky hand he put the earpiece back on the cradle of the upright phone and reached into the glass jar. That snivelling little Nazi weasel Moussa had the chutzpah to tell him that the Adlerflagge Syndicate no longer needed him. All diamonds, regardless of size or quality, would now go directly to Hamburg.

After twenty years of smuggling diamonds with his comrades, the fucking Nazis had cut him out. The business he had developed from nothing, his brainchild, his living, his life, stolen from him by jackboot fascists.

He took another sweet date from the jar. Bad news after bad news was eating away at him, consuming his very soul. Jesus, what had he done to deserve this? First the Tokolosh had returned and then the letter and now this.

He felt a hot tingle surge through his body, followed by dizziness and nausea, his heart trying to escape his chest. He put his head in his hands and rubbed his temples, trying to shut out the heavily accented voice of that little weasel. His shoulders started to shake, and tears rolled down his cheeks, disappearing into his grey beard, like a flash flood does in the sands of the Namib.

It had started the previous day. Amongst his mail had been a letter postmarked Amsterdam. He'd put it to one side, but when he looked at it again he recognised the handwriting. It was from his brother Michael. An overwhelming sense of dread had washed over him. His brother lived in Frankfurt. News of the pogroms in Germany, Austria and now Czechoslovakia were in the *Tangier Gazette* daily. He'd had a foreboding that it was only a matter of time until it touched his own family.

Michael had written to say that all Jewish bank accounts had been frozen, and the money stolen, including those of Zaber & Company and Indigo Trading. Their offices had been ransacked and the safe looted by Nazi Brownshirts. His mother had been robbed and evicted from her house, forced to walk through the streets in her underwear, being jeered at and beaten. She had been loaded onto a train, the destination unknown. Their beloved mother humiliated by evil, stupid brainwashed shmucks. Where had they taken her?

Michael and his other brother, Moshe, had escaped from Frankfurt by the skin of their teeth. They were now in hiding with relatives in Amsterdam and were planning to flee to London. Two of his cousins in Vienna had been detained and sent to a ghetto, again no one knew where. There were stories of beatings and deportations everywhere.

For months, Zaber had told Michael that the family should flee Frankfurt, but he was adamant that the Nazis would always need Jewish traders and bankers. Tens of thousands of Jews had fought for Germany in World War 1, as Michael had done. He'd proved his bravery on the battlefield, killed for his country, and would not entertain the notion that Germany would forsake them. He had been wrong.

Zaber had read the letter, over and over. Why had he not moved his money to Switzerland? He'd had more than enough time. And then he thought back to being taken prisoner in Luderitz more than twenty years ago. There also, he'd had more than enough time to escape. What the hell was wrong with him?

Shaking his head in disbelief and with his mouth agape, he let out the most harrowing lamentation. An outrage that burst from his soul, like the diamond-rich magma had when it exploded through to the surface, one hundred million years ago.

And now the phone call from Moussa. Zaber continued to rub his temples, trying to make the words go away. So, this is how they repay me? His livelihood ripped from him, his life's savings stolen, his life deprived of its sustenance. Would he ever see his family again? Or his money? It was all too terrible to contemplate. Things could not get any worse.

He reached into the glass jar. He couldn't trust the Nazis or his old friends in the Adlerflagge. He now needed to look after his own interests. But who could he trust, other than Fouad and Ahmed? For years they had done his dirty work with no questions asked.

He licked his fingers one by one, deep in thought. This was now about survival. Youssoufi had called to say that the Santa Maria was due to arrive in two days. If he could get to Wharf 5 with Fouad and Ahmed the moment she docked, perhaps there was a chance he could still offload the diamonds. He knew Captain Ferreira well, and it was unlikely that he would be aware of Moussa's new edict. If he took along a large roll of dollars, he might get access to the hold and rescue his future. And then he would get Ahmed to slit Moussa's throat.

The phone rang, and he picked up the earpiece.

'Yes? Hello, Fouad.'

Chapter 25

Medina Quarter, Tangier

Harvey Tremayne thought his lungs were on fire, sucking in air that turned to flame. Christ, he had to give up these bloody cigarettes. From Rue Khatami, he had run north, to get away from the Medina and the Straits Hotel, where he knew the police would be looking for him. Fouad must have informed Zaber, who would not hesitate to incriminate him. He weaved through the narrow alleyways, frightened rats and cats his only witness. He was utterly lost, but as the city started to fall away in front of him, he glimpsed the harbour below, and he knew the direction to take.

Bright lights led him to a small square overlooking the harbour close to the Sultan's Palace. In one corner, the Bab Haha Bar was full and noisy, with clientele spilling onto the street. Tremayne pushed his way in and shouted his order to the barman.

'Do you have a phone I can use?' he mouthed, mimicking with his little finger and thumb spread wide.

The barman pointed around the back of the bar. Tremayne downed the gin and tonic, punched some coins into the battered phone box, dialled and waited.

'Hello, Cartwright, it's Tremayne. Can you hear me? Well, actually I'm in a spot of bother!'

The consular car arrived at the bar fifteen minutes later with Cartwright at the wheel.

'Hello Tremayne. What the hell have you been up to this time?'

'Well, I was out for an evening stroll and one thing led to another, you know how it goes.'

'Tell me you weren't mixed up in that murder on Rue Khatami?'

'Now, I'd have expected you to be tucked up in bed with a cup of cocoa, Cartwright. How could you possibly know about that?'

'So, it was you … you stupid bastard!'

There was no further conversation during the journey.

Tremayne was dog-tired and he dozed, his head nodding around as the car cornered and braked. On their approach to the consulate, the gates swung open and they drove up the gravel drive and crunched to a halt outside the rear entrance. Tremayne followed Cartwright into the building.

'I have a message for you from Youssoufi. He says the ship you're interested in is the Santa Maria. She arrives at Wharf 5 the day after tomorrow, but you didn't hear that from me. Wait in there,' he said, pointing, 'I'll tell Richardson you're here. She's been trying to contact you.'

Tremayne sat down and thought about the message from Youssoufi. He didn't trust the man, but … his mind jumped back to the piece of paper he'd found in Ahmed's pocket. *Sanmar* … Could that be Santa Maria? *23* must be the date; he glanced at his watch, that was it. Today was the twenty-first.

He started to formulate a plan in his mind. Perhaps Youssoufi wasn't so bad after all?

Despite the late hour, Charlotte Richardson was smartly dressed and looked radiant. Seeing her, taking in her beauty and the smell of her perfume, Tremayne relaxed for the first time that evening.

She offered her hand and when they touched, a sense of warmth seemed to flow from her. He felt a tingle of energy and didn't want to let go. Richardson cleared her throat, withdrew her hand and sat down opposite him.

'So, Mr Tremayne, according to the gendarmes there is an arrest warrant taken out on you, for the murder of one Ahmed Allam.'

'What?' exclaimed Tremayne. 'The stupid bugger jumped off a roof without any help from me!'

'Were there any witnesses?'

'Yes. Zaber's other thug, Fouad. He'll have raised the alarm.'

'That's most unfortunate, but more to the point what on earth were you doing there?' she asked.

'I know that Salamon Zaber is a black-market dealer, but I haven't been able to confirm that he and Indigo are one and the same. What I do know is that Fouad and Ahmed are his fixers and I wanted to interrogate them.'

Tremayne sat back and ran his fingers through his hair, eyes shut tight. God, he was tired.

'Ahmed was at the flat on Rue Khatami. After a fight, I chased him along the front wall to the end of the block. He tried to jump across the alley to escape but didn't make it.'

'Did you go back to the flat?' she asked.

'Yes, I was going to leave the way I had come in, and that's when I

96

bumped into Zaber's other fixer, Fouad. He shot at me, the bloody bullet missed my head by inches. Then I made my escape.'

'The gendarmes found a broken gold cufflink at the scene. I take it HPT are your initials?'

'Well yes, Harvey Petroc ... I do have a pair of ... but ... that can't be mine.'

'That seems too much of a coincidence to the gendarmes, Mr Tremayne.'

He could see that. But how?

'They must have been stolen from my hotel room when I was robbed. I hadn't even noticed they were missing. Besides, why would I be wearing a long-sleeved shirt with cufflinks in this heat?' he added, taking off his jacket. 'This is what I'm wearing. It would be difficult to fit cufflinks to these.'

Charlotte Richardson looked at his brown muscular arms and the veins on the back of his large hands.

She leaned forward.

'Perhaps we can help one another, Mr Tremayne. You are in a world of trouble and you will not get to Zaber or his smuggling ring without help. I've got a proposition.'

She caught the sweep of his eyes.

'I'm listening,' he said.

'I've had a message from London. The British Government is concerned that the Nazis are planning to steal a large quantity of diamonds from South West Africa for their military rearmament. The South African Navy has picked up an increasing number of coded German communications along the coast. They want you down there to take charge of security, but not working for De Beers. You will work for the British Foreign Office, seconded to Section D of MI6. In that capacity you will have direct access to military support.'

Tremayne was dumbfounded.

'I have been authorised to sign you on as the attaché to the British Consulate in Tangier, backdated three days. In that way the local gendarmes won't be able to touch you.

'You'll have to ask Sir Ernest about all this Miss Richardson. That's a decision way above my station.'

'We already have. Churchill spoke with General Smuts, who talked to Oppenheimer, and he's in full agreement. They want you down there as soon as possible. I have the paperwork here,' she said, pointing to an envelope on the table.

So, that was what the old codger's telegram was about!

'What do I get in return?' he asked, with a suggestive smile.

The silence that followed was interrupted by a distant clock chiming the hour.

'The honour of serving your country, of course,' she said. 'Oh yes, and not being charged with murder, which if found guilty, has a mandatory death sentence in Morocco. Working for the Foreign Office you will have full diplomatic immunity.'

Tremayne thought back to Oppenheimer's telegram.

'Listen, I've got to find Zaber before I go down to South West Africa. If he is the man handling the smuggled diamonds, I need information about his contacts. I have one new lead, but I'll need a car with a driver. Someone armed and capable.'

She sat back in the chair.

'This is not just business, Miss Richardson, it's personal.'

'Alright Mr Tremayne, you can have Timpson, not the most endearing character but an impeccable military background, and he's been in MI6 for years.'

Tremayne signed the papers and handed them back to her.

'There is one string attached,' he added, and sat back and lit a cigarette.

'And that is?'

'Dinner with you at the Diplomatic Country Club tomorrow night,' he said, his gaze taking in the contours of her body.

'Mr Tremayne, you want a great deal, don't you?'

She felt a tingle of anticipation, but she knew what she had to do.

'I'm afraid that's totally out of the question. You're now an attaché to the British Consulate in Tangier, and I make it a point to never fraternise with my staff.'

Chapter 26

Guano Bay, Diaz Peninsula, South West Africa

Jager walked back to his cottage along the tideline. The seemingly endless white beach always provided a harvest of driftwood. For centuries, this treacherous coastline had been the graveyard of countless vessels heading around the Cape of Good Hope between Europe and the Far East. The Benguela Current brought the flotsam and jetsam from as far as Cape Town, six hundred miles to the south.

Jager reached his cottage just as the sun was setting. He opened the sturdy weather-scarred wooden door with his elbow and dropped the bundle of wood in the corner. He stoked the rusty cast-iron stove, put a heavy pot on top and half-filled it with seawater from a wooden bucket.

After lighting a candle from the smoking oil lamp on the table, he opened the wooden shutter on the north-facing window, spilled some wax on the sill and stuck the candle into it.

He put three glasses on the table and filled one with schnapps. Taking a swig, he screwed his eyes shut with relish.

'Hey Falkie, that's good stuff. Our comrades will like this.'

The falcon bobbed his head.

Jager lay back on his bed and waited, glass in one hand, bottle in the other. He was distracted. The expectation of Operation Benguela was soon to become a reality. Their country had been plundered for far too long and many of their loyal comrades still languished in jail. Enough was enough. They were now going to exact the ultimate revenge on those fat, belligerent British bastards. They had already made an example of the Tokolosh. He had been a serious threat to the Adlerflagge and Jager had done his duty. He smiled, remembering that night, and the terror in her eyes ... A loud bang brought him to his senses. Falkie flapped his wings in alarm. There was a clanking as the stone rolled down the galvanised roof. He relaxed.

'It's alright, Falkie. That's our comrades.'

He unbolted the door and greeted his visitors. They had been friends from childhood and, along with Indigo, were the original members of the Adlerflagge Syndicate. Now they were the three senior officers in what Abwehr II called Red Commando. This was the most important of the six commando groups the Nazis had set up across South West Africa.

Karl Bosman, codename Cobra, was a small, stocky, second generation 'South Wester'. His father had been a *Leutnant* in the *Deutsch-Südwestafrika Schutztruppe* fighting against the South African invasion in 1914. Having been an illegal diamond miner for years he now worked on the mine as a legitimate employee. He was a locomotive driver on the narrow-gauge railway, moving men and materials between Port Baleen and the Lewala Mine and Kolmanskop Camp. He was the one who smuggled the carrier pigeons into the mine and released them with the bag of diamonds attached.

Siegfried 'Siggie' Moritz was long, lean and bony. Years of prospecting for copper in Hereroland in the far north of the country had burned away any evidence of his European heritage. Three years ago, he had joined the mine and now worked in the sorting plant as a shift supervisor. He had the very finest gem diamonds passing within his reach on a daily basis. Because of this he was subject to 'search without notice' and so did not have a radio and hence no codename. His contact with Red Commando was by message drops via Karl Bosman. While in a position of trust, he was driven by the love for his land and a hatred of his paymasters.

'Jeez, man, it's good to see you again, Siggie,' Jager said. 'How was the journey?'

'No problem. We beached the boat on the far side of the peninsula and trekked across. I didn't want to risk getting fogged in.'

Jager closed the shutters and turned up the oil lamp and poured three schnapps.

'To the Führer,' he said, and they chinked glasses.

'So, Christo, what's all this about?' Bosman said.

'The Fatherland wants more diamonds. A lot more diamonds.'

'But there's going to be no more for a while. It's just too dangerous. Since those two policemen disappeared, security has brought the shutters down and everyone is being watched. There's no way to get a pigeon into the mine at the moment,' Bosman said.

Jager frowned. 'Ja, that was unfortunate. They were about to break my boat. I couldn't let that happen. I had no option.'

'I did wonder. What happened to them?' Bosman asked.

'They'll not be found. They went overboard north of Great White Point, gone in seconds.'

'Hell, I hate those fucking things,' Bosman said, shuddering.

'Not as much as me. Anyway, we're going to celebrate tonight. It's payday,' Jager said, throwing the leather wallet on the table.

Moritz counted the wad of notes and looked up and smiled. 'Now that's what I call a payday.'

'Well, Siggie, you pulled out some fabulous diamonds from the sorting plant, and Karl, you did a great job with the pigeons.'

'All those big diamonds are coming from the new Zach's Extension, east of the mine. I haven't seen crystals as good as those for a long time,' Moritz said.

Glasses were refilled and downed.

'So, what's this really about, Christo? I've never had a message from you before telling me to come over with Siggie. We should not be seen together,' Bosman said. 'This is very risky.'

'Comrades, it's good news. The best. The last rendezvous I had was not with Neptune, but with Moby,' he said, pausing for effect. 'And Sidewinder was on board.'

The two looked at him, grinning.

'And?' Bosman said, expectantly.

'He told me the Nazis are putting some spine back into the Fatherland after the humiliations of 1918. Germany is rapidly rearming and mobilising millions of men ahead of a big push to take back what is rightfully ours: Austria, Czechoslovakia and Poland. Sidewinder says that within two years Germany will control all of Europe. Our role is to support German arms manufacture by supplying diamonds. This comes right from the top, from Göring himself. They need at least two tons.'

There was a stunned silence.

'Fuck me,' Bosman said, with a huge grin. 'That's going to take a lot of pigeons!'

Hands banged on the table as they laughed. Jager topped up the glasses.

'Seriously, comrades, there are those in high places in De Beers and this puppet government that would do anything to make sure Germany doesn't get any diamonds. But these are our diamonds, this is our land, and we must make sure the Fatherland gets what it needs. This is our contribution.

'When Germany attacks Europe, the Allies will enforce a trade embargo and none of our diamonds will get to the Third Reich. When we've stolen the diamonds, Sidewinder wants us to sabotage Port Baleen. If Germany can't get our diamonds, no one will.'

There was silence around the table. The only sound was the water boiling in the pot. Bosman slid his glass forward expectantly.

'Fucking hell, this is the big one,' he said.

They looked at one another and the smiles faded. Realisation dawned on them that after this, their lives were going to be changed forever. For better or for worse.

Jager leaned forward and said, 'Sidewinder stressed the need for complete secrecy. He has given me his copy of the communication codes we are to use for Operation Benguela. Karl, we have to memorise them, then destroy his book.'

He handed him the maroon coloured book with the Nazi black eagle embossed on the front.

'We'll discuss the plan in detail tomorrow, but tonight we celebrate. I've got something special for us,' Jager said. 'I set some rock lobster pots yesterday. Even the Führer won't eat better tonight.'

Jager disappeared outside, then returned with a sack. One by one he pulled out large shiny blue crayfish and dropped them in the boiling water. Legs twitched and in seconds the shells were red. Bosman poured more schnapps.

'And what happens to our country after this war?' asked Moritz. 'Blowing up Port Baleen is easy, but we don't want to destroy our infrastructure.'

'None of us does, Siggie,' Jager said. 'When Europe is conquered, the Third Reich will help us retake South West Africa and then South Africa and all the British Protectorates to the north. We'll have a regional German colonial government, and we'll have helped to put them there. In return they will help us rebuild our nation.'

Jager pulled the cooked rock lobsters from the pot and put them on a large wooden tray.

'Here you go, boys. Fresh from the ocean this afternoon.'

Jager topped up the three glasses.

'If I retreat, kill me. If I die, avenge me. If I advance, follow me. To the Fatherland!' he roared, as they banged glasses.

There was a knock on the door. Bosman and Moritz reached for their guns but Jager put his hand up.

'Ja? Who is it?'

'It Joaba, Baas.'

Jager opened the door and the girl entered, not looking up, arms folded tightly across her chest. She had been crying.

'Good news, girl. You're going to earn lots more money tonight.'

Chapter 27

Lewala Mine, Forbidden Zone, South West Africa

Niels Kruger with Sergeant Samuel Ndakolo and Constable Isaak Japie returned to Respite Bay late in the morning. A train was waiting for them at the jetty and took them to the Lewala Mine where they met with the police commander, Nico Steenkamp.

'We found one important piece of evidence just above Great White Point,' Kruger said. 'We started searching the area north of where Corporal Gam and Constable Jurie were when they heard the gunshot. And Samuel found some evidence close to the beach.'

'So, that confirms he came in by sea?' Steenkamp said.

'It certainly looks like it. We found this,' Kruger said, handing Steenkamp the small leather hood.

'Bloody hell, it's a falcon's hood. They use them to keep the birds calm when they're transporting them. He must have been seriously distracted to drop this and not notice.'

'Nico, what this confirms is that we have someone smuggling carrier pigeons into Lewala, and that's a serious breach of security.'

'It certainly looks that way. I thought we had that under control,' Steenkamp said pensively. 'We had a spate of this many years ago when we were mining up at Kolmanskop. We had several high-grade areas right on the surface and someone smuggled in pigeons, force-fed some of them with small diamonds and attached small pouches of the larger stones to others. Apparently, it's easy to train pigeons to return to their home coop, regardless of where they are released. In this case we traced them back to a doctor working at Luderitz Hospital who kept pigeons in his back yard. Before we could question him he disappeared back to Germany, probably a very rich man!'

'Constable Jurie says he saw the hawk west of the Lewala Mine,' Kruger said. 'That means it wasn't released from the secure area but more likely from somewhere along the railway line. The thing I don't understand is why the smuggler would risk going that far south by boat, and miles into the desert, to hunt the pigeon that would return to its coop anyway.'

'Well, the stolen diamonds must have been very valuable to warrant such an undertaking,' Steenkamp said. 'They didn't want to risk the bird getting caught by a wild bird of prey, or it being seen flying in the Luderitz area and attracting attention.'

'That's a good point. So home is likely to be somewhere around Luderitz.'

'I think it has to be. Probably not in town, but in the area,' Steenkamp said.

'As for the smuggler, if he could beach at Great White Point it must be a small boat and he would not have journeyed too far. The next port north of us is Walvis Bay and that's nearly three hundred miles, much too far. My hunch is that he's local, Nico.'

'So,' Steenkamp said, 'we have a diamond thief who works on the mine and is selecting high-value stones from the restricted area. Another person who has smuggled a pigeon onto the property and attached the diamonds and released it.'

'Then we have the man with the falcon, who has sailed to Great White Point and walked over five miles into the desert to catch the pigeon,' Kruger said, scratching his chin. 'That requires good coordination.'

'So, there are definitely two, possibly three, men in this smuggling ring, plus those who handle the diamonds at the other end,' Steenkamp said. 'We can question everyone with access to the secure area. That's the easy bit. The hard bit is where will our falcon-flying friend be hiding?'

Kruger rolled the map out on the table. 'He won't be in Luderitz, I'm sure of that,' he said. 'He might be up here to the north of town around Penguin Island or Seal Island or west of town, somewhere around Diaz Point. There are some old fishermen's cottages on Halifax Island, but that's difficult to access by boat in bad weather. Guano Bay is a possibility. It has a beach and is protected from the south-west winds. The map shows some old cottages at the south end.'

'Right, Niels, you head back to town and check out Guano Bay immediately. If you find nothing there, check Penguin Island and Seal Island. We have to find out who's behind this.'

Outside a klaxon sounded. Kruger looked at Steenkamp.

'Don't worry,' Steenkamp continued. 'They're taking delivery of diamonds from the sorting plant and are about to open the Kaiser's Closet. That's why I'm here today, to check the security we have in place. Come. I'll show you.'

They walked to the back of the security office and an armed policeman unlocked and opened a steel door. There in front was the biggest safe door Kruger had ever seen. It was black, six feet high and the same width, and in the centre was a large stainless steel wheel, bigger than the steering wheel on his Fordor. The sorting plant manager dialled a number into the combination lock, grabbed the wheel and turned it anticlockwise, and with a satisfying clunk the two large locking bolts released.

'Welcome to the Kaiser's Closet,' Steenkamp said, as the door was pulled open. 'It's constructed of steel reinforced concrete and the door is two-inch-thick steel and the two bolts lock into these mortices in the steel door frame. It was built to order five years ago and stores the current quarter's diamond production until the drums are shipped to Cape Town. There was some debate as to whether it should be built at the port, but it was considered more secure to be located inland.'

Steenkamp nodded to Kruger, who followed him inside.

'This is three months' production?' Kruger asked, looking at the large stack of drums.

'Well, actually, more. The larger drums contain the diamonds of less than half a carat that are used by industry as an abrasive. They weren't shipped out last quarter, so there's about six months' worth of those. The smaller drums contain the larger diamonds produced this quarter that will go for cutting and polishing. The Eureka will be here on 1st September and will transfer everything to Cape Town.'

A man in white overalls wheeled in a drum looking like a small milk churn on a sack trolley, followed by another man pushing a trolley with two larger drums. Armed police accompanied them.

'As you can see,' Steenkamp continued, 'there is a clamp that holds the lid on each drum and that's been welded in place. The only way to get into the drum is to use an oxy-acetylene cutter.'

'What our smugglers wouldn't do to get their hands on this lot, eh Nico?' Kruger said.

'Well, they can try, but they'll not break into the Kaiser's Closet.'

Chapter 28

Wharf 5, Port of Tangier, Tangier

Harvey Tremayne waited in the shadows next to the warehouse on Wharf 5. In front of him, the three-masted barque, the Santa Maria, a sleek steel-hulled old lady, tugged at her moorings, the hemp ropes groaning with the exertion. Bats swooped and dived, preying on the swarms of insects attracted by the dockside lights.

Shortly after she had docked, two people climbed on board, but too far off for Tremayne to identify. Moving as close as he dared to the single gangplank, he waited for their return.

Thirty minutes later there was movement on deck. A small group of men huddled in conversation. Then two of them started down the gangplank. The first was large and lumbering, holding tightly to the handrails. He was followed by a thin, lithe man in a light-coloured suit, carrying a large bag in one hand.

'There you are, you lowlife,' Tremayne said, recognising the profile of Fouad. 'So, you must be Salamon Zaber!'

He was tempted to run out and confront them, but two men on the ship remained at the top of the gangplank, watching over the dock.

As they walked towards the warehouse, he slipped back inside and hid behind some crates. He pulled out his revolver and waited. But instead of entering they stopped outside in conversation. He cursed and wondered what to do. Glancing at the Santa Maria, he noticed that the men on deck had moved off, and he took his chance. He stepped out behind the two and armed his revolver with a loud click.

'Hands where I can see them. Inside, nice and slow,' Tremayne said, pointing towards the warehouse.

Fouad needed a sharp prod in the back to get him moving.

'On your knees, hands behind your back,' Tremayne said.

The Arab stooped to kneel but turned, reaching to his belt. Tremayne had a split second to act. The man's gun swung in Tremayne's direction, but before he could fire, Tremayne's revolver came down on his head. He fell to the ground, his gun clattering to the floor.

'You, stupid bastard. Don't you ever listen?' Tremayne said. He picked up the gun and with his foot rolled the unconscious man onto his back. Then he turned to confront the big man who had his hands as high as he could raise them. He poked him in the ribs with the point of his revolver.

'How nice to meet you at last Mr Zaber, or should I call you Indigo?'

Zaber recoiled at his approach, mouth open, eyes staring. He recognised him as the man at Café Taouz.

Tremayne searched him.

'Kneel. Hands behind your back,' he ordered.

Zaber was breathing heavily and did not attempt to move. Tremayne gave him a push and a sharp kick to the back of his right knee and he fell to the floor, landing heavily on his knees, letting out a squeal of pain.

'I'd advise you to do as I say, and answer my questions quickly and honestly, or it will get very painful.'

Zaber was mumbling. Tremayne opened the bag and pulled out one of several small sacks.

'So, tell me, what have you got in here?'

Zaber was silent, deliberately looking away. But what he did see, at the back of the warehouse, was a flash of light. Someone had opened a door, slipped inside and closed it again.

Tremayne pulled out one of the pouches from the bag and tipped the contents onto his palm and held it up to a shaft of light.

'Well there's a surprise, diamonds, from South West Africa if I'm not mistaken. What would you and your lowlife here be doing with these? Selling them for your Nazi friends?'

'You don't understand ... They've taken everything ... from me ... My family ... money ... everything ... I hate the fucking Nazis,' he said, between sobs.

'Oh, but I *do* understand. You get rich on smuggled diamonds, sell them to support the German resistance in South West Africa and they murder innocent people, including my wife.'

Tremayne kicked him hard in the kidney. He screamed and rolled onto his side.

'I think you're in a bad place, a very bad place,' he said, leaning over Zaber. 'I will take great pleasure in handing you over to the police. I wonder, do they hang murderers in Tangier or use Madame Guillotine?'

Zaber sobbed out loud, staring at Tremayne, shaking his head. 'You have to believe me, I had nothing to do with her murder.'

'But you sold the diamonds that paid for the guns,' Tremayne said, prodding him with his foot. 'Who murdered her?'

There was no response.

'Don't be a bloody fool, Zaber. A name. That's all I need, a name.'

Tremayne kicked him in the same kidney to make the point. As he stepped back, something metal was pressed into his back.

'Throw down the gun and kneel in front of the crates,' a man said, in thickly accented English.

'Thank God you're here, Moussa. Help me up,' Zaber said.

'Indigo, I told you there is a change of plan,' the man said.

So Indigo and Zaber were one and the same, but who was the man with the gun? Tremayne could sense the tension. He turned his head to try and get a glimpse.

'Face the crates, Tremayne. Do not look at me. Last time of telling.'

'Please, Moussa. There must be a mistake. Please, my friend, please,' Zaber said.

Tremayne racked his brains but couldn't recall having heard of anyone called Moussa. And how the hell did this man know his identity?

The man picked up the bag.

'I told you there would be no more diamonds. Everything now goes to Germany.'

'No, I have instructions to send them by air.'

'You lie,' Moussa said, spooning out the words. 'Sidewinder was right. You are a thieving, lying, dirty Jew.'

'Moussa, for God's sake, what has got into you?'

'You have become rich at the expense of our comrades in South West Africa and the Fatherland. You have been greedy, like all the Jews,' Moussa said.

'Look, we can share the diamonds, you and me.'

'So, is that what you were going to do, share the diamonds with me?'

'Moussa, there must be a mistake. We are partners.'

'Sidewinder said you had outlived your usefulness. You are going on a journey with Tremayne here. The boat goes to Hamburg, but you'll be dropped off halfway,' he said, with a chuckle. 'And we'll take along this little lowlife, as you so aptly describe him, Mr Tremayne. By the way, where's the other one?'

'He's dead,' Zaber said.

'Good, that's one less I have to worry about,' Moussa said.

Moussa kicked the prostrate figure of Fouad. But he was no longer unconscious. He had come around some time earlier and had been listening to the conversation, awaiting his moment. He sprang to his feet and lunged, knife in hand. Moussa fired at point-blank range and Fouad fell against him. Moussa cried out and stumbled back against a crate, clutching his chest. Zaber, scrambling for his life, tried to get up.

Moussa fired at him, and then again. Tremayne bolted for cover in the deep shadows as another shot rang out.

He gathered his thoughts. Fouad was down. Had Moussa been stabbed? He thought so. And Zaber? He took deep breaths, trying to control the thumping heartbeat in his ears. Initially he heard nothing. But then he picked up a monotone chanting.

Tremayne went down on one knee, peered around the crate and flashed the torch. A shot rang out, the bullet splintering some wood above him.

'Moussa, you look in a bad way. You need help. Let me go to—' and another shot rang out.

That's six bullets he's fired, Tremayne thought. If he's using a Luger there are probably three shots left. Too many to take a chance.

'Moussa! Is that your Nazi codename? What's your real name?'

'Fuck you, Tremayne. You should be dead!'

'But I'm very much alive, Moussa, and I want to help you. Just tell me, who is Sidewinder?'

Two more bullets hit the crate above him, causing a large splinter to embed itself in his cheek. He pulled it out and pushed a finger on the wound.

Glancing forward, in the light from the wharf, he could just make out Moussa, sat slumped against a crate. Throwing his torch to the side, Moussa fired at the noise. Tremayne leaped forward and grabbed Moussa's arm, smashing his hand on the floor, the gun clattering away.

Tremayne checked the scene. Moussa sat in a puddle of blood with a knife in his chest, head slumped to the side, now staring into infinity. Fouad was dead, shot through the heart, and Zaber was lying on the ground, chanting. His face was white, blood oozing from his shirt.

Tremayne knelt beside him.

'Listen, Zaber, I need to know. Moussa talked about someone called Sidewinder. Who is he? Did he kill my wife? Is he your contact in South West Africa?'

Zaber stared at him, his mouth moving, but no words came out.

'Who is Sidewinder? I must know.'

'Tokolosh,' Zaber said, his voice no more than a whisper. Tremayne looked at the blood pooling on the floor.

'I'm your friend. I'm not Tokolosh. I will help you. Tell me about Sidewinder. Is he your contact?'

'My country has sold me to the devil, Tokolosh.'

Zaber turned and stared at Tremayne as he expelled his last breath.

'God damn it!' Tremayne cursed. So many questions that would now remain unanswered.

There was shouting outside on the wharf and a quick glance revealed several men running towards the warehouse. Pulling out Fouad's revolver from his pocket, Tremayne fired two shots in their general direction and they retreated.

He searched all three men, taking their documents, picked up his revolver and grabbed the bag. Leaving from the back of the warehouse, he threw Fouad's revolver into the harbour and, keeping to the shadows of the buildings, sprinted towards the perimeter fence. After a few moments of searching, found the hole he'd cut on his way in and made for the rendezvous point. When he got there, Timpson and the car were gone.

Police sirens broke the quiet of the evening. Tremayne settled down to wait. He was sitting on the bag containing the diamonds, and it gave him a strange reassurance, a little bit of his beloved Forbidden Zone with him in Tangier. But the diamonds were a small consolation in the grand scheme of things.

He kept checking to see if the police or any of Moussa's thugs had found the hole in the fence. But he saw no one.

He thought through the events of the evening and cursed at having got nothing from Zaber. All those secrets gone to the grave. The only consolation was finding out about the person named Sidewinder. He was obviously a key figure and, given the anti-Semite rhetoric reported by Moussa, must surely be a Nazi based in Germany. In his experience the colonial Germans in South West Africa didn't hate Jews.

And Moussa – who the hell was he and where did he fit in? Clearly German and some associate of Zaber and involved in the diamond smuggling ring.

Headlights appeared at the top of the road and he ducked behind the wall. As the lights drew closer, he relaxed: it was the car from the consulate.

'Where the bloody hell have you been?' Tremayne said as he got in. 'I told you to wait here?'

'Yes, sorry about that. I went for a drive,' Timpson said, with a smile.

Tremayne stared at him, opened his mouth to give him a piece of his mind, but couldn't think of the appropriate words.

'You went for a bloody drive?' was all Tremayne could summon.

'A few minutes after the shooting started, a black Mercedes drove out the main gate in somewhat of a hurry. So, I followed it.'

'And did you see who was driving it?'

'No, but I saw where it went.'

Tremayne waited in anticipation, but Timpson just smiled.

'Well?' Tremayne prompted.

'It drove into the German Consulate. I hope you didn't shoot the German Consul-General. That wouldn't go down at all well.'

Tremayne sat back in the seat and ran his fingers through his hair. 'Oh shit,' he said wearily.

Chapter 29

Guano Bay, Diaz Peninsula, South West Africa

Joaba lay on the hard clay floor, listening to the three men snoring. With only a thin blanket around her she was cold, and her young body shivered, drawing in quiet sobs through her lips. She sat up, opened the stove door, threw in some wood and poked the embers back into life. Sitting, staring, hypnotised by the flames, she thought of what these drunken bastards had done to her, and how she would get her revenge. She was still bleeding.

Stirred by the crackling of the fire, Falkie bobbed his head from side to side. Joaba gingerly got up and ruffled his chest feathers, and he playfully pecked her. She removed his leather hood and his bright jet-black eyes reflected the orange of the flames.

'Waaik, waaik,' he cried.

'Quiet, Falkie,' she said, in a hushed voice, and gave him a piece of dried meat.

'Boil some water, girl. We need lots of coffee this morning,' Jager said, from under a pile of blankets.

Joaba opened the window shutters and shafts of light cut through the smoke-hazed room. She started to prepare breakfast.

Jager got out of bed and put on a pair of shorts. Joaba looked away, sickened at the sight.

'Hope you slept, Falkie. It got a bit noisy didn't it?' Jager said.

Joaba felt shame flush through her abused body. You'd scream too, if someone did that to you, she thought. As the black kettle started to boil, she glanced at Jager. He had his back to her. She lifted the kettle and flexed her arm, just as he turned around.

'What are you staring at? Make the fucking coffee,' he growled.

Climbing the ladder to the loft, Jager shouted at the two snoring bodies.

Joaba broke cormorant eggs into a pan and put it on the stove, stirring and turning as it cooked. She added the leftover lobster and laid slices of black bread on top of the stove. After serving it up on three plates, she added sugar to the pot of coffee. Gripping her arm, Jager said, 'Come back tonight, and make sure you're clean.'

The men all laughed and tried to grab her as she ran from the room and slammed the door. She couldn't take another night like that. Her voice came in gasps, words expelled between deep gulping breaths. 'I hate you, you bastards. I hate you.'

After breakfast, Jager cleared the table and unfolded a map of the northern sector of the Forbidden Zone.

'So, what's the plan for Operation Benguela, Christo?' Bosman said.

'We don't have much time to prepare.'

'As you know, De Beers didn't move the under half-carat industrial diamonds to Cape Town on the last shipment, so there's nearly six months of production sitting there. Probably a ton and a half, maybe more. Plus, of course, all the high-quality rough they've mined this quarter. We're going to steal the lot.

'There are a few critical activities. We have to cut the telephone lines to Luderitz, isolate Kolmanskop Camp, secure the port and mine, blow the Kaiser's Closet, load the diamonds onto a train and transport them down to Port Baleen. There we'll transfer them to Neptune and sail to Pomona Island and load them onto U-46,' Jager said.

'But that's going to take more than the ten men we have in Red Commando!' Bosman said.

'You're right, Karl,' Jager replied. Sidewinder has mobilised a further twenty men from Swakopmund and Walvis Bay. Including all of us, that will make thirty-four. I'll take everyone through the plan onboard Neptune when we rendezvous at Possession Island.'

'The fat cats won't know what's hit them,' Bosman said, with venom. 'When do we do this?'

'Sunday 27th,' Jager said. 'De Beers are due to ship the diamond stock to Cape Town on Friday 1st September, so that will mean there's close to maximum stock in the Kaiser's Closet. Sunrise will be at 6.26 am, so we'll set zero hour as 6 am for the start of the attack. That will cause confusion when we hit them in the dark and we'll be able to sort out any pockets of resistance at first light.'

'Let's not forget the fog at this time of year. That could delay us,' Bosman said.

'Ja, that's a potential problem, but we can't wait. The Fatherland needs the diamonds immediately. On the plus side, it's a Sunday. The mine doesn't work on that day so there will be no employees to get in the way.'

Bosman and Moritz nodded.

'So, Siggie, what have you got planned for Red Commando?' Jager asked.

'At dusk on the twenty-sixth, one of my men will cut the telephone lines, preventing any calls getting in or out of Luderitz. Then at 3 am, zero minus three hours, we'll drive the truck down the mine road towards Kolmanskop Camp. We'll park in this gully, a mile east of the camp, and at zero minus two hours me and two men will trek down to the bridge that crosses the Sandrivier Gorge. We'll attach charges to the steel arches under the bridge and run the blasting cable back to a safe place, south of the gorge.

'When you cut the power at zero hour, I'll send up a flare to confirm the bridge is ready to blow, and the truck will drive at full speed through the security barrier into the camp. With the lights out there should be total confusion. As soon as the truck is across the bridge, I'll detonate the charges. That will isolate the police north of the gorge. Even on horseback it'll take them hours to make the detour and follow us. We'll then drive down to the Lewala Mine railway spur at Mile 10, mopping up any Security Police patrols we meet on the way. We should be in position by 7.15 am at the latest,' Moritz said.

'That's good. We'll rendezvous with you at Mile 10 at 7.30 am,' Jager said. 'Karl and I will sail from Seal Harbour and land north-west of Port Baleen, the day before the raid. We'll spend the afternoon preparing for the attack. Karl will get the train ready and together we'll set time-delay charges at the security office and generating plant. They'll be set to explode at zero hour on the 27th. That will take out the power to the whole property.'

'How many Security Police are we expecting?' Moritz asked.

'There are about forty based at Kolmanskop Camp and at any point in time about half of those will be out patrolling,' Bosman said. 'Isolating the twenty in camp is the easy bit. There will be another five at the port and eight or nine at the mine that we'll have to deal with.'

Jager continued, 'When Karl and I have secured the port, I'll radio Neptune, who will be waiting offshore. She will dock at zero plus forty-five minutes. Blue and Green Commandos will transfer the drilling equipment, explosives and arms to the train. We'll load Blue Commando and half of Green Commando and Karl will take the train up to the Lewala Mine spur. That's where we'll meet up with you, Siggie. We'll load half your men, and the other half will guard the spur.

'We'll neutralise the Security Police at the mine and by zero plus three hours we'll blow open the Kaiser's Closet. Then we load the diamonds onto the train and pick up the remainder of Red Commando and return to the port.

'While we're doing that, the remaining five from Green Commando will set delayed charges at the jetty and around the port, so these facilities can be destroyed as we leave. We'll load the diamonds and commandos onto Neptune and sail to Pomona Island.'

Bosman wiped his lips with the back of his hand.

'What the hell will we all do after the raid?' he said. 'There'll be no jobs for us on the mine. And we won't be able to return home.'

Moritz nodded in agreement, having had the same thought.

'Sidewinder will give a big cash bonus on completion of the raid,' Jager said. 'The families of any men killed or injured will be taken care of. The three of us and any wounded will transfer to Moby with the diamonds and head to Lobito Bay. Sidewinder will support us there for as long as necessary. As for the other commandos, Neptune will sail north to Swakopmund. Our contacts there will smuggle them out to the old German fort at Nonidas in the desert. They'll use that as a safe house.'

Jager got up from the table and fetched three glasses and the bottle of Bavarian cherry schnapps. 'So, on to more important matters,' he said. 'Let's raise a glass.'

They all stood to attention, raising their glasses. 'If I retreat, kill me. If I die, avenge me. If I advance, follow me. To the Fatherland,' they said in unison.

'Heil Hitler,' Jager barked, giving the Nazi salute.

Bosman and Moritz glanced at one another.

Chapter 30

British Consulate, Rue Amerique du Sud, Tangier

Driving away from the port, Timpson took a circuitous route to the British Consulate. He scoured the road in front and behind for any sign of being followed. Zaber or the Germans might have associates upset at losing their bag full of diamonds. Tremayne had it on his lap and his revolver at the ready.

Arriving at the consulate, they drove to the back of the building.

'Right, I don't know about you, but I need a stiff drink. I've got Scotch,' Timpson said.

'Yes, a large one please.'

The office was cluttered: a desk at both ends, one wall dedicated to shelves of box files, the opposite wall lined with filing cabinets. Cartwright was seated at the far desk in front of a large grey radio, wearing headphones.

'Hello, Phil. You missed a good show this evening,' Timpson said.

'I know. Three dead at the docks. I've been following it on the radio,' he said.

'Hello, Cartwright,' Tremayne said.

Cartwright turned in surprise at the voice.

'You remember the invitation you gave me to meet the Santa Maria at Wharf 5?' he said, keeping eye contact. 'Well, it all ended rather badly, I'm afraid.'

Timpson smiled and put three glasses and a bottle of whiskey on the desk.

'How were the three killed?' Cartwright said.

'Zaber's thug, Fouad, knifed Moussa in the chest, and Moussa shot Fouad and then Zaber.'

'And you didn't fire a shot?'

Tremayne passed his revolver to Cartwright. 'Check for yourself.'

He opened the revolver and sniffed it.

'You don't trust anyone, do you?' Tremayne said.

'Nothing personal. It's my job. Given your track record you'll have left a trail a blind person can follow.'

'Give me those personal papers and I'll see what they tell us,'

Timpson said. 'You need to take an inventory of those diamonds and search the bag for further clues.'

Tremayne cleared papers from the table and poured out each bag into separate piles. He was surprised to see how well they had been sorted, each bag containing similar value stones. Zaber hadn't had the time to do that, so this was done by a smuggler with expert knowledge in South West Africa. That was a big concern.

He double-checked two of the piles containing the larger and more perfect crystals. These had almost certainly been smuggled from the sorting room – or even the strong room where the diamonds were temporarily held until they were moved to the Kaiser's Closet. He shook his head at the sheer audacity of the theft.

At that moment Cartwright said, 'I hope you didn't leave any evidence at the scene?'

'No, I don't think so. Why?' Tremayne said.

'Well the man they called Moussa is Leopold Wenger. He's the top Nazi at the German Consulate in Tangier.'

Tremayne sat back and looked at Timpson.

'Well, at least it's not the German Consul-General,' Tremayne said, with an apologetic smile.

'This is no joke, Tremayne. There are going to be serious repercussions. He's a senior official of the German Consulate,' Cartwright snapped. 'I need to speak with the boss and bring her up to speed.'

Tremayne finished assessing the diamonds and totted up his scribbled figures. Nearly fifteen thousand carats. Zaber could have retired anywhere in the world on that, he thought.

'The boss wants to speak with you,' Cartwright said, sticking his head around the door. 'Leave the bag. I'll check it for clues.'

Timpson gave Tremayne a wink.

Tremayne put the last packages back in the bag, slung it over his shoulder and picked up his revolver from the desk. Cartwright eyed the bag.

'Nothing personal. It's my job,' Tremayne said, smiling.

They walked down a marble-tiled hall to a door with a plaque that read *British Vice Consul*.

'Mr Tremayne is here, ma'am, and he's got a gun,' Cartwright said, with a smirk.

Charlotte Richardson smiled brightly and walked forward.

'Oh, you've cut your face. Are you alright?' she said, offering her hand.

For Tremayne, it seemed that all the stress and danger of the day somehow concentrated into this moment.

117

'A penny for your thoughts, Mr Tremayne,' she said.

'Can we drop the formality? Call me Harvey,' he said.

She held his gaze for a few seconds before withdrawing her hand.

'I think you need a drink,' she said, walking over to a large cabinet against the wall.

She poured him a large Scotch and put the glass in his hand.

'Sorry I don't have any gin,' she said, with an apologetic smile. 'From what I hear, I'd say you had a pretty eventful evening.'

Tremayne took a deep swig of the Scotch and leaned back with his eyes closed and downed the remainder.

She took the empty glass and refilled it.

'Are you alright … Harvey?' she said.

Tremayne cocked his head and looked at her from under his eyebrows.

'Well, I've been shot at several times,' he said, with emotion in his voice.

He felt the warmth from the Scotch pulsing through his system, chasing away the demons. What the hell must she think of me? Pull yourself together, man. He cleared his throat, sat forward and smiled at her.

'Thanks, just what I needed,' he said, raising the glass.

'So, tell me. What did you find out?' she said.

'Well, I finally met with Salamon Zaber. He's the Tangier dealer, otherwise known as Indigo. He's been handling the smuggled diamonds, but it seems he's fallen out of favour with the Nazis and they have cut him out of the smuggling ring. Zaber planned to steal one last consignment from the Santa Maria and then disappear. I was questioning him when a man jumped me. Zaber called him Moussa and it he turns out his name is Leopold Wenger. He said he'd told Zaber there would be no more diamonds for him, and everything now goes to Germany. He must have been the Nazi overseeing the Tangier smuggling ring. He talked about orders from someone called Sidewinder. Does that name mean anything to you?'

'Well, we know Wenger. He's head of Nazi propaganda at the German Consulate, a real fascist. I've never heard of Sidewinder, but I'll get it checked. It's a strange codename. Sounds like a type of clock,' she said.

Tremayne smiled. 'Well I rather suspect this Sidewinder is named after one of nature's malicious creations. It's a type of adder that lies buried in the dunes in the Namib Desert, until its prey steps on it and then it strikes. I've known a couple of people bitten by them. Fortunately they didn't die, but the pain was so excruciating, they wished they had.'

'So, if Wenger is taking his lead from Sidewinder perhaps he's his Nazi boss in Berlin, rather than Zaber's contact in South West Africa?' she said.

'I'm inclined to agree, yet Sidewinder being the name of a snake from the Namib Desert, could also be somebody based there, rather than Berlin! Anyway, it seems Sidewinder had given Moussa orders to kill both Zaber and me. I think they planned to throw us overboard on the way to Hamburg!'

Charlotte Richardson sat deep in thought, staring at an imaginary spot on the wall.

'So how did Wenger know you were going to be there?' she said.

'That's a very good question. And more to the point he called me by my name. Sergeant Youssoufi gave me the information on the Santa Maria's arrival, via Cartwright. That means Youssoufi is somehow involved in the smuggling ring. I think we need to ask Timpson to watch him.'

'That should be Cartwright's job,' she said.

'They are too close and, frankly, I don't trust Cartwright,' he said.

Richardson stared at Tremayne and was about to say something, but just nodded.

'And where are the diamonds that Zaber was stealing?' she asked, changing the subject.

'Right here,' he said, patting the bag. 'Around fifteen thousand carats of top-quality rough from the Lewala Mine. Whoever smuggled these knew their diamonds and had access to restricted areas. Sir Ernest Oppenheimer needs to know about this. Can I send a telegram from here?'

'Write down your message and I'll get it sent,' she said.

He reached into the bag and pulled out one of the small pouches and tipped the contents onto her desk. The stones rattled as they hit the glass top and sparkled as they rolled.

She looked at them, open-mouthed. 'My God, they're so beautiful.'

'Ten stones, each around ten carats and of the best blue-white quality.'

She picked one up and held it to the light.

'Gosh, that is amazing.'

He pictured a large cut diamond on a fine gold chain hanging in the 'V' of her white blouse.

'I need to secure these diamonds in the consulate safe until they can be shipped. Can you organise for them to be sent to De Beers in London for me, via the diplomatic bag? I'll give you the details.'

'We can transfer them to my safe right now if you like.'

Tremayne scooped them together to return them to the pouch, but Richardson still held one, which she placed gently in his hand. He closed his fingers around hers and softly brushed his thumb across the back of her hand. He knew he shouldn't have done it, and looked up to check her reaction.

There was a loud knock on the door and she hurriedly pulled back, arranging her hair and brushing down her skirt.

'Who is it?' she said.

'Cartwright, ma'am, it's important.'

As he stepped into the office his eyes fell to the small pouch in Tremayne's hand, and the open bag on the chair.

'Sorry to interrupt, ma'am, but I need to speak with you on a matter of some urgency.'

'Mr Tremayne, will you wait through there please?' Richardson pointed to a door. 'I won't be a moment.'

He picked up the pouch and the bag and walked through into a bright, airy room overlooking the floodlit consulate garden. On the table was an ice bucket with a bottle of champagne and two glasses.

A few minutes later she returned.

'Oh good, do open the bottle. I thought we should toast your appointment to the Foreign Office.'

Surprised, he just stared at her.

'You do know how to open a bottle of champagne, don't you?' she said, mocking him.

'Yes, of course.'

He poured, they touched glasses, both took a sip and sat back.

'So, Charlotte, you haven't told me anything about yourself. I should really like to know who I'm working for.'

She cocked her head at the use of her first name. It was a long time since a man had addressed her in that way.

'I don't discuss my personal life with staff, Harvey,' she said with a smile.

She studied him.

'Well, I was born in Henley, studied Greek History at Oxford and then joined the Foreign Office in London. I was posted here two years ago.'

'Are there many old Greeks to study in Tangier?' he asked, with a lopsided grin. Her smile faded, and she looked down.

'Sorry,' he said. 'That was supposed to be a joke.'

They both sipped their drinks.

'Is there a Mr Richardson?'

She looked at him and shook her head. The phone rang.

'Yes?' she said. 'When will the plane be ready? Thank you.'

As she turned back, Tremayne was standing beside her, bottle in hand. He held her arm steady and carefully refilled her glass.

'Mr Tremayne, we are now colleagues and we have to behave accordingly,' she said, putting on a formal air.

'I could resign,' he said, his eyes sparkling.

She looked at him, taking another sip of champagne. 'Or I could fire you for misconduct!' she said.

'Charlotte, will you have dinner with me tomorrow night?' he said, in a whisper.

She took a few sips of her champagne and shook her head. 'I'm sorry, Harvey. I'm afraid that is out of the question.'

Tremayne looked at her, disconsolate.

'We have to get you out of the country tonight. The police have issued a warrant for your arrest for the murder of Leopold Wenger. Someone from the German Consulate has put you at the scene of the shooting at the docks.'

'But no one else saw me,' he said, holding his head with his free hand.

'Someone knew he was going to meet you tonight, so they've put two and two together. We have confirmed that you have diplomatic immunity and that we are expelling you with immediate effect. An RAF plane will leave in three hours to take you to Cairo. From there you take a scheduled Imperial Airways flight to Cape Town. Timpson will take you to the airport.'

There was silence at the finality of her words. Tremayne knocked back the remainder of his Scotch.

'Make sure these diamonds are sent to Dr Andrew Davey, at De Beers, 17 Charterhouse Street, EC1. Please tell no one that they're here, not even your closest colleagues. Diamonds have a habit of bringing out the worst in people.'

She nodded but said nothing.

'I'll go and make arrangements with Timpson,' he said, turning for the door.

He didn't look back.

PART 2

Chapter 31

Respite Bay, Forbidden Zone, South West Africa

As HMSAS Table Bay sailed south from Luderitz, Captain Ernest Denning surveyed the deep swells that climbed over the jagged reefs and crashed against the rocky shore. Here, where the mighty Benguela Current splits, and flows either side of Possession Island, it formed powerful currents and eddies that lay in wait for any unsuspecting sailor.

Affectionately known as The Stinker after years in the Southern Ocean as a whaler, the vessel was delivering an RDF system plus two naval radio technicians to Port Baleen at Respite Bay. With an identical receiver being installed in Luderitz, it was part of the diamond coast security network being set up by Commander Mike Crosson to track and intercept radio messages. With the two stations installed, plus The Stinker offshore, the location of any transmission could be quickly triangulated.

Today, negotiating the rips and eddies off the coast was particularly hazardous. The starboard engine of The Stinker was overheating and Captain Denning had it shut down as a precaution. The old steel-hulled twin-screw whaler was well past her best.

Ernest Denning was forty-two years of age and joined the Navy as a boy sailor at fourteen. In World War 1 he had been a gunner on the light cruiser HMS Galatea. By the end of the war he had risen through the ranks to petty officer. When hostilities ended, Britain had a surplus of war ships and the decision was made to provide these on permanent loan to the various British Dominions around the world. They were manned by Royal Navy volunteers, who provided the necessary expertise and experience to help train a new crew under their new flag. Denning had jumped at the chance for adventure. The prospect of returning to civilian life, with a menial job at best, was not to his liking. He signed a two-year contract and sailed to South Africa. There he enlisted in the South African Naval Service in 1921, got married, had children and never returned to Britain.

He was initially assigned to HMSAS Protea, a hydrographic survey vessel, mapping the three thousand miles of territorial waters for shipping hazards and future port locations. Then, in early 1939 with the growing threat of war with Germany, the South African coast was deemed vulnerable and poorly protected. Fishing trawlers and whalers were commandeered and hurriedly converted for intelligence gathering and for harbour and shipping lane protection. Denning had been appointed captain of HMSAS Table Bay, one of four listening and intelligence-gathering vessels. She was fitted with a powerful RDF and armed with two 20 mm cannons, one fore and one aft. For anti-submarine defence she had a 1920s vintage depth charge rack at the stern. This model was obsolete in the Royal Navy but still part of the arsenal in the far-flung corners of Empire. The system, recently installed, had never been tested and everyone agreed it was only for show. It was designed to take six cylinders, but with munitions in short supply she carried just two. Denning acknowledged their inadequacy. He rather wished the harpoon gun remaining on the bow could still be fired.

His knowledge of the South African coastline and its shipping routes made him an ideal choice to captain her. Originally based in Simonstown on the Cape Peninsula, he had patrolled the west coast of South Africa. Later he and his crew were assigned to Walvis Bay, nearly nine hundred miles to the north, to monitor maritime shipping and radio transmissions off the coast of South West Africa. And that is where The Stinker now patrolled; with the fore and aft cannons cloaked in tarpaulins and her harpoon standing prominently on the bow, she looked just like the whaler she had once been.

Within days of arriving at Walvis Bay they had intercepted Morse code messages. The problem was that they were usually encrypted, and this raised the authority's suspicions. No one went to the trouble of coding messages unless they had something to hide, and that was invariably the military. But these were not British military codes.

Several weeks before, they had picked up an encrypted message just north of Luderitz, and the radio operator recognised one of the words, *Abwehr*, the name of the German Secret Service. There was uncertainty as to whether it was a code word, but when this was communicated to the authorities it was like throwing a stone at a hornet's nest. Within days Commander Mike Crosson of British Naval Intelligence in Cape Town was relocated to Luderitz and The Stinker was also transferred there from Walvis Bay.

The problem was they could not locate the point of transmission based on a single receiving station. Crosson had immediately requisitioned two RDFs. The first was being installed in Luderitz and The Stinker was delivering the second to Respite Bay. It was housed in three wooden crates lashed to the foredeck. One for the radio receiver, one for the direction finder and mast and the third for the batteries necessary to operate the system for up to twelve hours in the event of a power failure.

Denning shouted speed and direction changes into a mouthpiece on the bridge. With one engine shut down, the old trawler was sluggish and slow to respond. Not ideal when negotiating this treacherous coastline, but this was a top-priority delivery.

To the north of Respite Bay lay Great White Point, a headland jutting out in to the Benguela Current. To the south of this, a strong swirling rip was created. Denning kept The Stinker well offshore, but as she sailed past the point she slowed and wallowed under its influence. He steered her hard to starboard and rang Full Ahead, but she barely responded. He ordered the overheated starboard engine to be restarted, much to the chief engineer's irritation, and set it Half Ahead. That did the trick.

Making it into the quieter waters of Respite Bay, Denning made a mental note not to risk getting that close to Great White Point in an underpowered boat.

The Stinker tied up at the wooden jetty, directly beside the single dock crane, which was used to transfer heavy materials from a vessel to wagons on the narrow-gauge railway. But today it was a short journey to the top of the hill where the RDF was to be installed. The elevated location had clear views to the north and to the south along the coast. A dedicated power line ran from the generator house.

With the three crates safely offloaded, Bill Williams and Jimmy Britt, the naval radio technicians, disembarked. They were responsible for setting up and commissioning the system. Captain Denning bade farewell to the two and headed back out into the bay.

To his surprise, three motor torpedo boats appeared from the south, travelling at speed, their sleek bows slicing through the rough water with ease. Radio communication confirmed they were the MTBs that Commander Crosson had requisitioned from Simonstown. They were making an unscheduled stop to refuel. They roared past The Stinker at high speed.

Shaking his head at their apparent recklessness, Denning sailed slowly out of Respite Bay, planning to give Great White Point a wide berth on the return journey.

Chapter 32

Guano Bay, Diaz Peninsula, South West Africa

Captain Niels Kruger, with his trusted trackers Sergeant Samuel Ndakolo and Constable Isaak Japie, departed Luderitz at first light in the pilot's launch. An offshore wind had picked up overnight, driving the fog away, leaving the promise of a scorching day. They gave the treacherous Diaz Point a wide berth and motored out into the fifteen-foot swell driving in off the South Atlantic. As they turned south towards Guano Bay and into the lee of Halifax Island, the sea calmed.

Kruger scoured the bay with his binoculars. At the north end the beach was brown with seals, the silver of the sand almost completely hidden. The smell being driven offshore did nothing to calm their uneasy stomachs.

At the far south end of the beach was a huddle of fishermen's cottages, set back above the tideline. After the guano had been mined out, a few fishermen would spend the season here catching and salting snoek. The arrival of the new fishing fleet based in Walvis Bay had caused that market to collapse. Even the clear turquoise water lapping the silver-white sand was not enough to overcome the air of neglect.

'Well, there's no boat. If he does stay here, he's not here today,' Kruger said, surveying the beach with his binoculars. Then he stopped. 'Well, well, there's a tall pole on the end of the farthest cottage that could be used to take an aerial. We'll check that one first. Arm your rifles. The man we are looking for probably killed Jan and Hendrik.'

As the boat scrunched onto the soft sand, the two policemen jumped out and secured the anchor. Kruger followed them, revolver in hand.

'We'll start with the house, and then the outbuildings. Isaak, you stay by the boat and cover us. If you see anything, one shot in the air.'

As Kruger approached the cottage, he pointed to Samuel to circle around the other side. The windows were shuttered, and the only door was bolted and padlocked. The wooden pole at the end of the cottage had a wire attached to it.

'Samuel, search the shed,' Kruger said. 'Isaak, get the sledgehammer and crowbar from the boat. We'll have to knock the lock off.'

'The bastard not here,' came a distant voice. It floated on the air, from no discernible direction.

Kruger armed his revolver and looked around. 'Who's there?' he said in an authoritative tone. 'This is the police.'

There was no reply. The only sound was the waves tumbling on the beach.

'Where did that come from, Samuel?' he asked.

'Over there, I think, Captain,' he replied, pointing towards the tumble of boulders at the bottom of Black Ridge.

'I shan't ask again. Who's there?' he demanded, walking forward, revolver at the ready.

'The bastard not here,' the voice repeated, echoing off the rock face like the siren call of seafaring legend.

Samuel, suspecting a wicked spirit, backed away. Even Kruger hesitated. As he approached, he could make out something amongst the rocks, moving but without form.

'Who is not here?' Kruger asked.

'The bastard what live here,' said the voice.

The featureless bundle moved again and a figure materialised, and slowly walked out into the sunlight. It was a young girl, with an old brown blanket over her shoulders. Kruger relaxed.

'Come here, girl. What's your name?' he asked, in a kindly voice, putting away his revolver.

'Joaba. I live there,' she said, pointing further along the beach.

'Well, Joaba, I'd like to ask you some questions.'

She nodded.

'Where is the man who lives here?'

'I told you, he not here. They gone this morning.'

'They?'

'He took the other bastard with him…. They hurt me.'

Kruger could hear anguish in her voice.

'What's his name?'

'I don't know. I call him bastard.'

'Joaba, he must have a name?'

'The other bastards call him Christo.'

A loud bang broke the quiet of the beach as Constable Isaak started to smash off the padlock with the sledgehammer. Birds lifted from Black Ridge in their thousands, all screeching a warning. Samuel was now convinced there was an evil spirit at work.

Saying nothing, Joaba walked over to the shed and pulled something out from the wall.

'Here,' she said, holding out two keys on a ring.

Kruger chuckled and shook his head. 'Isaak, stop. Here are the keys.'

Entering the cottage, Isaak unbolted the shutters and opened the windows. Shafts of light brightened the darkest corners.

A sudden flapping of wings caused dust and feathers to rise, catching in the shafts of light, accompanied by a high-pitched 'kak-kak-kak-kak-kak'. Constable Isaak was outside in a split second, wide-eyed and two shades paler.

'That Falkie,' Joaba said, laughing.

Isaak, thinking it was something evil, kept a safe distance.

'He a bird,' she added, to the amusement of all present except Constable Isaak.

'I look after him when that bastard gone.'

She entered the cottage and a minute later came out with Falkie on her gloved arm.

'That must be the falcon he uses when he's smuggling diamonds,' Kruger said. 'Rather a handsome chap, aren't you?'

Isaak studied the bird from a distance and nodded. Joaba launched him into the air and he flew off towards Black Ridge. Samuel raised his rifle but Falkie was fast and disappeared from view.

'He come back later,' Joaba said.

'Alright, get searching. The cupboards, the stove, the chimney.'

The limited number of hiding places in the cottage was soon exhausted. The only thing found was a small hessian bag of coffee and several tins of food.

'Right, search the sheds. There's got to be something here,' Kruger said.

'You look for the crystals, mister?'

All eyes turned to Joaba.

'Yes, we are. Do you know where he keeps them?'

She knelt and lifted a black stone from under the stove, exposing a wood-lined cubby. Kruger shook his head and smiled at the simplicity of it. He put his hand in and cautiously felt around. This would be a favoured place for scorpions, he thought. At one end he found a metal object. It was made of steel, the length of a pencil, but twice the diameter, with four cuts at one end and a point at the other. He knew immediately what it was.

'Joaba, does this Christo have a crossbow to fire these?'

'He shoots a flat-handed bow over there,' she said, pointing towards Black Ridge.

'Isaak, take the girl over there and see what you can find. Samuel, search these sheds, then we'll check the other cottages.'

Kruger reached into the hole under the stove to give it one last check.

'Captain, look at this,' Isaak said, holding a heavy piece of driftwood with four steel bolts deeply embedded.

'Look at the flight feathers on these. They are the same colour and size as the piece we found,' Kruger said.

He pulled an envelope from his top pocket and tipped out the cut feather they had found at Great White Point. It was identical.

'This Christo person is definitely our man. And with a crossbow and steel bolts he's very dangerous.'

The reason for the disappearance of Jan Gamab and Hendrik Tseib began to take shape in Kruger's mind.

'Joaba, I'd like you to come to Luderitz with us to help answer some questions. We have somewhere for you to sleep and eat and we'll get you something to wear. You are my key witness. I need to tell your mother. Where can I find her?'

Joaba pointed further along the beach.

'Captain look at this,' Samuel shouted, from one of the outbuildings.

Kruger found him in a small wooden hut and from the smell he knew its purpose.

'Down there, Captain,' Samuel said, pointing into the long drop.

To one side, there was something rectangular sticking out of the mess.

'Find something to get it out, Samuel.'

He returned moments later with a ladle from the cottage.

'Lift it out carefully, don't drop it.'

Samuel took a deep breath and leaning in and retrieved the article.

Kruger held it at arm's length by the corner and started to scrape off the worst of the mess on the door frame. It was a small, maroon coloured soft-backed notebook. It had some sort of black motif on the front. As he opened it, he could see pages of words, letters and numbers. It had to be a codebook. On the inside of the front cover, handwritten in pencil at the top, was a single word: Sidewinder.

Chapter 33

Tangier, Morocco

Three days after the death of Leopold Wenger, MI6 got word of an unscheduled German Luftwaffe flight arriving in Tangier. Two passengers were listed. It was too much of a coincidence, given that Wenger, alias Moussa, was a senior Nazi official and had just been killed. And he was implicated in the German diamond smuggling ring. Mark Timpson was assigned the job of shadowing them and had been at the airport to witness their arrival.

It was on the second day that he saw the two leave the German Consulate in an old black Mercedes. Timpson discreetly followed them to the harbour, where they stopped in a side street. A tall, slightly stooped man in a white suit, walking with long stilt-like strides, appeared and got in.

Timpson banged the steering wheel. It was Youssoufi! Tremayne's intuition had been right, and now there was no doubt of his connection with the Nazis. The question was, in what capacity?

He followed them along the coast road, west of the city, to a big house on Route Sidi Masmoudi, overlooking the beach. He drove slowly past the whitewashed sheet steel gates just as they were closing and parked further up the road.

The property was surrounded by a high stone wall and Timpson needed to see what was inside and, if possible, gain access. He walked back down the road to inspect the gates. There was a gap between them, and he peered through. In his limited field of view, all he could see was part of the house, and the black car parked in front.

To the side of the property he climbed a tree to get a better view. Two uniformed men with sidearms patrolled the grounds, one with a guard dog. There was no way he could gain access on his own. He'd just have to wait.

After nearly three hours in the hot car, Timpson had dozed off when the sound of the steel gates clanking open woke him. The black Mercedes turned onto the road and headed in his direction, and he had to slump sideways onto the passenger seat to keep out of sight.

He followed the car into the foothills of the Rif Mountains, keeping it in sight about two or three bends ahead. When the car disappeared, he thought it might have turned off and was about to backtrack, when he saw it appear on a promontory high above. He drove to the next bend and pulled over. A few minutes later the Mercedes came back down the hill at speed. Why was it in such a hurry?

He drove on, and the road ended at a viewing point. Seeing nothing, he swung around to follow them, but hesitated. Why the hell would the Germans drive to the viewpoint and come straight back down? It wouldn't be to take photos of the scenery. Something didn't add up.

He searched the area, looking over the edge and down the steep cliff face that ended in a boulder field far below. Then he saw the body, wedged behind a stunted tree, about twenty feet down. He scrambled down and saw the man's face. It was indeed Youssoufi. He was bruised and battered, and his eyes were closed and his hands tied behind his back. He was still breathing.

Timpson climbed back up to the car and fetched his knife and water bottle. After he'd freed him, he let Youssoufi drink and washed the worst of the blood from his face.

Youssoufi opened his eyes, looked at Timpson and gave him the most heartfelt 'Thank you' Timpson had ever heard.

It took nearly half an hour to get him back up to the car and onto the back seat.

In silence Timpson drove down the mountain towards the city, in a hurry to get to the British Consulate. He wanted to question Youssoufi while the Germans still believed him dead, and then he'd take him to hospital.

With a mile to go, the Tangier traffic conspired against him and they came to a halt. The impatient drivers all around blared their horns in a futile gesture of rage. While it might help ease their frustration it was giving Timpson a headache.

Five minutes later when the traffic finally started to move, he saw the culprit: an overturned cart and the police and passers-by trying to subdue a rebellious donkey, its eyes manic and back legs lashing out at its would-be captors like steam pistons on a train.

When they arrived, he helped Youssoufi clean up the cuts on his face, and two cups of strong coffee and half a bar of chocolate later the rescued man was sitting up in a chair.

'You are most kind. I thank you. Where exactly am I?' Youssoufi said.

'You are safe in the British Consulate. My name's Mark Timpson. And you are …?'

'Sergeant Mustafa Youssoufi.'

Timpson nodded and said, 'I'd like to ask you some questions, and then I'll take you to the hospital.'

Youssoufi put his hands up and shook his head, dismissing the offer.

'Who were your two friends in the black Mercedes?'

Youssoufi chortled, then winced with the pain.

'No friends of mine, I assure you. They are from the Abwehr, investigating the death of Moussa.'

'Why did they want to speak with you?'

Youssoufi looked away and was silent.

'What you say here stays here,' Timpson said. 'You have my word.'

Youssoufi looked Timpson in the eye for several seconds and cocked his head in acceptance. 'I was a fool. I had dealings with Moussa. I took money in exchange for giving him information. May Allah forgive me.'

'What was Moussa's role in Tangier?'

'He made sure illegal cargoes bound for Germany received safe passage through the port, including the diamonds hidden on the Santa Maria. He also ensured that Zaber only got the diamonds that were allocated to him. The Nazis didn't trust him because he was Jewish.'

'And who did Moussa work for?'

'The top Nazi in Abwehr.'

'Wilhelm Canaris?' Timpson asked, with a doubtful frown.

'I don't know that name. The man I heard talk of is Sidewinder.'

Timpson was astonished. That was the name Tremayne had learned from Wenger.

'Have you met this Sidewinder?'

Youssoufi shook his head.

'So, why did these Abwehr men try to kill you?'

'The Santa Maria with all her cargo was impounded by Tangier customs and they lost all their diamonds. They thought I was responsible.'

'And are you?'

Youssoufi looked him in the eye and said, 'No. The request came from the British Consulate.'

'But why does the impounding of the Santa Maria warrant two Abwehr agents to fly from Hamburg? There must be something else, something to do with Wenger?'

'I think Sidewinder is planning a raid and Moussa knew about it. They wanted to make sure the information hadn't been leaked before he was killed.'

'If Moussa was part of the smuggling ring it must involve diamonds. Where will this take place?'

'I do not know. I am not involved in it,' Youssoufi said, immediately looking down. Timpson could see the shame washing over his face at the realisation that this was a lie.

'There must be something more you can tell me.'

Youssoufi shook his head.

'Damn it, Mustafa, you must remember names, places, dates?' Timpson said, exasperated.

Youssoufi looked up, startled at his tone, and thought for a moment. 'They asked me if I had heard of ...' he trailed off and rubbed his chin in thought. 'If I'd heard of Bengala, no, Benguela, yes, Benguela, that's it.'

'Who is Benguela?' Timpson said.

'I do not know,' Youssoufi said, shaking his head. 'They asked me if Moussa had spoken of Operation Benguela on the 27th.'

Timpson looked at his watch, picked up the phone and dialled.

'Begging your pardon, ma'am. There's something important you need to know.'

Charlotte Richardson went over Youssoufi's story, clarifying points and scribbling notes. They still had no idea of where or who Benguela was. It was the *Encyclopedia Britannica* that gave them the answer.

'The Benguela Current runs up the west coast of Southern Africa, right past South West Africa,' Timpson read out loud.

Richardson turned to Youssoufi and said, 'How can I be sure you're telling the truth, Sergeant Youssoufi?' She looked him in the eye pointedly.

Youssoufi held her gaze and said, 'Because Mr Timpson saved my life and I am in his debt.'

'Timpson, take Sergeant Youssoufi to the kitchen and give him some food and get Services to organise him a room and call for the doctor. He will stay with us for a few days.'

Youssoufi smiled and nodded his thanks to her as Timpson helped him out.

As the door closed, Richardson put her head in her hands. Harvey Tremayne was unknowingly walking into a Nazi raid. What could she do? She picked up the phone.

'Get me MI6 in London. It's urgent.'

Chapter 34

Police Headquarters, Luderitz, South West Africa

At the Diamond Police headquarters in Luderitz, Joaba was relishing a plate of *mielie pap and wors*, the local staple of stiff corn porridge and sausage. Dressed in a pair of police overalls several sizes too big, she cleaned the plate to a shine with a chunk of black bread.

Kruger's heart went out to her. Fatherless, uneducated, vulnerable and abused, yet she was a bright girl with a sharp mind. She was his prime witness, the only one who could identify Christo and, from the codebook they'd found, alias Sidewinder.

Returning from Guano Bay in the early afternoon, Kruger had spent the rest of the day writing down Joaba's story. Her eye for detail and her grasp of what was important painted a detailed picture of Sidewinder's life, his smuggling activity and his personal life.

It was beyond doubt that he was responsible for the murder of the two policemen near Great White Point. He had a steel bolt crossbow and a peregrine falcon for intercepting carrier pigeons, and Joaba had seen the diamonds and a transmitter, plus the description of his sailing boat matched the type that could be used for a beach landing. Importantly, Joaba confirmed he had sailed off early with his falcon the day the policemen went missing, and only returned at dusk. The following day she'd had to wash what looked like blood from the bottom of the boat. He said he'd been fishing, but Joaba knew that was a lie. Why would he take Falkie fishing?

That had to be the reason why they had not found any trace of the two bodies. He probably killed Constable Hendrik with a crossbow bolt, losing a flight feather in the process. Sergeant Jan must have had time to take a shot before he too was killed. It explained why Sidewinder had dropped the falcon hood. He was in a hurry to escape in his sailing boat after the noise of the rifle shots from Corporal Gam.

Joaba also confirmed that he had no wound marks on his body. The fact that she knew this made him cringe.

She was certainly on the mark as far as her name for him was concerned. That bastard must have loaded the bodies of the two policemen into his boat and dumped them at sea, without ceremony, without decency, to be fed to the sharks. Bile rose in his throat and he had to swallow hard to avoid retching. He cleared his throat loudly, his eyes watering. Joaba looked up at him, her head to one side.

'You alright mister? You need some of Ma's thunderclap?'

Kruger nodded and smiled. He could well imagine that would sort out any number of ailments.

What troubled him now was where Sidewinder and his accomplice Karl had gone. According to Joaba they'd sailed out of Guano Bay at first light this morning, heading north. Did that mean he was heading up the coast, or had he sailed out around Halifax Island and then gone south? That made most sense. As a smuggler he'd head for the Forbidden Zone, along the diamond coast.

He picked up the phone and dialled.

'Hello Commander Crosson, its Kruger here.'

Chapter 35

Seal Harbour, Possession Island, South West Africa

Forty miles south of Luderitz, Jager and Bosman arrived off Seal Harbour on the sheltered east coast of Possession Island. A mile long and a few hundred yards wide, it was flat, wind-swept and almost devoid of vegetation. For countless millennia, seabirds and seals had raised their young here, surrounded by the plankton and fish-rich Benguela Current. In the nineteenth century Europeans culled the seals for their skin and blubber and mined the layers of guano for fertiliser. But with the deposits exhausted and with no fresh water, the island was abandoned.

They had sailed down the west coast of the island to avoid the choppy waters of Rip Strait, that part of the Benguela Current that squeezed between the mainland and the island. They had rounded the southern tip and turned north, scanning the heat-hazed, shimmering shoreline. Although it was an isolated location, Jager still needed to make sure there were no seal hunters or fishermen to spoil the rendezvous. All he could see were birds, tens of thousands of them, boobies, gannets and pelicans nesting noisily on the low rocky cliffs.

He lowered the mast, engaged the oars and rowed into the harbour. Two curious seals followed the boat, bobbing up, snorting and staring. An old crumbling timber jetty and the remnant walls of the guano miners' homes were all that remained, stark white in the bright sunlight.

As they neared the shore the stench of the nesting birds was overpowering, heightening the sense of decay. They landed in a little cove out of sight of the harbour that had a small flooded cave at the back. It wasn't natural: it had been excavated during the guano mining, and it made an ideal hiding place.

With the boat secure, they walked to the high point that had an uninterrupted view all around the island. They were alone.

Back at the cove they offloaded the canvas-covered box containing the transceiver. Bosman rolled out the aerial and ran it up the hill, while Jager fitted the handle and wound it hard to charge the battery. He put on the headphones and started to tap.

Scorpion to Neptune.

Five minutes later he tried again. *Scorpion to Neptune.*

Neptune receiving.

Your status.

Eight miles south west of target.

Target clear.

Confirmed ETA in 60.

Await signal.

Confirmed out.

Jager felt a rush of excitement at the impending rendezvous and meeting again with his old friend Horst Nissen. At last there was a rekindling of their colonial pride. The Fatherland was asking for their help, the sort of help only loyal South Westers could provide. And in return, their self-determination would be restored.

With the sun dropping into the distant fog bank, an orange glow lit the western horizon. Jager climbed up to a promontory overlooking the harbour. In the fading light, looming out of the first wisps of fog, he saw Neptune, looking like a ghost ship from an old sea dog's story. She was a trawler named Octopus, a fishing boat typical of this coast. She had been deliberately chosen so as not to raise suspicion if spotted by the authorities. Her armaments were carefully hidden.

With his torch he flashed a Morse signal to say it was all clear. He watched as she turned into the bay and dropped anchor in Seal Harbour.

Five minutes later a small inflatable boat rowed over to the jetty and picked up Jager and Bosman. As they pulled up alongside, there were shouts of welcome and jocular abuse and many friendly hands to help them on board.

'The first person to greet them was Nissen, in scruffy, well-worn sailor's clothes and a black woolly hat.

'So, what do you think of the disguise, Christo? Do I get the part?' he said, laughing.

'A parrot and a beard and you'd be perfect,' Jager said.

'Christo, you remember Nico Bronkhorst from the Walvis Bay, Green Commando, he trained with us two years ago,' Nissen said.

Jager and Bronkhorst slapped each other on the back. They had known one another since childhood.

With the introductions and pleasantries over, they went below deck for the debrief. Nissen spoke about the Third Reich's mission to bring pride back to German-speaking people, wherever they were but particularly here in South West Africa.

'Generalfeldmarschall Göring has given his blessing for this operation because his father Heinrich Göring, was the Imperial Commissioner of German South West Africa in 1885. The Generalfeldmarschall has a personal interest in getting your country back under German control,' Nissen said, almost shouting the words.

There was a rousing cheer and glasses of schnapps were downed and banged noisily on whatever hard surface came to hand.

Jager then went through the operation in meticulous detail, highlighting what was expected of each company and each person in that company. The final thing was to have everyone hand in documents and items that could identify them, to be retrieved when they returned to Neptune.

'To Operation Benguela and success!' Jager shouted.

'If I retreat, kill me. If I die, avenge me. If I advance, follow me. To the Fatherland!' they all shouted in unison, downing more schnapps.

Chapter 36

Robert Harbour, Luderitz, South West Africa

Joaba accompanied Captain Niels Kruger on the fifteen-minute walk from police headquarters to Robert Harbour. He was going to introduce her to an old friend who was flying in that morning, all the way from Tangier. Joaba had no idea where Tangier was. She'd heard of Cape Town and thought it might be near there.

They stopped to look at the motor torpedo boats, newly arrived from Simonstown. They were sleek, grey predators, their designations – ST14, ST15 and ST20 – showing on their bows. Two had been pulled onto the slipway, covers off, with cables and pipes feeding into their inner workings. The third was still in the water.

'Hello, Niels,' Crosson said. 'These MTBs are a sight for sore eyes, aren't they?'

'Well, they certainly look the part,' Kruger said.

'Eighteen hundred horsepower, top speed of thirty-three knots, fitted with twin Lewis machine guns mounted fore and aft and twin 18-inch torpedo launchers. They'll be the scourge of the smugglers along this coast.'

Overhead there was the deep throbbing drone of a large plane.

'Shit, that a big bastard,' Joaba said in astonishment.

'Isn't she a beauty,' Kruger said.

The Short Sunderland flying boat, with its red, white and blue RAF decals clearly visible, flew north and made a long, leisurely turn back towards Luderitz. Minutes later she touched down gracefully on Robert Harbour. Amidst spray and engine noise, the flamingos on the far shore lifted off in unison, forming a pink panicky cloud. With one of the four Bristol Pegasus engines throbbing gently, she motored slowly to shallow water and tied up to the floating pontoon. Within minutes the pilot launch returned with the passengers and ropes were thrown up and tied off. Harvey Tremayne was first at the top of the walkway and shook Kruger's hand and slapped him on the back.

'Hello, Niels. It's been a long time. How the hell are you? Promoted, I see,' he said, eyeing the epaulettes on his white shirt.

'All the better for seeing you, Harvey. It's been, what, more than three years? I was sorry to hear about what happened ... you know.'

Tremayne nodded. 'I've got a score to settle, Niels, and I'll need your help,' he said, in a low voice, putting his head next to Kruger's.

'Harvey, can I introduce you to Commander Mike Crosson. Commander, this is Harvey Tremayne,' Kruger said.

'Tremayne, your timing is perfect,' Crosson said. 'We've just had our first positive lead on the recent coded communications. Let's go to my salubrious office for a debrief. I have some coffee brewing.'

Kruger broke away and told Joaba to wait at the harbour and when he was finished he'd come and collect her. Joaba folded her arms and stared at him as he walked off. She let out an expletive, but Kruger was too far away to hear.

When Tremayne saw where they were heading, he thought they must have the wrong building, and when he walked inside he was sure.

'Welcome to Pilchard Hall,' Crosson said with a wry smile, gesturing to the walls of the former fishing-net shack they now stood in. 'Sorry about this. I've just moved in. Anyway, think of it as home while you're here. That's your desk over there.'

'That's alright. I've been in worse,' Tremayne said, recoiling at the smell none the less.

'I won't embarrass you by asking where that was,' Crosson said, with a chuckle. 'Coffee?'

He handed Tremayne a chipped enamel mug containing hot brown liquid.

'The mug goes with the décor,' Crosson said, smiling, anticipating what Tremayne was thinking.

'So, Harvey, what brings you back? It's all been very hush-hush,' Kruger said.

'Niels, there's a situation developing. MI6 in London has new intelligence that indicates the Germans are running short of diamonds to support their military rearmament. The British Government is concerned they will resort to just about anything, to get hold of more. We're not just talking about smuggling here. We're talking about military-style theft of substantial quantities. South West Africa, with its German sympathisers, is an obvious target. It could potentially be an attack on the Eureka taking the quarterly diamond production to Cape Town or even an attack on the mine itself. I'm here to coordinate the Navy, De Beers and the Diamond Security Police on behalf of the Foreign Office to ensure that this does not happen. General Smuts and Sir Ernest have sanctioned this.'

'You're with the Secret Intelligence Service?' Kruger said, eyes wide and forehead wrinkled.

'Something like that. But no one needs to know – is that clear?' he replied.

'This sounds serious,' Kruger said, and then added, 'but surely the Germans wouldn't attack South West Africa directly. If they did, there'd be international condemnation!'

'Well, Niels, I doubt they'd worry about that. The Nazis are devious and belligerent. I'm sure they'll be actively fermenting trouble with our local colonials as we speak. We know they have been involved in illicit mining and smuggling, and all the diamonds, except the top-quality ones, have been going to German industry. A ship called the Santa Maria has been taking the diamonds from Swakopmund via Tangier to Hamburg. Tangier customs impounded her a few days ago and confiscated the illicit diamonds, but the Germans will find an alternative ship very quickly. What we don't know is how they get diamonds from here to Swakopmund, and I hope you can shed some light on that, Commander – you said you had some new intelligence?'

'There's been an increase in radio communications in recent weeks, and we had been unable to decode them until now. Captain Kruger here traced a suspected smuggler back to Guano Bay and was able to recover a German codebook that confirms him as a German agent. On the inside cover is the name Sidewinder,' Crosson said.

'Sidewinder?' Tremayne said, standing up. 'Are you sure?'

'Positive. Here's the book.'

Tremayne studied it. A black Nazi eagle was embossed on the maroon cover, and inside there were columns of words, letters and numbers. A brown stain partially covered the bottom half of the book. On the inside of the front cover, at the top, was a single handwritten word: Sidewinder.

'Well, I'll be damned. That's the name I got out of a shady diamond trader by the name of Salamon Zaber in Tangier. Niels, you'll know him better as Indigo. His name came up several times during interrogation after the shooting. I thought it was his boss in Berlin, not his contact here in the Forbidden Zone. I guess you've proved me wrong on that,' Tremayne said.

'Did you find out anything else from Indigo?' Kruger asked.

'No, he died before I could get anything more out of him.'

Kruger and Crosson glanced at one another.

'Look, I've got to find this Sidewinder. What do we know about him?'

'Well, his friends call him Christo, he has a falcon to catch carrier pigeons, he's been seen with diamonds in his house out at Guano Bay and he's personally responsible for the recent death of two policemen in the Forbidden Zone. We also know he has a radio set and the codebook you've seen,' Kruger said. 'He must have memorised the important codes and tried to destroy the evidence.'

Crosson nodded. 'Using the coding that is legible, the boffins in Cape Town have compared this with the earlier messages we intercepted. Although it's a different code, it is similar enough to establish a number of common call-signs. The names they've deciphered are, Neptune, Moby, Scorpion and Cobra.'

'What about Sidewinder?' Tremayne said.

'No, that's the odd thing. It hasn't come up so far, I'm afraid. But they are still working on it. What we have established is that Neptune and Moby communicate directly with each other. Moby does not communicate with any of the others. Neptune has two-way communication with Scorpion but none with Cobra. Scorpion and Cobra communicate with one another only occasionally.'

'Neptune and Moby sound like maritime names, don't you think? From memory, Neptune was the Roman god of the sea, and Moby is the whale in Herman Melville's novel,' Kruger said.

'We think the two maritime names might refer to ships used for transporting the smuggled diamonds,' Crosson said.

'Scorpion and Cobra are both deadly local residents,' Kruger said, 'as is the Sidewinder, our very own viper. All in all, they make up a venomous trio.'

'But, you say Sidewinder has a transmitter. So why doesn't he send any messages?' Tremayne said.

No one replied, furrows showing on their respective brows.

'So, do we know where this Sidewinder character is?' Tremayne asked.

'He sailed from Guano Bay yesterday morning, last seen going north towards Diaz Point, but after that we don't know. He had one other person with him, someone he calls Karl,' Kruger said. 'I've cross-checked against the list of mine employees and there are three with that name. Two are at work on the mine and the third, a Karl Bosman, is on a week off. If he clocks in, he'll be automatically detained.'

'Well, until we get updated information, Sidewinder is the chief suspect, implicated by his name in the codebook. I don't care what it takes, I want him alive. I have a score to settle,' Tremayne said.

He sat back and ran his fingers through his hair. Kruger looked at him, coming to terms with the change in his old friend. He was a different person. Harder, impatient and angry.

'Sorry, it's been a long journey,' Tremayne said, taking a swig of the now cold brown liquid.

'Harvey, he murdered two of our officers. I want to get him as much as you do—'

'Were they family, Niels?' Tremayne snapped.

Kruger said nothing. He knew it was personal, the rawness exposed like a bleeding rash.

'They'll have gone south, towards the diamond coast, but what are they planning, and what is their destination?' Tremayne said, talking more to himself than the others.

'Remember they've taken a transceiver,' Kruger said.

'Yes of course,' Tremayne said. 'Commander, have we picked up any transmissions in the last twenty-four hours?'

'Yes, The Stinker picked up one yesterday afternoon at 16.23, but the duration was very short,' Crosson said.

'The Stinker?'

'Sorry, that's our surveillance ship. A converted whaler, HMSAS Table Bay. She's fitted with a powerful RDF,' Crosson said.

'So, what direction did the transmission come from?' Tremayne asked.

Crosson shook his head. 'We didn't get a direction. She was in harbour undergoing maintenance at the time. Truth be told, she's an old rust bucket.'

'Are there are no other receiver stations?'

'I've just taken delivery of two RDFs. One of them was installed here in Luderitz today and the one at Port Baleen should be ready tomorrow. With those operational, plus The Stinker patrolling the coast, we'll be able to triangulate the location of any future radio signals and then intercept them with one of the MTBs.'

'Well, if Sidewinder is after diamonds, two men aren't going to do much on their own. They must have help on the way, and that's why they sent a message. When is the Eureka scheduled to take the next shipment of diamonds to Cape Town?' Tremayne said.

'She arrives on the 1st September,' Kruger said, checking his watch. 'Six days' time.'

'Well, that's certainly a possibility. Niels, message Cape Town and Kimberley and have the Eureka pick-up brought forward so she arrives as soon as possible. And she must have an armed escort. Then, if they are planning to attack her on the 1st they'll be on the back foot. If they plan to attack the mine, the sooner we have all the diamonds in the vaults in Cape Town the better,' Tremayne said.

'If Sidewinder is arranging to meet someone, the only hiding places along the coast would be in the lee of Possession Island or further south at Pomona Island?' Kruger said.

'Agreed, we need to get down there as fast as possible. When can we leave, Commander?' Tremayne asked.

'The first MTB will be ready late tomorrow morning. They've just arrived from Simonstown and took quite a beating rounding the Cape of Good Hope. We don't have our full complement of maintenance engineers and spare parts yet so the repairs are taking longer than they should.'

'Damn it, that's not soon enough, what about HMS what's its name?' Tremayne said.

'Table Bay. She'll be back in action tomorrow morning,' Crosson said, 'but she's slow, fifteen knots tops.'

'Niels, phone Kolmanskop and the Lewala Mine and tell them to double-check everyone coming on-shift and if they're in any way suspicious they must hold them until we can get down there. My guess is that Sidewinder and his poisonous accomplices are mine employees. The last parcel of smuggled diamonds I saw in Tangier can only have come from someone with access to the secure area.'

'Here, use my phone,' Crosson said.

'Niels, this may be a stupid suggestion, but can't we drive down to Respite Bay?' Tremayne said.

'We can, but it's nearly a six-hour drive in daylight to Kolmanskop Camp, twice that at night and then another hour to Port Baleen. We'll get there faster by taking an MTB tomorrow morning, plus we'll be able to check out Possession Island on the way. Assuming this fog doesn't get any worse,' Kruger said.

There was a knock on the door.

'Come,' Crosson said.

An officer entered, holding a wriggling Joaba by the scruff of her overalls.

'Begging your pardon, Commander. Lieutenant Maxwell reporting, sir. I caught this girl snooping around on ST14, but she swears blind that she's with Captain Kruger.'

Kruger looked up from dialling a number. 'Yes, that's correct, she's with me,' he said. 'Joaba, what have you been up to?'

Joaba wriggled from the sailor's grasp and studied the ground.

'If I might say, sir, you need to keep an eye on this one. She had opened the emergency equipment locker and was waving the signal pistol about like she was at a fairground shoot. If it had been loaded, she could have killed someone, sir.'

'Jus looking. I wasn't doing nothing,' Joaba said, staring at her feet.

'Joaba, I told you to wait at the harbour, not get on a boat. What you did was dangerous.'

'Lieutenant have someone take the girl to the canteen and get her some food,' Crosson said, 'and they do not let her out of their sight.'

Kruger was still busy on the phone, dialling and redialling.

'Hello, operator, I'm trying to call Kolmanskop Camp ... Are you sure? ... When did that happen?'

Kruger put the phone down. All eyes were on him.

'All telephone lines out of Luderitz have just gone down.'

'Shit. I'll go and see how quickly we can get the first boat ready,' Crosson said.

Chapter 37

Port Baleen, Forbidden Zone, South West Africa

At first light Jager and Bosman set sail from Seal Harbour and headed north across Rip Strait towards the mainland. A bank of fog had rolled in overnight making visibility poor, and in these waters that was dangerous. Sailors needed to read the waves and the eddies and correct accordingly. The boat was soon lurching in the short choppy waves and within minutes they were soaked. The sail flapped in the light breeze.

'If the wind doesn't pick up the fog is going to make it difficult for Neptune to dock on schedule tomorrow,' Bosman shouted.

Jager nodded and wiped spray from his face.

They kept north of the entrance to Respite Bay, heading for Jackass Cove, one of the more easily accessible beaches. They were thirty minutes behind schedule when the boat scrunched onto the soft sand. Having offloaded their supplies, they pushed the boat higher up the beach, disturbing a group of penguins, for which the cove was named. Jager wrapped the sail over the back of the boat to provide some camouflage.

They helped one another put on their heavy packs and then, Bosman with his MP38 submachine gun and Jager with his crossbow, climbed the rocky cliff and headed east.

The cool foggy air was ideal for their march towards the port and within an hour they topped the ridge on the west side of Respite Bay. Jager scoured the area with his binoculars but the poor visibility obscured any detail.

They cautiously approached the western perimeter, which consisted of two chain mesh fences, ten feet high and twenty feet apart, both topped with barbed wire. As Bosman took the first cut of the wire, a loud crack sounded as though it must be heard across the whole harbour. A dog barked somewhere in the distance, followed by a second. Jager armed his crossbow, and they both lay still and waited. When the barking stopped, ten more precise cuts were all that was needed for Bosman to be able to crawl through. Jager passed through the packs and slipped through the gap. He lay down, aiming his crossbow up through no man's land between the two fences, two further steel bolts between his teeth in readiness. The Diamond Security Police patrolled no man's land with Alsatian dogs and sometimes let them run free. Jager was taking no chances.

Bosman was quickly through the second fence, pulling the two bags behind him. Jager pushed back the cut flaps of the first fence and wired them closed. Then, with the inner fence secured, they climbed down the rocky slope towards the harbour.

The fog was now burning off, affording Jager a clearer view. No boats, just a few men going about their normal duties.

A dog barked above them but was hidden from view by the rock slope. It made a deep-noted snarl.

'Must have picked up our scent,' Bosman whispered.

Jager nodded. 'Cover me,' he said, slipping off his pack and crawling up the slope. As he peered over the top, he could see the dog busily pacing up and down where they had crossed, nose to the ground and growling. There was no policeman. He could have killed the dog with a bolt, but then he'd have to open up the fence again to remove it from no man's land. He waited, undecided.

Then a siren sounded, and he quickly slithered back down the slope to the beach.

'Fuck, they must be on to us,' Jager said, breathing heavily and pulling out his Luger.

But Bosman was smiling and shook his head.

'No, that's the midday siren. It's lunch break.'

'Fuck, I thought we'd been spotted,' Jager said, rolling on his back and laughing with relief.

'The dog will be hungry and he knows he'll get food. He'll be long gone,' Bosman said.

'Right, let's get going while they're distracted,' Jager said.

They quickly moved to a disused building set on the shore. Bosman pulled out a key, unlocked the padlock and they went inside.

'Good work, Karl. This is ideal. We've got a perfect view of the jetty from here,' Jager said.

The building was the old pump station once used to pump sea water to the separation plant. It was now empty of machinery, apart from four lead acid batteries attached to a charging unit and a black canvas bag hanging on the wall. Emptying the bag, which Bosman had stashed earlier, they both put on the dirty mine overalls and fastened on mine security passes. Jager's was forged.

'Right, take a diesel loco, covered wagon and brake van from the maintenance area and move them to the ready siding. Then immobilise the loco,' Jager said. 'We'll meet back here in two hours, and then set the explosives at the power plant and the security gate. I'll prepare the charges and timers in the meantime.'

From the jetty the narrow-gauge railway ran twenty-five miles north to Kolmanskop Camp. It was a single-track line with passing points and a branch off to the Lewala Mine. At the port there were two sidings where the locos and rolling stock were held in readiness and a third that held the equipment requiring maintenance. As Bosman approached the siding, he cursed. There were no locos. He walked across to the maintenance shed and greeted the foreman.

'I've got orders from Lewala to ready a loco and guard's van,' Bosman said.

'First I've heard about it,' the foreman said.

'What about these two?' Bosman enquired. 'Are either of them ready to take out?'

'Well, this one is due an engine change and the other one is about to have the brakes overhauled.'

'Let me take this one then, before you butcher it for good,' Bosman said with a laugh.

'If the brakes fail while you're coming back down the steep grade, God help you!' the foreman said, absolving himself of any responsibility. 'Did you see those Navy boats the other day?'

'No, what boats?'

'They were right here at the jetty, the day before yesterday. They needed fuel for their final leg up to Luderitz.'

'What boats were these?'

'Three MTBs being relocated from Simonstown, to patrol the coast for diamond smugglers.'

'Three of them, you say? What size?'

'Big, 1,800 horsepower, fast and well-armed.'

Bosman's mind raced to the implications. He felt a tingling, as if an icy hand had touched his neck.

Chapter 38

Robert Harbour, Luderitz, South West Africa

It was after dark by the time Commander Mike Crosson returned to the office.

'I've allocated all my maintenance men to work on ST14. She has the least amount of work left, and she'll be operational by 8 am. We'll then have you down at Respite Bay in just over an hour. The bad news is that thick fog has moved in, and visibility is already barely ten paces. We may not be able to get away until later in the morning.'

'Shit,' Tremayne said, 'that's too late. We need an alternative plan, Niels. We can't be beholden to the fog clearing. We have to get down there as early as we can.'

'I'm not sure we have a viable alternative. If we drive down, we will have to leave after sunrise to even see the road, and we'd only get there early in the afternoon,' Kruger said. 'We can't fly, because there's no airstrip at the mine.'

'You're right, Niels,' Tremayne said, smiling. 'That's a very good idea.'

Kruger looked at him and wondered if he was taking the piss.

Tremayne and Kruger walked through fogbound Luderitz to an address on Woermann Straat. It was pitch-black and Tremayne had to use his cigarette lighter to read the street signs. When they arrived, he hammered on the door and a big dog started barking, jumping up against the inside of the door. Tremayne instinctively put his hand on his revolver. For a moment he was back in the trenches in France, with the sound of the German dogs hunting in no man's land in the dead of night. And the screams.

He banged the door again. This time the outside light came on and a very belligerent man wielding a shotgun appeared, swearing and cursing at them in unison with the dog. When he saw Tremayne he froze.

'Fuck me. Is that you, Harvey?'

'It's me, Sebastien, alive and well.'

'Fuck, I thought you were dead,' he said, kissing Tremayne on both cheeks and kicking the dog into silence.

They hugged one another and laughed.

'Come, let's open some good Gallic brandy.'

'Thanks, Sebastien. This is Niels Kruger. He's with the Diamond Police,' Tremayne said.

'Come in, come in,' Sebastien said and ushered them inside, the dog losing interest and flopping back on its blanket.

'Listen, do you still do those beach charter flights, Sebastien?'

'Yes, I've still got Marie Antoinette. She has no radio, but she's airworthy. Where do you want to go?'

'Pomona Beach.'

Sebastien laughed raucously. 'You're still fucking crazy, Harvey. You always were. I remember some of the places we landed in the Forbidden Zone!'

He searched Tremayne's expression for any hint that he was joking.

'Fuck me, you're serious! Listen, I told you after Chamaais Bay I would never fly you again.'

'I'm deadly serious, Sebastien. This is a matter of international importance. But I must warn you, we believe there are armed smugglers near the mine, and they will not take kindly to a flyover.'

'Well, we'll die landing on that fucking beach, so what're a few fucking bullets?' Sebastien said, pouring them all another brandy.

'What's the earliest we can leave?'

'06.15 from the airstrip. It's outside the fog belt so there'll be no problem, but there is no guarantee that Pomona Beach will be clear. If this fog persists, a crash landing is guaranteed.'

Tremayne and Kruger returned to the harbour and met Crosson in the canteen.

'Sebastien will fly us down to Pomona Beach at first light tomorrow. That's about two miles south of Port Baleen and we'll make our way back up the coast,' Tremayne said. 'Commander, you need to depart in ST14 as early as possible and have the other two boats and The Stinker follow as soon as they're ready. Bring ST14 around the top of Possession Island and check down the east coast for any boats taking shelter, then wait out in Respite Bay and look for my signal. I'll send up a white flare.'

'I want to come. I know the bastard, I want to shoot him in the cock,' Joaba said, mimicking the shooting with her hand.

The three men turned to her, not even realising she was in the room.

'No, Joaba, it's too dangerous,' Kruger said. 'I'll arrange for someone to take you back to Guano Bay tomorrow. I'm going to be busy for a few days. I know where to find you when I need you.'

'I want to watch the bastard die!' Joaba yelled, throwing her head forward as if she was spitting. 'You can't leave me.'

One of the orderlies grabbed Joaba and dragged her kicking and screaming from the room.

'I want to shoot that bastard! Noooooo! Misterrrrr ...!' she screamed.

When Tremayne, Kruger and Crosson left the canteen an hour later, it was like walking into a cold, clammy spider's web. The foghorn of the Luderitz lighthouse boomed its warning, and in the far distance the Diaz Point foghorn joined in, making for a melancholy duet. It didn't bode well for an early start.

Chapter 39

Sunday Morning, 27th August 1939

Sandrivier Gorge Bridge   4 am

At zero minus two hours, Moritz and two men from Red Commando made a wide detour around Kolmanskop Camp and trekked south towards the bridge over the Sandrivier Gorge. They quickly got into a rhythm, running a hundred paces and marching the next one hundred. On foot it was easy to find the road that ran beside the railway line, even though the fog was unusually thick for that far inland.

Vehicle lights appeared in the gloom, travelling north towards the camp. That was unexpected. They moved off the road and lay low. As it passed them, Moritz saw it was a small flatbed lorry of some description. He hadn't seen it before. That was a potential problem but there was nothing he could do about it now.

In less than forty minutes, they had covered the three miles and saw the row of large white-painted boulders on either side of the road to funnel drivers onto the bridge during dust storms, rather than ending up in the gorge. He thought it particularly poignant, given that their truck had to cross the bridge tonight in fog.

While one of the soldiers cut the telephone line to the mine and port, Moritz climbed down the short inspection ladder on the north side of the bridge. He packed the explosives he carried against the riveted joints of the steel arches and tied them securely. After inserting the electric detonators into the soft, putty-like explosives, he connected the wires to the reel of electric blasting cable. He looped the wire around the top of the ladder, to avoid it being pulled loose, and one of the commandos ran across the bridge, unreeling the cable. Moritz did the same on the south side of the bridge. At a safe distance from the planned explosion, he connected the two pairs of wires to an electrical shot blaster. All he had to do was pull up the T-bar handle, turn it ninety degrees to make the contact, and then plunge it down. The current generated would set off the detonators, which in turn initiated the explosives. They were ready well ahead of time.

Swartpan Airstrip 5.30 am

An hour before first light, Kruger picked up Tremayne and Sebastien in the police's Ford Model A Fordor. The baggage space was loaded with guns, munitions and water. Constable Isaak sat beside Kruger in the front.

They were heading to the Swartpan airstrip, six miles inland from Luderitz. It was situated outside the fog belt so could be used all year round by small planes but only during daylight hours.

They left town in thick fog, Kruger driving at a snail's pace with the headlights reflecting a blinding white glare. He switched them off and drove slowly on sidelights, now able to see ten feet in front, but the dirt road was indistinguishable from the sand and rock on either side. Kruger kept steering side to side trying to keep to the centre.

'How long will it be to the airstrip in this fog?' Tremayne asked, anxious at their slow progress.

'Mon amie, it will take us at least thirty minutes, but at this speed we stay alive,' Sebastien said.

'Well, the good news is that this fog will also hinder Sidewinder and his friends,' Kruger said. 'It will be even thicker down at Respite Bay.'

As they progressed inland, the hot desert air had finally blocked the advance of the fog bank, thinning the incursion to wisps that swirled as the Ford sliced through them. Then, as if someone had flicked a switch, the majesty of the Milky Way appeared. It sparkled from horizon to horizon, millions and millions of stars and galaxies, seemingly so close you could reach up and touch them. Tremayne gazed up, remembering the last time he'd witnessed this spectacle, and it brought back precious memories of his last moments with Eleanor. Was this an omen or just a coincidence? His momentary musing was broken when Kruger braked hard to avoid a startled porcupine scurrying across the road, appearing like a ghostly white tumbleweed.

At the airstrip, Kruger parked with the lights shining on the galvanised hanger and as the doors were opened, the small size of Marie Antoinette hit him.

'What is she, Sebastien?' Kruger asked.

'She's a de Havilland Puss Moth, just like the one Beryl Markham used when she was the first person to fly east to west across the Atlantic in 1936. Hers was modified to carry fuel and not much else. This one's standard, apart from extra-large sand tyres.'

'Is that going to take three men, guns, munitions and water?' Kruger asked, looking doubtful.

Sebastien viewed the pile of guns and provisions and rubbed his chin.

'You know, you might have a point there. If we can't gain altitude we'll have to jettison a passenger. You should decide between you which one is going to jump. It avoids argument when we're airborne.'

Kruger caught Tremayne's grin.

'Help me push Marie Antoinette out of the hanger,' Sebastien said.

While Sebastien was busy attending to the engine, Kruger and Isaak loaded the munitions and water into the small baggage hold behind the back seats.

'Drive up and down the airstrip twice on main beam and sound the horn. We don't want to hit any wildlife on take-off,' Sebastien said. 'Did I tell you about the time I hit a kudu on the airstrip up at Etosha Pan? I had enough biltong to last the year!' He laughed loudly at his own joke.

'Yes, we've heard it before,' Tremayne said. 'I seem to remember the kudu started out as a jackrabbit!'

'OK, stand clear,' Sebastien said, and Tremayne tugged the propeller until he felt the coiled resistance and pulled down. The engine sputtered and gave the strangled phlegmy cough of a dedicated smoker, and stopped. The second time it did the same, and Sebastien got out and stuck his head under the engine cover and cursed. The third time it revved, engulfing the plane in a cloud of smoke.

When Kruger returned, he gave the thumbs-up.

'Isaak, go to that end of the airstrip and shine the headlights down the right-hand side of the runway. When we're gone, drive straight to Commander Crosson's office and tell him what time we took off …' he checked his watch in the car headlight. 'At 6.30 am, making for Pomona Beach.'

Sebastien beckoned and Kruger and Tremayne squeezed into the back seat of the plane, behind the single pilot seat.

At the end of the runway, Sebastien turned the Puss Moth, put on the brakes and applied full power. It bounced on the spot like someone desperate for the toilet. When he released the brakes, the plane lurched forward and slowly gained speed. As the end of the airstrip approached, Kruger braced for impact, convinced the plane didn't have enough speed. At the very last second, Sebastien pulled back on the control column, and the plane hopped a few feet and then droned up into the early morning sky. Over several minutes they climbed to a thousand feet and levelled out. The first light of dawn appeared over the port wing and the inland extremity of the fog bank over the starboard wing.

'That was lucky,' Sebastien shouted over his shoulder, above the roar of the engine. 'No one needed to jump.'

Port Baleen RDF Station   6 am

Bill Williams and Jimmy Britt, the two Royal Navy radio technicians from Simonstown, were fast asleep in their hammocks. They had been on-site for two days, installing the new RDF equipment at Port Baleen. Late last night, they had commissioned the system. An empty whiskey bottle lay on the floor.

The building that housed the equipment was one of the old German-built houses used before World War 1. Arguably it had the best view of any RDF station in the world, looking out for miles to the north and to the south, along the rugged South Atlantic coast.

In the kitchen there were a few blackened utensils, an electric hotplate, a shelf full of tinned food and a temporary fifty-gallon drum on the roof filled with slightly brackish drinking water. The original contents of the drum still formed an iridescent sheen on top of their many cups of black, sweet tea. A hammock was slung in each bedroom and a bucket was the sole source of water, for use in the shared sink.

Last night Williams had made radio contact with the RDF station at Luderitz and confirmed they were now operational. They were ready to receive the permanent radio operators and would then return to Luderitz. They agreed to speak again at seven o'clock that morning.

Both men were woken from a deep whiskey-enhanced sleep by a loud noise that rattled the house, threatening to lift the galvanised sheets from the roof.

'What the hell was that?' Williams shouted, toppling out of his hammock.

'Sounded like an explosion,' Britt said, making through the pitch-black kitchen to the back door. It was still dark, and the area was shrouded in a cold, damp fog. Down below, in the port, an orange light flickered in the gloom and dogs barked.

'There's a fire. We need to get down there and—' but before Williams could finish the sentence there was a second explosion followed by the noise of gunfire echoing around the port.

'Shit, it sounds like a bloody war,' Williams said.

The gunfire grew louder and there were a series of smaller explosions and then it went quiet. The dogs stopped barking.

'That sounded like hand grenades,' Williams said, breathless. 'We need to report this to Luderitz. Something is seriously wrong.'

Britt felt his way to the RDF room and flicked the light switch several times.

'Shit, we've lost power. The explosion must have been at the generator plant,' Britt said.

It was then that they realised the backup lead acid batteries, intended for such emergencies, were being charged down in the old pump station. After manufacture, they required a long, slow charge to bring them up to full power. They'd been due to collect and install them that morning. It was the last job on the list.

'Well, we've got to radio Luderitz. We'll just have to go down and fetch the batteries. In this fog it's unlikely anyone will see us,' Williams said.

'Christ, they weigh a ton, Bill. We'll have to bring them up one at a time, and there's four of the buggers,' Britt said.

'Listen, we only need to use the radio, not the direction finder. I reckon two batteries should be enough for that. Maybe just one if it's fully charged.'

Sandrivier Gorge Bridge   6 am

One mile east of Kolmanskop Camp and three miles from the bridge, the driver of the truck carrying the other members of Red Commando looked nervously at his watch, counting down the minutes to zero hour. Right on schedule the camp lights went out. He switched on the engine and waited for the flare.

Because of the fog, Moritz did not have a visual on the camp lights so, double-checking his watch with the two commandos, he fired the magnesium flare at exactly 6 am. He knew immediately that there was a problem. It disappeared up into the fog, and when it ignited it produced no more than a dull glow. There was not a snowball's chance in hell that it would be seen by the truck, three miles away.

The driver waited nervously. Should he move off regardless? Moritz had made it clear that the signal was crucial. When they drove through the camp the alarm would be raised and if the bridge was not ready to be blown the police could follow them across. He waited.

At zero plus ten minutes voices from the back of the truck shouted to get moving, and he revved the engine and crunched it into gear. As they drove through the camp security barrier, the police scattered and then fired at the disappearing truck. By the time they got into the camp the headlights picked up just two policemen standing next to a flatbed lorry, who watched them drive past. They had not associated the gunfire with the commando's vehicle.

But a third policeman had. He stepped in front of them and levelled his rifle. The driver ducked and a bullet zinged through the windshield

157

exactly where his head had been. He stared through the shattered spiderweb of glass into the blinding reflection of the headlights off the fog. He had to stop the truck and tried to knock out the window with the butt of his rifle, but all he managed was a small hole. Being yelled at by the commandos in the back, he drove on with his head stuck out the driver's door window so he could see. Someone in the back shouted, 'there's a vehicle following us,' and with that the commandos opened fire at the distant headlights.

At the bridge Moritz could hear the gunfight, a mixture of rifle and semiautomatic fire. He glanced at his watch. It was zero plus twelve minutes. The shooting was getting closer.

The truck headlights finally appeared on the far side of the gorge, but it was too far to the right. They had lost the track. He fired another flare low across the bridge and along the road. To his relief the truck turned in that direction. He could make out the lights of another vehicle trying to cut off the commandos' approach. Moritz and his two men ran across the bridge to intercept them. One policeman went down, but the firing continued. Moritz ran back to the shot blaster. The truck started onto the bridge in a hail of gunfire and swerved off the road and onto the railway track and hit the side railing. It stopped dead, flames leaping from underneath.

Moritz's two commandos gave covering fire as the men on board bailed out and ran for their lives across the bridge. The last man made it to safety just as the flare extinguished. Moritz pulled up the T-bar, twisted it and pushed down hard. There was a tremendous explosion with steel and debris rising into the air. The truck lifted in a ball of flame and then everything fell back and disappeared from sight into the gorge.

Port Baleen Railway   6.30 am

At the port, Karl Bosman inched the Schwarzkopf loco out of the ready siding and around the loop that joined with the mainline between the port and the Lewala Mine. Behind the engine was a double-bogie covered goods wagon, and at the back, an old German-built brake van with a veranda at both ends. The loco rattled over the points and when the brake van was clear Karl stopped.

He walked back to the points that were always set to take down-traffic into the loop, a safety feature in case trains or rolling stock ran away on the mainline. If that happened the runaway would be directed into the loop and to safety, rather than onto the jetty and off the end into the sea.

To activate the lever that switched the points, a special key was required. These were entrusted only to the senior loco drivers and had to be returned to a check-out at the end of shift. Bosman had made a copy. He twisted the key, pulled back the release catch and heaved the lever forward. The points moved with a clunk, giving the train a clear run down to the jetty. Regulation required that the driver reset the points after passing, but today he needed unrestricted access to the jetty on the return journey. If something went wrong, switching the points might waste valuable time.

In poor visibility, he slowly reversed down the gradient and rumbled onto the timber jetty and stopped. Pocketing the key, he returned to the railway sidings to disable all the other locos.

Old Pumping Station, Port Baleen   6.30 am

Williams and Britt clambered directly down the rock slope from the RDF towards the old pump station, avoiding the main track. The shooting had stopped, and it was eerily quiet.

At the bottom they worked their way towards the flames and found the area littered with sheets of galvanised iron, splintered wood and a dead policeman. The fire burned unchallenged. A pall of acrid smoke hung over the area, mixing with the fog to form a noxious black veil. As they reached the old pump station, Williams pulled the padlock key from his pocket.

'Shit, the bloody lock's gone!' he said. 'Someone's been here.'

He put his ear to the door and eased it open. It gave a high-pitched resentful squeak that made them flinch. Inside he flicked his lighter and, to his relief, could make out the four batteries. On the far side, there was a canvas-covered box and some bags that he was sure hadn't been there two days ago. He opened the lid and flicked his lighter.

'Fuck me, it's a portable Morse transceiver, German army issue if I'm not mistaken!' Williams said in a loud whisper.

'What the hell is that doing here?' Britt asked, but as soon as he'd said it, the answer dawned on them both. The explosions and the gunfire started to make sense.

'Check the bags over there. I'll disable the radio,' Williams said.

Britt came back with boxes of bullets and a bag of stick-handle grenades.

'Shit, I remember these from the Great War,' Britt said.

'We've got to get rid of this stuff, including the radio. We'll dump it in the harbour,' Williams said.

Checking all was clear, they walked quickly around the back of the building and down the side of the railway to the jetty. The splash when the transceiver hit the water was so loud they froze. As they listened, there was a faint noise, a distant rumble. Williams instinctively put his hand on the rail.

'Fuck, there's a train coming,' he said.

They ran back to the old pump station as if their lives depended on it, and each grabbed a battery. They had no intention of making a return trip. Adrenalin had kicked in.

Old Pumping Station, Port Baleen   6.40 am

After checking the port for any remaining Security Police, Jager returned to the old pump station to radio Neptune that it was safe to enter port. When he had first peered out of the old pump station window earlier that morning he couldn't even see the lights on the jetty, just a hundred yards away. He was worried that Neptune would be delayed, and there was no way to communicate with Siggie and Red Commando. But now, at first light, he was more optimistic. The visibility was still poor but improving.

When he entered the pump station, he went straight for the radio. He looked around, perplexed, thinking he must be in the wrong building. But no, their bags and spare clothes were right there. He couldn't help a furtive glance over his shoulder.

'Where the fuck is it?' he hissed.

He wondered how he could have been so stupid as to not hide it. The radio was critical to the success of the raid. Panic started to build. How the hell was he going to communicate with Neptune without a radio?

He could picture Sidewinder on the deck of the trawler, impatiently glancing at his watch. It was now gone 6.30 am, and she would be holding off Port Baleen, awaiting the all-clear from him. The choppy water out there would be making it an uncomfortable wait for those on board. The last thing they needed was seasick commandos.

He took deep breaths and cleared his mind. Someone had stolen the radio. Could it have been the Security Police? He went to check the bags. Their spare ammunition and the grenades were also missing.

He looked around the room and saw that where there had been four batteries on charge there were now just two. He inspected them and immediately suspected their purpose. He knew what he had to look for.

It was then that Jager heard a high-pitched engine noise. As he listened the direction changed, and the noise became a drone. It was a plane!

His sixth sense kicked in. There was no reason for a plane to be flying in fog over Respite Bay that early in the morning. This, plus the three MTBs in Luderitz, spelled danger. Was the plane spotting for them?

Heading South to Mile 17   6.40 am

At the Sandrivier Gorge, Moritz took stock of the situation. He had blown the bridge in the nick of time and all but two of his men on the truck had made it to safety. According to the survivors, both were already dead.

The bad news was that they were without transport, thirteen miles north of the railway junction to the Lewala Mine, with their supplies at the bottom of the gorge. The only good news was the police were stranded on the north side of the gorge, at least for now. They would be preparing a mounted patrol to follow them, but to circumvent the gorge would take them at least three hours. With their transport destroyed, that now seemed a worryingly short time.

They had enough ammunition for a good firefight plus several grenades and emergency flares. But they had no spare water. That was at the bottom of the gorge. Each commando carried a canteen on their person, but most had already consumed half of that. There was no way they were going to get to the rendezvous at Mile 10, in the heat of the day, without additional water. There was a hut at Mile 17 that held an emergency stash, but that was six miles down the track. If they took advantage of the fog while it still lasted, they could be there in under two hours and replenish.

South to Pomona Beach   6.45 am

Sebastien scoured the fog bank that sat stubbornly along the coast. Out to sea, he saw a clear area where the waves reflected the morning light. He banked hard to starboard, reduced the throttle and the plane dropped. They descended into the middle of the clear area and levelled out about one hundred feet above the waves.

'I'll see if we can get in under it,' Sebastien shouted.

The plane dropped even lower and Kruger dug his fingers into his seat, his knuckles white.

It was like going into a tunnel. From the first rays of the morning sun, they plunged into almost total darkness. Sebastien reduced throttle and flew ever lower, his eyes flicking between the altimeter and where the waves should be. After what seemed the longest minute of Kruger's life, Sebastien banked the plane and flew back towards the clearing. The plane re-emerged into daylight and he pointed forward, indicating he was going to try the other side. Kruger wanted to shout out not to, but one glance at Tremayne, who was quietly dozing, stifled his outburst. Perhaps I should have had a few gins last night as well, he thought.

As they flew north, the fog was just as thick.

'No beach landing possible,' Sebastien shouted, giving a Gallic shrug. Tremayne, roused from his doze, looked around.

'We can't wait for the fog to clear. How close can you get us? Somewhere they won't hear us coming in.'

'I can probably get you to the flats, about three miles east of the port. It will be just inside the fog belt but if I come in from the desert side, we might just get underneath it to land. You'll have to tighten your seatbelts though.'

Tremayne gave the thumbs-up and Kruger pulled vigorously on his seatbelt. It wouldn't tighten any further.

Flying well south of Respite Bay, they turned inland and followed the edge of the fog bank north, losing altitude all the time. Sebastien stared out the side windows looking for landmarks.

'Look!' he shouted, pointing out the window. 'Ten o'clock.'

Tremayne and Kruger looked in that direction and saw the plume of black smoke rising out of the fog.

'That's at Port Baleen,' Sebastien said.

Port Baleen RDF Station   6.50 am

Williams and Britt carried one battery between them up the last and steepest part of the track to the RDF station. They were breathless by the time they heaved it onto the rack.

'Let's see if it works with just this one, Bill,' Britt said, regretting the previous night's celebrations.

Williams connected it and flicked the switch. Lights came on and they grinned at one another. He checked the frequency and put on the headphones.

'Port Baleen to Luderitz, come in,' he said. 'Port Baleen RDF to Luderitz RDF, come in.' He waited. 'SOS at Port Baleen, repeat SOS at Port Baleen, come in.'

Britt pressed the headphones to his ears, trying to hear the faint response.

'SOS at Port Baleen, repeat SOS, come in Luderitz.'

Williams listened intently but shook his head and checked the dials.

'There'll be a stronger signal if we get the second battery, Jimmy.'

'You keep trying. I'll bring it up,' Britt said, and disappeared.

'Port Baleen RDF to Luderitz, come in. SOS at Port Baleen, repeat SOS, come in Luderitz.'

Boegenfels Salt Pan   6.55 am

Tremayne and Kruger stared in disbelief at the plume of black smoke rising above the port.

'That means the harbour has already been attacked and we have to assume they are making for the Kaiser's Closet,' Tremayne said. 'Sebastien, how close can you get us to the Lewala Mine?'

Sebastien looked over his shoulder. 'There is a small salt pan to the east, but the area around it is rough. None of us will be of any use if we're dead, mon amie.'

Kruger wanted to pat him on the shoulder in support of common sense, but Sebastien banked the plane, cut the throttle and dropped into the fog. Pilot and passengers stared out, looking for the reassurance of land, but there was nothing but grey.

The plane bounced, lower and lower, and then, at full throttle, banked back around to the east.

'I'll try further north,' Sebastien said, the wrinkles normally around his smiling mouth gone, now relocated to his forehead.

The second attempt had them fog blind again, just a few feet above the desert. Boulders and red dirt fleetingly appeared and disappeared, and then it turned white and Sebastien dropped the plane hard onto the desert floor and cut the engine. They bucked and bounced, lifted off momentarily and hit the ground again and, finally slowing down, hit a salt hummock with the left wheel. The plane spun through ninety degrees, stopped dead and tipped forward onto its nose.

For several seconds there was complete silence.

'Ladies and gentlemen, welcome to Boegenfels salt pan,' Sebastien said, wiping blood from his nose.

Luderitz RDF 6.55 am

At 6.55 am, Luderitz RDF station picked up a weak radio signal, and from the bearing the operator knew it was Port Baleen. He checked his watch and realised it must be the call scheduled for 7 am. He tried to fine-tune the wavelength and remove the static, but it was still barely audible.

He listened intently, trying to catch the words. There was an urgency to the voice, the same message being repeated, over and over. Each phrase seemed to include a three-syllable word.

'Baleen RDF this is Luderitz, you are breaking up,' he enunciated carefully into the receiver. 'Baleen RDF, repeat, you are breaking up.'

The faint reply was still garbled.

'Luderitz to Baleen RDF, I cannot hear you.'

After several minutes they stopped sending.

Port Baleen RDF Station   7 am

Williams was still transmitting when he heard Britt return and drop the battery on the rack. The power level had fallen into the red, but even so he tried.

'You took your time, Jimmy,' he said.

When there was no reply he glanced up to see Jimmy was accompanied by a tall man in dirty overalls, a mine security pass hanging from a pocket. At first glance he looked like any other mine employee, but on closer examination Williams saw he was holding a Luger pistol with a long silencer attached. He had a desert-burned face and cracked, scabby lips. And had a crossbow slung over his shoulder.

'So, you threw my radio in the sea,' the man said, and hit Williams across the cheek with the Luger, gashing the flesh.

Britt, with a cut forehead and bloody nose, could not look his friend in the eye.

'Connect the second battery and get the radio working. Any tricks and this one gets a bullet,' Jager said, pointing the gun at Britt's head.

Williams did as ordered.

Boegenfels Salt Pan   7.20

Tremayne and Kruger helped Sebastien right the plane so they could access the munitions and water in the hold.

Sebastien then assessed the damage. The left wheel strut was bent but not broken and the tyre was still inflated. Miraculously the propeller was undamaged. He'd shut off the engine in the nick of time.

'Well, Marie Antoinette is going no further today,' Sebastien said, like someone about to put down an injured horse. 'I'll come with you.'

'This has turned into a military operation, Sebastien,' Kruger said. 'We'll have to send someone out to help you.'

Sebastien bristled with indignation.

'Mon dieu, you want me to stay out in this fucking desert, on my own?'

Kruger was about to say, yes, this will be dangerous, but he caught Tremayne's eye.

'We'll be able to carry more supplies if there are three of us,' Tremayne added.

'Merde, I was shot down behind enemy lines in France. It took me three weeks to get back to my squadron,' Sebastien shouted, in defence of his injured Gallic pride. 'I didn't sit by my plane and wait to be fucking rescued.'

In stony silence they packed their weapons and provisions.

'Roland Garros, our great fighter ace, was a friend of mine, may he rest in peace,' Sebastien said, crossing himself. His final word on the subject.

By the time they were ready to start, the fog was starting to burn off and the blue sky that showed presaged another blistering day. Sebastien tied some cloth around his head, Arab-style, and Kruger put on his slouch hat. Tremayne cursed himself: he'd left his hat in Kruger's Fordor. His head and face were going to be cremated. Seeing his predicament, Sebastien found an old canvas water bottle in the hold and slit open the bottom and one side. It looked like an old coif, the simple bonnets used by women in medieval times, but it would serve the purpose.

They took a compass bearing and headed south-west, walked for thirty minutes, stopped and took a mouthful of water, walked for twenty minutes and did the same. Tremayne loved the desert but realised in the years he'd lived here he'd always been prepared and in control. This time was different: he was on the back foot and at the desert's mercy. It was unforgiving, and it sizzled and shimmered around them in warning. There was not so much as a thumbnail of shade. They were like three ants on a griddle.

The heat sapped them and the loads they carried became heavier by the minute. He thought of the Diamond Security Police on their long patrols, hour after hour, day after day, in this insane heat. He had a new admiration for them and made a mental note to make sure they were better rewarded.

By the third stop, they were exhausted. If they didn't get to the mine in the next thirty minutes, they would have to start lightening their loads and leave valuable munitions behind. If they didn't make the mine in the next hour, they would be at serious risk of heat exhaustion.

Luderitz RDF   7.23 am

At 7.23 am, the Luderitz RDF operator picked up a strong radio message that was located fifty miles due south, the same location as the previous message. It was the Port Baleen RDF.

The operator was about to acknowledge the message when he realised the voice was speaking in German. Using the code from Sidewinder's book, he scribbled down the message and stared at it. Scorpion had sent a message to Neptune.

This could only mean one thing. He picked up the phone and dialled Commander Crosson.

Mile 20   7.30 am

The seven remaining members of Red Commando took advantage of the fog and quickly got into their rhythm, running a hundred paces and marching the next one hundred. As the sun began to win its daily battle with the fog, Moritz reduced the running time and finally abandoned it. After fifty minutes they rested and had a mouthful of water.

In the next hour they covered half the distance as the sun blistered them mercilessly, searing their exposed skin, sapping their morale and soaking them in sweat. Two of the commandos ran out of water. When they came to a stack of wooden sleepers at Mile 20, they sat and rested.

Moritz realised that if they were to stand any chance of making it to the hut at Mile 17, they would have to pool their remaining water and let two men go forward and bring the water back. Moritz chose the youngest commando, Petrus Johannes, to go with him. The others rearranged the sleepers to create a hint of shade and resigned themselves to a long, hot and thirsty wait.

Robert Harbour, Luderitz   7.30 am

Commander Mike Crosson had a spring in his step as he walked along the harbour to his office. Luderitz RDF was actively monitoring transmissions, and today the Port Baleen RDF would be commissioned. He could now locate the transmitters of the coded German messages, and with his three MTBs he would soon be able to respond very quickly. ST14 was ready for testing in Robert Harbour and The Stinker's starboard engine had been fixed and she had just left port with orders to patrol Possession Island.

As he walked into his office the phone was ringing.

'Commander Crosson,' he said. 'Yes, I've been at the harbour checking on the repairs. Say that again? What time was that? Shit.' Crosson's mind raced. 'Radio The Stinker, update Denning and tell him to proceed to Port Baleen at full speed. I'm scheduled to leave on ST14 in a couple of hours and we'll rendezvous with her there.'

Port Baleen   7.30 am

Jager was relieved at the turn of events. When he'd discovered his transceiver missing, he'd feared the raid was in jeopardy. But now his plans were back on track and he had successfully contacted Neptune.

He had found out from the two Royal Navy technicians that Luderitz had also commissioned the latest RDF and that the old whaler was already fitted. Even with Port Baleen RDF out of action, the other two would still be able to plot his transmissions. He'd need to keep any messages as short as possible.

It hadn't taken him long to work out that the lead acid batteries were a power backup for something like a radio. That would have to be located on top of a hill and with the weight of the batteries it wouldn't be far away from where they were being charged. He had located the RDF station within ten minutes. He ejected the magazine from the grip of his Luger and squeezed in two replacement 9 mm bullets and reinserted it, with a satisfying click.

But he was still troubled by the news of the MTBs. They were fast and well-armed and between them and the ship Table Bay, the U-boat was in potential danger. He would warn Nissen when Neptune docked and would let Moby know when he radioed to confirm their rendezvous time.

The word was that the MTBs were in a poor mechanical state when they refuelled at Port Baleen. They were probably still under repair at this very moment. In any case, in six hours it would be all over, and Moby would be submerged far out to sea, sailing north with two tons of diamonds destined for the Fatherland.

Port Baleen   7.45 am

Over an hour late, Neptune nudged against the jetty and tied up. After bobbing like a cork in Rip Strait, the commandos were relieved to be on solid ground and busied themselves with the job in hand. The ammunition and guns were quickly transferred to the covered wagon, and a belt-fed MG34 machine gun was set up on the forward-facing veranda of the brake van.

Also loaded into the wagon were rockdrills, drill steels, lengths of hose, two diesel-powered portable air compressors, detonators, explosives and blasting fuse.

Jager pulled Nissen to one side.

'Horst, there's a problem you should know about. Three MTBs stopped here en route from Simonstown to Robert Harbour, two days ago.'

Nissen thought of the consequences this might pose. They were well-armed and fitted with torpedoes and more to the point they were very fast. The big question was the status of those MTBs. He had to assume that at least one would be out patrolling, and Moby had to be warned. Sohler was not going to be pleased.

'What is our revised time for the rendezvous?' Nissen asked.

'We should be back here in three hours, and by the time we've transferred the cargo, we'll sail at around twelve noon. Then three hours down to Pomona Island, so ETA 15.00,' Jager said.

Nissen radioed Moby with the revised rendezvous time and the warning of possible MTB patrols.

After he had sent the message, his mind started working through this new information and what the potential impact might be on Operation Benguela. Even as a boy on his first single-handed sailing trip around Heligoland, he had exercised his mind by thinking about what might go wrong and how he'd avoid it happening. What if the thunderstorm on the far side of the island drifted towards him? How would he avoid cargo boats at night? His mind had churned through the permutations of the threats around him, and it had saved his life.

As the summer sun dipped, he had reefed the mainsail and backed the foresail, so that the boat hove to in the evening breeze. He took a turn of the foresail sheet around the tiller and dozed. Any change in wind direction would tug the sail, causing the tiller to move.

In the early hours, the tiller pulled at his arm and he was instantly awake. Lightning flashed in the jet-black night sky, a prelude to a summer storm. He dropped both sails and rode out the squall.

He used the same thought processes now. The delayed arrival of Neptune had been regrettable, but the train was being loaded, the fog was clearing and Moby had been warned. The status of Moritz and Red Commando was unknown, but he had to assume that they were at Mile 10.

Then there was the small plane that Jager had heard fly over just after the raid. This played on his mind, more than the MTBs. It couldn't have seen anything on the ground because of the fog and there was nowhere for it to land. But it was too much of a coincidence and had to mean something. He looked up at the sun starting to show through the fog – and saw the pall of black smoke billowing high into the sky.

Luderitz RDF   8.06 am

Both Luderitz RDF and The Stinker picked up the message at 8.06. They identified the caller as Neptune, this time messaging Moby. It was the first time that Moby had been heard of for some time and brought another piece to the baffling jigsaw. Where the hell had he been and why had he appeared now?

Thanks to Sidewinder's codebook, they could now decode numbers. Denning pondered what the 1500 in the message meant. Probably a rendezvous time. He checked his watch. That was in just under seven hours.

With The Stinker now sailing south past Halifax Island, she and the Luderitz RDF were able to estimate the location of the transmission from Moby to about eight nautical miles west of Possession Island.

Denning was convinced that Moby was a submarine. He radioed Crosson on ST14.

Railway to Mile 10   8.15 am

The hooter of the Swartzkopff loco gave two blasts and the train jolted forward on its twelve-mile journey to the Lewala Mine. As they passed through the port security gate the commandos eyed the demolished security office and the human debris that remained. Bosman felt a twinge of remorse. He had known some of them.

Nissen found progress tediously slow, with the clickety-clack of the iron wheels across the rail joints acting like a metronome beating a soporific rhythm. Every mile from the jetty was marked with a board by the track. He counted each one, and that made the journey even slower. As they passed the Mile 7 board a rifle shot rang out and the train stopped. Bosman leaped from the right-hand side of his cab and dived to the ground.

'Shot, left hand side!' he yelled.

Nissen ran forward and said, 'Where did it come from?'

Bosman pointed. 'Some bastard up on that ridge tried to shoot me. Put a fucking big blister in my door. Any closer it would have gone straight through the steel plate.'

Nissen surveyed the area with his binoculars.

'He might have moved off when he saw what he was up against,' he said.

Another shot rang out and the man behind the machine gun on the front veranda of the brake van slumped back, hit in the chest. Two more bullets hit the brake van and those inside bailed out, dragging one wounded man with them.

'They're Security Police marksmen and there's more than one of them,' Nissen said. 'Blue Commando, on my signal you go forward, five each side, up the hill and work around behind them. I want them dead. Green Commando, provide covering fire.'

Another shot sounded.

'Fire!' Nissen yelled.

Rifles and the machine gun opened up and the bullets kicked up dust on the ridge. The two groups of men spread out and ran either side and within a minute had disappeared over the rise.

'Ceasefire!' Nissen yelled.

A series of distant rifle shots rang out and a few minutes later the company returned, jogging back down the hill.

'Diamond Police, sir. Two on horseback heading north. We might have hit one of them, but they were too far off to be sure.'

Nissen hoped that it was an opportunistic encounter, a routine patrol. With their powerful binoculars they'd have seen the pall of smoke over the port and the machine gun on the brake van and put two and two together.

'Load up, get the wounded on board, everyone on alert,' Nissen shouted.

One hundred yards short of the Mile 10 board, Bosman slowed to a stop and flashed the lights on the loco. He peered into the distance and flashed again.

Nissen and Jager joined him.

'No sign of Siggie and Red Commando,' Bosman said, peering ahead through his binoculars.

Nissen was tempted to fire two shots in the air but didn't want to give the Security Police at the mine any more warning than they already had.

They waited, all binoculars focused on the railway junction.

After several more minutes Jager said, 'This isn't right. Red Commando must have a problem.'

Mile 10 to the Lewala Mine   8.55 am

Nissen decided they couldn't wait. Their sole purpose was to secure two tons of diamonds. They would just have to manage without the additional commandos.

As Bosman took the train into the Lewala spur he increased speed to ascend the rise to the mine. The commandos retreated into the brake van with the machine gun and those in the covered wagon closed the sliding doors. His heart sank when he saw that the track was blocked by the dead bar, a large thick-walled steel pipe hinged at one end with a heavy counterweight. Both ends fitted into slots in the steel reinforced concrete bollards and even at full speed the train would not be able to break through it. They were going to have to fight their way in.

Bosman was greeted by two Security policemen, who walked forward, rifles held at the ready. A further two were positioned behind the bollards, one each side.

'So, what's happened at the port, Karl?' the sergeant said. 'We heard a loud bang a couple of hours ago and we've been without power ever since. And the telephones are down.'

'Ja, there's a fuck-up at the power plant. Some problem with a transformer short circuit. It caused a surge and it blew up,' Bosman said.

'Why are you here on a Sunday?' the sergeant asked.

'It's a special job. There's some priority pump that has to go down to the workshop for repair first thing tomorrow, and I was told to leave these at the siding for them.'

'We weren't notified about that.'

'Perhaps because the phone's down?' Bosman ventured.

The sergeant walked back to the control hut, picked up the phone and put it to his ear, then put it down again and waved the train forward. The barrier was raised, and with two blasts of the horn the train pulled forward.

One policeman remained standing by the track and would see the commandos on the back of the brake van at any second. As they came level, Jager aimed his crossbow at the man and fired. He fell backwards onto the ground, his body twitching, but silent. Bosman shouted his thanks and waved as he passed. The other policemen were oblivious to the fate of their colleague.

As the brake van passed the barrier, commandos leaped from the back. One constable hit the alarm button at the control hut, but without power it remained silent. They were all dead in seconds.

As the train approached the mine buildings, there was further gunfire. Security Police in the plant had been alerted by the shooting. Within minutes, carefully aimed hand grenades had silenced them.

Given the all-clear, Bosman pulled forward into the siding, stopping just short of the doors that led to the Kaiser's Closet.

Kaiser's Closet   9.15 am

Two men ran forward and fixed explosives to the hinges of the two outer steel doors. A loud crack and the doors were on the ground. When the debris was cleared, Bosman pulled the train forward and stopped outside the gaping hole. Peering through the dust, he grinned. He could see the huge black door of the Kaiser's Closet.

The sliding doors on the covered wagon were rolled back and the tools and explosives offloaded. A compressed air hose was fitted to each compressor and rolled out into the building and connected to the two jackhammers. Tungsten carbide tipped drill steels were fixed into position, the two diesel-powered air compressors were cranked-up, and the drills coughed into action.

The steel reinforcement made drilling slow and arduous. The tips on the drills soon blunted and several drill steels jammed in the hole,

171

requiring a new hole to be drilled next to it. Nissen became concerned they hadn't brought sufficient drill steels with them.

Within the hour twenty holes had been drilled into the frame that engaged the huge locking bolts. Sticks of explosives were put into each hole and rammed in hard with a wooden pole, with the last stick being more carefully placed because it was fitted with a detonator and safety fuse. Men and materials were removed to a safe place and Bosman reversed the train a short distance down the track. The safety fuse was lit, and they waited.

An ear-cracking explosion threw bits of concrete and steel out through the doors and onto the track, followed by a billow of smoke. It was several minutes before it cleared, and they could inspect their handiwork. The lower of the two locking bolts was in mid-air with just the upper one still partially engaged. Sledgehammers made quick work of it and the rubble was cleared away. Then they heaved on the door and, helped by a crowbar, it reluctantly eased open.

Zach's Extension, Lewala Mine   9.25 am

Kruger stopped and pointed forward at something that appeared through the shimmering colourless flame rising from the desert floor. It was out of keeping with the flat terrain, like a tree trunk pointing skyward, except that there were no trees. They walked towards it.

'That's Zach's Extension,' Tremayne said. 'Christ, they've come a long way east in six months.'

What they had seen in the mirage was the boom of a huge steam shovel, now softly hissing the last of its steam. It sat between a twenty-foot-high bank and the narrow-gauge railway track. It was used to dig the diamond-bearing sand and gravel. The shovel filled the wagons that were then taken to the diamond processing plant at the Lewala Mine.

To the west, the railway track, with its attendant telegraph poles, snaked across the desolate landscape and disappeared into the shimmering haze.

'There'll be a telephone in here,' Tremayne said, pointing to a hut where the line ended.

As they approached, a shot rang out and a spit of dust kicked up next to Tremayne's right foot. The three were in the open with no cover. Even if there had been some cover close by, their heavy packs would render them sitting ducks.

'This is Captain Niels Kruger of the Diamond Security Police. Who's there?' he shouted.

'Baas?' came the high-pitched reply.

'Who's there?' Kruger demanded.

The door opened wider and a police constable appeared, pointing his rifle. When he saw Kruger, he stood to attention and saluted. 'Constable Frikkie, Baas,' he said. 'Am sorry. I thought you was the smugglers.'

Mile 17   9.30 am

Through his binoculars, Moritz surveyed the hut at Mile 17 and, to his surprise, saw two horses tied up outside under a shelter canopy. It was a Security Police patrol. Now, that was a stroke of luck. If they could kill the policemen without stampeding the horses, they still had a chance. He could ride south and raise the alarm with Jager. Petrus Johannes could take water back to Red Commando at Mile 20 on the other horse. Perhaps all was not lost.

They both took a large swig of water, armed their rifles and moved forward, keeping the hut between them and the horses so as not to spook them. All was quiet at the hut. Moritz crept up to peer in a window, but it was boarded up. One of the horses whinnied in warning and there was a clatter from inside. Petrus Johannes fired through the timber wall as Moritz approached the door. Looking in from the blinding desert, he could see nothing but blackness and fired indiscriminately inside. The horses reared up, pulling violently on their reins, snorting and neighing. With Johannes covering the door, Moritz pacified them.

Both policemen were dead, but one had a blood-stained bandage around his right thigh and had clearly been wounded that day. That had to be as a result of contact with Sidewinder's commando units. It was the first indication he'd had of the attack. Checking both horses, he found one had a wound on its right shoulder. The bullet had gone through the policeman's leg and into the horse.

They quickly filled their canteens from the water barrel, plus two large canvas water bags they found hanging on the wall. Johannes filled the small drinking trough outside for the horses.

They loaded the injured horse with the large water bags. Johannes was to ride as fast and as far as he could, he might even get all the way back to Mile 20 on horseback. The commandos were to continue marching south as soon as they'd had water. Moritz climbed on the other horse and cantered off, making for Mile 10.

Zach's Extension to Lewala Mine   10 am

Constable Frikkie had been the only policeman at Zach's Extension that morning. A constable from the Lewala Mine had phoned nearly two hours before to say that there was gunfire and they were under attack. He had waited in the hut in case there was another call and then, half an hour ago, heard a big explosion at the plant.

'Merde, why would they blow up the processing plant?' Sebastien said.

'They didn't,' Tremayne said with certainty. 'It was the Kaiser's Closet. It means they've got the diamonds.'

Tremayne looked at his watch and guessed that the attackers were well on their way back to the port. They could still try and thwart the robbery if they could get down there quickly. He looked around for any form of transport, but there was no truck, no train, no horse, nothing.

'Could we use this?' Sebastien said, looking at a heap of iron at the end of the siding.

Tremayne looked at it dismissively.

'Look underneath, Harvey. It's a pump-action rail cart,' Sebastien said.

They cleared away the detritus and manhandled the cart onto the rails, burning their hands on the sun-scorched metal. The pump-action arm had lost its wooden handles and Sebastien found lengths of iron pipe that fitted. They tried the pump handle, but the cart was seized. Tremayne ran to the steam shovel and rooted around in the engine compartment and came back with a tin of grease and a grease gun. Five minutes of energetic greasing and the cart's moving parts were as free as they were going to be. Loading their packs and weapons, the four jumped on and, pumping hard, headed down the track towards the Lewala Mine. The pump-action screeched in defiance like an angry donkey. The wheels squealed like demented piglets.

It was a ludicrous sight. Four dust-covered men in assorted headgear bobbing up and down two by two, like Jews praying at the Wailing Wall, on a squealing cart in the blowtorch heat of the late morning.

Lewala Mine   10.25 am

They stopped well short of the processing plant and studied the scene. It was surrounded by two lines of steel mesh fencing ten feet high, topped with barbed wire. Where the rail line entered the mine there was an inner and outer gate made of the same materials. They were chained and padlocked. The adjacent security hut was empty.

'We can blow the chains off, but we'll have to do the outer one first and then the inner. If any of the attackers are still here, they'll be on to us,' Tremayne said.

'Or we can reverse the cart up the track, load on some rocks and send her down at full speed,' Sebastien said.

Constable Frikkie pulled out a bunch of keys from his pocket and looked at the three expectantly.

'On the other hand, that might be a better idea,' Sebastien said, his old grin returning.

Constable Frikkie was sent forward to unlock the gates and find his police colleagues. He was the only one they would recognise. After some time, he returned with two constables.

They reported that about twenty men had come in by train. They were German-speaking locals and seemed familiar with the mine. The Security Police at the control gate had been taken by surprise and all four had been killed. Two more constables were killed with hand grenades and the two survivors had hidden in the old tool store.

Then they had heard drilling, followed by an explosion. It had been the Kaiser's Closet. The men had loaded everything onto the train and departed.

Tremayne looked into the safe and his stomach turned. It was empty. The equipment they used was littered around, the drilling machines still hot. There were four boxes of explosives stacked beside the railway track. They had obviously been well prepared.

Tremayne knew they would already be at the port, loading the diamond drums onto a ship. Sidewinder was just twelve miles away. His mind flashed back to the hotel room, a stabbing pain … and the bastards involved were just twelve fucking miles away! He let out a shout that drew on all the pain and anguish of the last six months, put his hands to his face and bent forward. Kruger thought he'd been shot; Sebastien ran to him, thinking he'd had a stroke. The three constables looked on in alarm. When Tremayne straightened up, something had changed; his eyes were different.

Return to Port Baleen   10.30 am

When the train had departed the Lewala Mine there was relief all round. The most difficult and dangerous part of the operation was over. They had completely emptied the contents of the Kaiser's Closet and there was a sense of elation.

But when they reached the junction with the mainline there was still no sign of Moritz and Red Commando. Bosman stood on the roof of the loco, his binoculars searching the horizon. Nissen and Jager joined him and there was a heated debate as to whether they should take the

175

train north to search for them. Bosman was adamant they should try as he knew Siggie would do the same for them. Nissen said he would not jeopardise the operation. For all they knew, Siggie and his men might be captured, or even killed. They had the diamonds, Neptune was ready, U-46 was holding offshore and the Fatherland demanded they do their duty. Jager also wanted to search for Siggie but said nothing.

At the Mile 8 board, Bosman was still troubled about abandoning his friend. He slowed the train for the tightest curve and steepest gradient on the line, which then led into a cutting. With the loco at the rear on the return journey, he had to ensure that the brake van in front didn't jump the track. Certainly not today.

He had driven this line a thousand times and always felt excitement at this point because it was where he released the pigeons. The train was hidden from view and he could stop, attach the leather pouch containing diamonds, and release the bird in less than a minute. But not today; indeed, never again. They were embarking on a quest from which there was no return, at least until their land was back under German rule. He felt troubled. He'd miss the routine of driving the line each day and the nerve-jangling bird release. In a couple of days, he would be in Lobito Bay. What the fuck was he going to do there? He hated that hot, stinking tropical port with its vexatious biting insects. It suddenly occurred to him that the expectation of the raid and serving the Fatherland far outweighed the reality. And with his friend Siggie possibly captured, what was the point? If Red Commando had killed any policemen, they'd all get the death sentence. Nothing was worth that.

Port Baleen   10.40 am

Nissen was also in a contemplative mood on the journey to the port. He thought through the possible consequences of Red Commando going missing. He had to assume the worst, that they'd been captured. If they had, the Security Police interrogation would be harsh, and they'd quickly find out about the plan to transport the diamonds to Lobito Bay by U-boat. The element of surprise would be gone and the MTBs and naval trawler at Luderitz would be alerted and pose a real threat to U-46 as she sailed north through that area later tonight. He needed a contingency plan.

If their initial intelligence was correct, the MTBs were undergoing repair in Robert Harbour. If they could somehow put them out of action before U-46 sailed north, that risk would be eliminated. When the train arrived at the jetty, Nissen told Jager to join him on board Neptune.

'Christo, if any of Siggie's men have been captured, the Security Police will soon know about U-46 and the authorities will be on to her. If we can neutralise the MTBs in Robert Harbour, she'll have a better chance of safe passage. There's a security launch tied up in front of us. We could load that with explosives, sail it up to Luderitz and detonate it close to the MTBs and put them out of action. What do you think?'

Jager looked at Nissen, taking in the concept and working through the practicalities. The appearance of the security launch in Robert Harbour would be a surprise, but it was an official vessel, so it was unlikely to be challenged.

He nodded. 'It's certainly feasible. But it will take over three hours and will require someone familiar with the coast and the harbour,' Jager said.

'Who do we have that can do this?' Nissen asked.

Jager thought for a few seconds. 'There's no one who knows these waters better than me.'

'I can't risk sending you, Christo,' Nissen said. 'That's out of the question.'

'Look, if the weather's right, I know how to cut between Halifax Island and the Diaz Peninsula and get there even quicker. The sooner I arrive, the more likely we are to catch the MTBs in port.'

Nissen looked at him for several seconds. And then nodded. 'What weight of explosives can she carry?' he said.

'With spare fuel and me, the launch can take two passengers, so let's say that's around three hundred pounds. But there's none left on Neptune, so we'll have to reclaim the explosives that Green Commando have laid to sabotage the port.'

'The Fatherland will not forget this, Christo,' Nissen said, putting a hand on his friend's shoulder.

Jager nodded. But at that moment the pledge sounded hollow.

Lewala Mine   11 am

Harvey Tremayne was only just holding it together. Sidewinder, with his murdering, thieving accomplices, was just twelve miles south, but with him stuck at the mine it might as well have been a hundred.

'Is there any rolling stock, something big enough to take the six of us plus these boxes of explosives down to the port?' Tremayne said.

'There's a wagon over there,' Sebastien said.

In the siding by the mine store building was a double-bogie flatbed wagon, piled high with steel pipes. Both sides of the wagon had four steel uprights to hold the pipes in place and a series of ropes lashed them to the base. Behind it was a brake van. That was more like it, he thought.

'Constable Frikkie, take someone with you and clear those rocks from the track,' Tremayne said.

'This wagon must weigh nearly twenty tons,' Sebastien said.

'We'll have to uncouple the wagon and let it go. We'd never be able to control the speed with just the brake van,' Tremayne said.

Sebastien unhooked the coupling between the wagon and the brake van and released the manual brake. It didn't move.

'Find something we can use as a lever,' Tremayne shouted.

Using a long piece of pipe, they pushed and heaved.

'The brakes are seized. We'll need to give it a shock. Bring that bag of explosives and fuses over here, Niels,' Tremayne said.

He cut off a quarter of a stick of dynamite, inserted a detonator and wedged it between the buffers of the wagon and the brake van. He cut the fuse short and lit it.

'Take cover!' he shouted.

Seconds later there was a sharp crack and a cloud of dust, rust and sand. They returned and started to lever with all their might. With a reluctant screech, the wheels started to turn, and the wagon slowly moved forward, picking up speed as the gradient increased until it disappeared from sight. They listened as the clickety-clack of iron wheels on rail joints faded into the distance.

'Well, if that doesn't derail at Mile 10, it's going to give them one hell of a surprise when it arrives at the port,' Tremayne said.

Mile 10   11.30 am

Moritz had to keep kicking his heels into the horse to keep up the canter. The beast must have been ridden hard that day and was exhausted. Moritz didn't care. He had one purpose in mind.

At Mile 11, the desert dropped away in a gentle slope and he stopped and pulled out his binoculars. He could make out the buildings at the Lewala Mine and glancing at his watch, resigning himself to riding all the way to the port. Even then, if Sidewinder was on schedule, he stood little chance of getting there before they sailed. He began to wonder if he should have accompanied Petrus Johannes back to the waiting commandos and then taken their chance to escape north. But that wasn't an option any longer, and he spurred the horse on.

As he passed the Mile 10 post and cantered on down the track, he heard a distant rumble. It sounded like thunder, but that was impossible. He looked back and saw a wagon coming down the Lewala spur. His

178

heart leaped. It must be his comrades departing the mine. They were late. He turned and galloped back to the junction.

When the wagon got closer he could see it was loaded with pipes, and as it clattered through the points he realised it was a single wagon with nothing attached. That didn't make sense.

He immediately realised the danger it posed to the port. More to the point, there had to be someone up at the mine who had sent that wagon down. That hadn't happened on its own. He was about to head to the mine when he saw movement. There was now a brake van coming down the line. He armed his rifle and waited.

Chapter 40

Sunday Afternoon, 27th August 1939

Leaving Lewala Mine 12.10 pm

The policemen loaded the boxes of explosives onto the brake van and Sebastien released the manual brake. With some persuasive levering with the pipe, it started to move.

'Everyone on board,' Tremayne shouted. 'I want two constables in front and one on the back. Niels, you're our eyes, and Sebastien, you're our brakeman.'

As they rolled towards the junction with the mainline, Tremayne prepared the explosives. He removed the sticks of explosives he had in his bag, tightly bound them together with wire and embedded two detonators. He took the two fuses that were secured to the detonators and tied them together and cut them to the same length and secured his makeshift bomb into the top case of explosives. When the fuses were lit, they would explode within thirty seconds and the top case would detonate the other three. It was going to be one hell of an explosion.

'Harvey, there's someone on horseback at the junction!' Kruger shouted.

Tremayne jumped up and stuck his head out the side window. It had to be a police patrol. The man took off his slouch hat and waved at them to stop.

'Take cover and only fire if fired on!' Tremayne yelled. 'Sebastien, slow us down.'

Sebastien applied some braking as they approached the points and Tremayne stuck his head out the window again. The man raised his hand, signalling them to stop, but as the brake van drew level he froze, eyes staring, mouth aghast. It was like he'd seen a ghost. It took him a few seconds to recover his composure and then he raised his rifle and fired. The bullet hit the woodwork above Sebastien's head.

'Fire!' Tremayne yelled, and the three constables started shooting. The horse staggered back and fell, legs kicking, trying to get up. A further three shots and the horse was still, but the man was out of sight. Tremayne wasn't sure if the man had been hit, but if he was a marksman they were still well within range.

'Keep firing!' he shouted.

They only ceased when they disappeared over the rise.

'Who the fuck was that?' Sebastien said.

'I recognised him,' Kruger said. 'His name is Moritz. He's a supervisor in the sorting plant. Did you see his face when he recognised you, Harvey?'

'I remember him. If he's still alive, he's a marked man,' Tremayne said.

The journey down the mainline was exhilarating: The screech of wheels against track on the corners and the clickety-clack across the rail joints. Sebastien imagined he was back in the cockpit of his Escadrille biplane in 1918. There was the same rush of adrenalin, the excitement and danger, the wind in his face.

Port Baleen   12.15 pm

At the port, the commandos were busy loading the diamond drums onto Neptune, and Jager, with two commandos, set off to reclaim explosives to load into the security launch. They had stripped the jetty and marine diesel tanks; now they were going to strip the powerplant.

Jager had been reluctant to remove all the explosives as this was their only opportunity to render the port unusable. But he knew Nissen was right. Safe passage for the diamonds had to be the top priority.

Karl Bosman offered them a lift on his loco. He had to go up and switch the points back to the safety loop now that the diamonds had been safely delivered. The jetty felt vulnerable with the mainline open all the way to the mine.

When he'd dropped them off, he was still in a reflective mood. It was the end of an era and the next phase of his life had no direction or plan. He felt as if he was in a rowing boat, caught in the rapids at the top of a waterfall. There was no turning back and only one way to go: the unknown. He looked back up the railway line, his line, that disappeared over the rise into his desert.

Stopping short of the points, he walked to the hand-operated lever and reached into his pocket for the driver's key. It wasn't there. Where the hell was it? As he walked back to check in the cab, he heard the screech of steel wheels on steel track. He looked up. Four hundred yards ahead he saw a flatbed wagon coming down the line.

A wave of panic consumed him. He had to switch the points to redirect the wagon; he could now see that the wagon was fully loaded. He ran to the loco and searched for the key. It was on the floor. He grabbed it and ran back to the points. His hand was shaking and he couldn't fit the key. He could now hear the wagon clickety-clacking and he didn't have to

181

look up to know it was nearly on him. The key slipped in and he released the lever and pulled. There was a clunk as the points changed. He ran back towards the loco to watch the wagon enter safely into the loop. At the last second he realised it was travelling too fast. As it entered the points, the wagon jumped the rails and twisted to one side.

Instead of bulldozing to a stop in the soft sand, the front bogie was ripped off, the wagon's chassis ploughed into the track sleepers, and it stopped dead. The pipes did not. They snapped the fastening ropes and continued at the same speed, shooting through the air like projectiles.

The last thing Bosman saw was steel pipes coming at him like a salvo of spears. Several sliced through him and embedded themselves deep in the sand. When the dust cleared, it was reminiscent of a scene from the Bayeux tapestry where soldiers lay dead in the English countryside, impaled with spears. But in this scene, it was Karl Bosman and stainless steel pipes in the sands of the Namib Desert.

∞

From the brake van Tremayne saw a plume of smoke rise at the port and was elated. But not for long. It was not smoke, but a billow of dust, and it quickly cleared to reveal a boat tied up to the jetty.

'Either the wagon has derailed, or they've sabotaged the track,' Tremayne yelled. 'Sebastien, stop us five hundred yards above it.'

Around the next bend, and now in sight of the derailed wagon, Sebastien wound the brake handle like a man possessed, and the brake van screeched to an indecisive halt.

'On my signal, Sebastien, let the brake off, light the fuses and jump. The explosion will cause a distraction and give us a chance to surprise them. Niels, you and two constables go right to the high ground and try and cover us from that building. Frikkie and I will make for the workshops.'

Tremayne was galvanised into action. He was just a few hundred yards from his nemesis. He signalled Sebastien, who turned the brake handle and disappeared inside the brake van.

'Let's go!' yelled Tremayne, as gunfire started up from the direction of the jetty.

Tremayne glanced back and saw the old timber-constructed brake van disintegrating under the withering fire from a machine gun.

'Jump, Sebastien!' Tremayne shouted, and seconds later there was a crash and grating of mangled metal as the brake van hit the back of the derailed wagon. Then there was silence.

Seconds ticked by and Tremayne wondered if Sebastien had managed to light the fuses.

∞

While removing explosives from the powerplant, Jager had heard the grinding of metal as the flatbed wagon derailed. Looking up, he saw pipes cascade all around Karl's loco. He hoped to God that he was not inside it. He ran forward, shouting his friends name. Then he saw the brake van rolling towards the derailment. Seconds later it crashed into the back of the wagon.

Jager ran forward again to search for his friend but before he got halfway a shockwave smacked into the front of him. It lifted him bodily into the air and threw him back thirty feet. He was unconscious before he hit the ground.

∞

When the explosives detonated, the shockwave was enormous. Sheets of galvanised iron were ripped from the roofs of nearby buildings. What was left of the brake van was blown into a thousand pieces, mushrooming into the sky and fluttering down like confetti.

Tremayne and Constable Frikkie were slightly concussed, and their ears were ringing. Tremayne thought of Sebastien, but immediately focused again. Kruger, on the hill to his right, opened fire towards the boat and Tremayne saw the men on the jetty scatter.

With bullets ricocheting around them, he and Constable Frikkie made it to the back of the workshop. They couldn't go any further forward; they were pinned down by the machine gun on the trawler.

∞

Kruger and the two constables returned fire as best they could but had to withdraw and take cover behind some old concrete foundations. There they found Sebastien, injured after leaping from the brake van, deaf as a post, but not wounded.

Tremayne and Constable Frikkie were sheltering behind some heavy machinery as bullets pierced the galvanised iron cladding. Tremayne realised it would be suicide to attack from here and his mind flashed back to the attack on Y Ravine at Beaumont Hamel in 1918. A moving barrage kept the enemy's heads down while they advanced across no man's land, and a smokescreen on both flanks hid them from the enemy further along the line. He didn't have a moving barrage, but perhaps …!

He ran across the workshop and looked through one of the side windows. A dead policeman and his dog lay in full view, already bloating in the heat of the day. The building next door was the power plant, and beyond that stood the diesel storage tank. Between the two there was still a small fire flickering with the black smoke drifting towards the jetty. Perhaps there was a way to stop or at least delay the boat. He shouted to the constable to give him covering fire.

Constable Frikkie fired bullet after bullet at the boat, repeatedly replenishing the magazine. Kruger and the other constables were again firing from the hill. Under this cover, Tremayne slipped out the back of the workshop and ran to the diesel tank. The valve at the base had a circular steel handle, secured with a padlocked and chain. He looked in his bag and cursed at having no more explosives. All he had was one hand grenade and a signal pistol with two cartridges. He placed the grenade on the pipe between the tank and the valve and weighed it down with a piece of splintered timber, pulled the pin and ran.

There was a sharp crack, and shrapnel clanked off the metal sheeting. He looked back and smiled: the pipe was leaking a stream of diesel, but it spread very slowly, most of it appeared to be soaking into the sand. It was acting like blotting paper. He couldn't wait for it to reach the fire. He loaded a cartridge into the signal pistol, aimed at the leaking diesel, confident that the high temperature of the burning magnesium would set it off. He pulled the trigger and the flare whooshed forward and, with a clank, ricocheted off something metal and shot off at an angle and landed harmlessly. Cursing, he loaded the last cartridge and aimed a little lower and squeezed the trigger. This time the flare buried itself in the puddle of diesel and when it ignited there was a loud *whoomph*, and a large orange and black oily ball of flame leaped into the sky and up the side of the diesel tank. A plume of thick black acrid smoke drifted towards the jetty.

Under the continuing covering fire from Constable Frikkie and Kruger and his men, Tremayne sprinted across the open ground towards the jetty, firing his revolver point-blank at a man who appeared out of the gloom and, vaulting over the railing, he dived head-first into the harbour.

Tremayne hit the water awkwardly and was winded. He had been unaware that the security launch was tied up in front of the boat and he skinned his right shin against the gunwale as he went in. He cried out at the sharp pain, losing valuable air, and he turned turtle and swam back to the launch to catch his breath. But all he got was a lungful of acrid smoke that made him cough and splutter. There were shouts above and gunfire started. Taking a deep breath, he dived and swam below the launch and heard the *zyung zyung*, as bullets came through the bottom of the boat, probing the depths like shimmering glassy spears. He swam away until he felt the hull of the moored boat. His old wound was stabbing, his lungs burning and his shin stinging.

The boat had a deeper draft than he'd expected, and when he cleared the bottom he was desperate for air and kicked with his legs and drifted up towards the light. As he broke surface on the far side of the boat, he gulped more acrid air. He heard shouts above, and within seconds they had pinpointed him again. He was a sitting duck, and the crack of gunfire started again.

Taking a deep breath, he tumbled, kicked and dived. He swam deep into the icy cold water and, in what felt like slow motion, bullets whipped around him, accompanied by their eerie phantom spears. How long could he hold his breath? Bloody cigarettes! He knew he had to keep going. He swam along the seemingly endless keel, foot by agonising foot. How much further? Another foot, then another. Oh God, he needed to take a breath. His lungs were empty, his strokes slowed, his arms wouldn't function, his legs felt like lead. The last bubbles of air drifted from his open mouth, his body went limp and he started to rise. Something hit his head, then his shoulder. He grabbed at it and broke surface, taking in huge gulps of air, coughing and spluttering. It was the boat's port propeller. He held on tightly, his head spinning.

When he had recovered sufficiently, he swam under the jetty, looking for somewhere safe to hide, but everywhere seemed hopelessly exposed. The timbers covering the jetty were spaced apart and he could see someone moving towards him, firing through the gaps, down into the water. On one of the upright timbers a coil of thick rope was hanging from an iron bracket. He hid underneath it, and as the gunman passed overhead he felt the rope jolt as a bullet hit it. He looked at the rope that had just saved him and had an idea.

∞

When Jager reached the jetty, men were running around, shooting over the side. One of the commandos said there was a policeman in the water.

Just minutes before, when he had started to come around, the pain had been intense. With difficulty he sat up and assessed his injuries. His shirt and trousers had been ripped and he was spattered with spots of blood from flying sand and gravel. His face felt as if it were on fire.

An explosion at the diesel storage tank brought him to his feet and he stumbled back towards the jetty. He had a job to do.

Jager looked over the side of the jetty and to his relief he saw the security launch was intact and full of explosives. He climbed down and checked the detonators and safety fuse that the commandos had attached. He took off his crossbow, checked the box of matches in his pocket, untied the mooring rope and motored off into Respite Bay.

∞

Tremayne heard the engine of the launch start up, and immediately thought they were going to use it to search for him. As it chugged by, he moved behind the thick upright timber to avoid being seen. Then the engine pitch changed, and it headed away from the jetty and out into Respite Bay.

I wonder if he knows about the bullet holes, he reflected.

His arms and legs were now numb with the cold and his fingers wouldn't function. He recognised the first signs of hypothermia and knew he had to keep moving. Managing to pull the rope off the bracket and holding onto one end, he swam to the back of the boat.

He tried to visualise what the trawler would do when it sailed. The starboard engine would be put in reverse to pull the boat back and away from the jetty. That meant it would turn backwards, and he studied the pitch of the propeller. With painfully stiff hands he wound the rope half a dozen times clockwise around the shaft and tied the end to one of the blades. The other end he threaded through the gap between the rudder and the hull and tied it off. He left the remaining rope floating in the water. As it started to turn, the rope would wrap around the propeller shaft and seize it; at least that was the theory.

With his body about to shut down, he had to get out of the water. At the end of the jetty there was a steel ladder and he swam to it. He barely had the strength but managed to get his torso clear and clung there. He could feel the scorch of the sun on his back, and it felt good, its energy flowing into him.

Knowing he was exposed, he climbed further. Six feet from the top there was a large horizontal timber that provided support for the uprights. He climbed on, sitting with one leg dangling either side, and waited.

He thought he must have passed out because the next thing he heard was the trawler's engines. The starboard propeller churned and the rope he'd attached snaked through the water and went taught but, seemingly oblivious to his ploy, the boat pulled away from the jetty.

Leaving Respite Bay 1 pm

As Neptune sailed out of Respite Bay, the starboard engine seemed to be labouring and the captain reduced it to half throttle. Ten minutes later the engine stopped and could not be restarted. Continuing with just the port engine, he tried to adjust the rudder to compensate, but she responded very slowly.

He suspected he'd caught on some discarded fishing tackle and wanted to return to port to check. Nissen would have none of it. He was worried about being able to make the rendezvous with Moby.

'How long will it take to get to Pomona Island on one engine?' Nissen asked, studying the chart.

'At least five hours,' the captain said. He was about to add that he wasn't even sure they could make it but kept that thought to himself.

'Shit, it will be nearly dark by then and the fog will be returning. We'll have to change the rendezvous to Seal Harbour. How long to get there?' Nissen said.

'We'll have to go around the top of the island and sail down the Atlantic side. We can't risk sailing down against Rip Strait with her in this state.'

'I said, what time can we be there?' Nissen snapped.

'In just over an hour, sir, so make the rendezvous 14.30.'

'Damn it! Sohler is going to be fucking pissed off,' Nissen said.

Nissen knew that Seal Harbour was too close to Port Baleen, but there was no alternative. It was the only sheltered place that they could reach in daylight to transfer the diamonds to Moby. And now he had the added complication of what to do with all the commandos. Neptune certainly wasn't going to get to Swakopmund on one engine. In addition to two tons of diamonds, Moby could take the wounded and maybe another five at most. If they couldn't fix Neptune, the remaining commandos would have to be left on board in the harbour and hopefully rescued later. What a fuck-up! But the Third Reich would have the diamonds. That was the important thing.

He reached for the radio.

'Sidewinder to Moby, over.' He waited. 'Sidewinder to Moby, over.'

'Moby receiving, over.'

'New rendezvous at 14.30, over.'

'Confirm location, over.'

'Seal Harbour, over.'

'Confirmed. Moby out.'

Leaving Robert Harbour   1.10 pm

ST14 finally left Robert Harbour at just after 1 pm. There had been a delay due to an incorrectly fitted bearing. Crosson had cursed and cajoled his men for two hours until it was finished. At last, the 1,800-horsepower motor roared into life and, ignoring the speed restriction in the harbour, they departed at full throttle.

Flamingos along the north shore took flight and in the forward hold of ST14 Joaba, who had found a warm and safe place to sleep overnight, took fright. She had never heard such a noise. Opening the small door, she was met with a wall of noise, heat and fumes, and quickly shut it. She was terrified.

Crosson remained in radio communication with Luderitz and The Stinker on their journey south. There was no good news, only uncertainty. They had failed to raise Port Baleen RDF, and the fact that the last message was transmitted in German was serious cause for concern. What about the two naval technicians?

They'd heard nothing from Tremayne. Constable Isaak had reported that they had taken off at 6.30, destined for Pomona Beach, but the fog had been persistent, and they would not have been able to land there. He wondered where they had landed, because he would have to organise a search party.

Then at 13.23, Luderitz RDF radioed to say that they had picked up another message sent to Moby, but this time from Sidewinder. It was the first time they'd heard Sidewinder transmit, and now they'd heard Moby twice in one day. The first message sent at 8.06 had been Neptune contacting Moby, and now at 13.23 it was Sidewinder. Were Sidewinder and Neptune together?

The transmission from Moby was estimated to be about ten nautical miles south of Possession Island. Crosson gave new instructions to Denning to locate Moby. If it was a Kriegsmarine vessel, in South African territorial waters, he should take her into custody, using force if necessary.

As for Sidewinder, his signal was located north-east of Possession Island. It meant that he had left Port Baleen, presumably on board Neptune. ST14 would first check if Tremayne and Kruger were at the port, and if so, find out what intelligence they had gathered. They would then search for Neptune.

'Make for Respite Bay, full speed!' Crosson yelled to Lieutenant Maxwell. 'We have to locate Tremayne.'

Port Baleen   1.15 pm

Tremayne was angry when Neptune sailed from Respite Bay. He'd been so close to thwarting the diamond theft, and his one chance at vengeance had slipped from his grasp. Now they had no radio, no flares, no way of communicating with the outside world. They couldn't even take a loco up to Kolmanskop Camp because of the derailment.

His bandaged shin was stinging like hell and his old wound ached from the day's exertion. It was a reminder of that fateful night and it added further insult to the injury. And Sidewinder and the diamonds were making their escape to the Fatherland. A wave of exhaustion washed over him.

'Listen, I'm going up to the headland to see if the boat has gone north or south. Although she'll probably be long gone by now,' Tremayne said.

Kruger moved to join him but was stopped by a raised hand.

'I need to be alone. I have someone to meet. Someone I haven't seen for a while,' he said.

Kruger nodded. He knew where he was going. It was no wonder he acted the way he did.

Tremayne limped up the small track that zigzagged to the hill directly above the jetty. At the top he passed the old derelict German houses and made his way to a small area with railings around it. The view was stunning, with an endless panorama to the north and the south. Lifting his binoculars, he was surprised that he could just make out the trawler, heading west around the top of Possession Island. Perhaps he had slowed her down after all.

He stood there, taking in the scene, remembering the happy times that were gone for ever. With that thought, exhaustion seeped from his aching body into his troubled mind, weakening his resolve. Tears rolled down his cheeks and his shoulders shook. Eleanor had loved this place so much. That is why he'd asked Sir Ernest to have her interred here, where she was happiest. Sir Ernest had lost his wife, Mary, just five years earlier and knew the tragedy of losing a best friend, confidant and lover.

He opened the small gate and entered. There were three old headstones, now sandblasted and barely legible. The fourth one was new, cut from Cornish granite. Tremayne part knelt, part stumbled, his eyes blurred with tears. He ran his fingers over the inscription, caressing the letters, seeking their energy.

Eleanor Beatrice Tremayne
16 January 1909 – 25 March 1939
Loving wife of
Harvey Petroc Tremayne

For ever in the place she loved

He told her how much he missed her, how sorry he was that he'd let this happen. How he wished and prayed that he could rewind time, how … how he would see justice done for her, if it was the last thing he did. He knelt there until no more tears came, and then left.

In the distance he saw Kruger standing by the old German house closest to the cliffs. He noticed it had a double aerial in front and realised that it must be the new RDF station. His heart lifted.

'Is the radio working?' he shouted.

Kruger shook his head. 'It's been destroyed, and both technicians are dead.'

Tremayne shouted something to the sky.

'Are you alright, Harvey? You don't look well.'

'I'll warn you now, Niels, I am going to kill that bastard Sidewinder, or die trying.'

They returned to the jetty in silence.

South of Seal Harbour   1.15 pm

U-46 came up to periscope depth south of Possession Island. Kapitän-leutnant Herbert Sohler searched the horizon for any sign of shipping but saw nothing. With the change of rendezvous, he was early and would use the time to charge the U-boat's batteries. They had a long journey ahead and had to use battery-powered propulsion when submerged. He needed them fully charged in order to remain underwater for as long as possible.

The U-boat remained at periscope depth with the engines slow in reverse to compensate for the Benguela Current pushing them north.

'Any activity?' Sohler asked his sonar operator.

The boy pressed his headphones tight to his ears and shook his head.

Sohler took one more look through the periscope and ordered U-46 to surface.

Respite Bay   1.20 pm

ST14 turned into Respite Bay and reduced speed. Crosson surveyed the shore with his binoculars. The port was shrouded in a haze of black smoke but there didn't appear to be any boats at the jetty. Neptune, whoever she was, had gone.

With the engine noise decreased, Joaba opened the door of the forward hold and scurried past the engines as if they were tethered guard dogs, and quickly climbed the short ladder to the deck and hid.

'Send up a flare,' Crosson said.

One of the ratings pulled out the signal flare box from the emergency equipment locker, took what appeared to be an oversize revolver and loaded a large red cylindrical cartridge. He cocked it, pointed it up in the air and pulled the trigger. With a loud crack the flare soared high into the sky and burst into an intense white light, leaving a white smoke trail. Joaba was mesmerised.

Crosson scoured the jetty and foreshore for any response, but there was none.

South West of Possession Island   1.25 pm

The Stinker had left Robert Harbour to the boom of the Luderitz lighthouse and Diaz Point fog horns. But now they sailed at full speed under a clear blue sky over a turquoise sea with the west coast of Possession Island off their port bow.

Denning had ordered action stations and was making sure each crew member knew exactly what to do if they did come across a U-boat. He started below decks, checking with the RDF operator as he scoured the airways for any messages.

The fore and aft 20 mm cannons were loaded, and spare ammunition was stacked to one side. The two depth charges at the stern were armed and the release mechanism engaged. The Stinker's first officer, Lieutenant Hugo Ricks, was anxious about these old, untested munitions and would have gladly ditched them given half the chance.

A klaxon sounded and Denning rushed back to the bridge.

'Sir, target one thousand yards straight ahead!' the helmsman shouted.

South of Seal Harbour   1.25 pm

On U-46, the sonar operator pressed his headphones to his ears, listening to an approaching ship. 'Captain, twin-screw marine diesel approaching, nine hundred yards,' he said.

'Is it the Neptune?' Sohler asked, checking his watch, realising that if it was, she was early.

The sonar operator was flustered. The captain was a man of fearsome reputation and demanded fast, accurate information.

'It's a twin-screw, sir, similar to a trawler,' the operator said, wanting to add that he'd not heard Neptune's propulsion signature.

'Action stations, action stations,' Sohler ordered, and the crew went to work like an army of soldier ants.

His mind was racing. He had orders that on no account was U-46 to be captured, and that it should defend itself with lethal force if necessary.

He raced up the conning tower and searched the eastern horizon, expecting to see Neptune sailing towards him. Nothing! Where the hell was she? Then he looked behind.

A trawler was rounding the southern tip of the island, coming from the west at full speed towards him. He felt momentary relief, but then doubt. He had expected her to come from the east.

'Prepare the 88!' he yelled, and ratings swarmed over the top of the conning tower and down the ladder to the foredeck.

They released the 88 mm deck gun from its secure position, removing the protective cover from the nozzle, and rammed a long rod down the barrel to clear out any marine debris. They feverishly retrieved ammunition from a small watertight locker placed near the gun that held a few rounds ready for immediate use. Sailors' arms spun as they brought the gun to bear on the approaching boat.

'Hold your fire!' Sohler yelled.

He stared at the vessel, looking for a clue that it was indeed Neptune. He had not seen her before, but the description seemed to fit. He could see no other boats behind her. She slowed as she approached.

It was then that he saw the Royal Ensign flying, and her forward deck cannon.

'Aim for the bow,' Sohler yelled.

'Stand down, U-46,' an authoritative voice shouted over a loudhailer. 'Prepare to be boarded by His Majesty's vessel Table Bay.'

'Fire!' Sohler yelled.

U-46's deck gun fired as a large swell hit her obliquely. The lethal projectile went high and sliced through the front window of the bridge and exited the back, smashing the engine order telegraph and radio. It went between the helmsman and Denning, splattering them both with bits of metal and shards of glass.

The swell washed over the U-boat deck and knocked the gun crew off their feet. They were hanging on for dear life.

Denning grabbed the loudhailer and yelled, 'Fire!'

The Stinker's front-mounted cannon opened up, shells smashing into the deck gun and slicing through the hapless sailors trying to recover their footing. Then they targeted the conning tower, forcing Sohler to make a hasty retreat into the safety of the submarine. Denning slid down the ladder to the deck. Without the engine telegraph he had to shout instructions directly to the engine room. He glanced around the base of the bridge towards the U-boat. The submarine's deck gun had no steel plate protection and the gunners had been the unintended victims of its necessary destruction.

He then saw that the U-boat was moving backwards, the sea already starting to lap her stern. 'Oh no you don't,' he said. Holding the loudhailer, Denning yelled down into the engine room, 'Full ahead port, half ahead starboard.'

The Stinker turned on a collision course.

'Full ahead both,' Denning yelled. 'Prepare to drop anchor.'

The Number One looked around in astonishment, thinking he'd misheard the order.

U-46 picked up speed and now only the conning tower and bow were above water. But she wasn't fast enough. The Stinker crunched over the stern of U-46. As she continued to slide over her, the screech of grinding steel was ear-piercing. The port bow of The Stinker caught behind the conning tower.

'Drop anchor!' Denning yelled.

It landed on the submarine's deck, but as The Stinker rode up over her it slid off the far side.

'Raise anchor,' Denning yelled.'

The capstan groaned as the anchor was raised and finally stalled as it fouled on the hull of U-46. The Stinker was being taken for a slow ride out into Rip Strait.

Port Baleen   1.30 pm

Sebastien was sitting in the brake van at the jetty with his injured leg resting on the bench seat. Gazing across Respite Bay, he was thinking about Marie Antoinette. He needed to remove the bent strut and bring it to the mine to have it straightened. With some labour, he could clear a strip across the salt pan and fly to Windhoek to make a permanent repair. He took another swig of brandy from his hip flask.

Out at sea he saw a light flash, and he sat up. It must be the sun reflecting off a plane. Perhaps it was searching for them? He had seen that many times in World War 1 when behind enemy lines. But this was different. The light seemed to hover and then drop.

'Mon dieu! Look, it's a flare!' he shouted.

'That'll be Crosson,' Tremayne said. 'Shit, how do we let him know we're here?'

'Break the glass in that window and bring me the biggest pieces,' Sebastien said, climbing off the brake van and hobbling towards the end of the jetty.

They all hesitated. What the hell was he going to do with broken glass?

'Merde, fetch me some fucking glass, you useless bastards!' he yelled.

Constable Frikkie was the first to bring some pieces, each about the size of a small plate.

'Look, another flare,' Sebastien said. 'Point the glass midway between the sun and the horizon directly below the flare and twist it on its horizontal axis.'

Tremayne and Kruger understood immediately and copied him. The three kept this up even after the flare had vanished.

'Look!' Kruger yelled. 'There's a boat.'

'That's an MTB,' Tremayne said, with palpable relief. 'You clever bugger, Sebastien.'

'That's how we communicated between planes in the war,' Sebastien said. 'When I went down behind enemy lines in 1918, weather permitting they'd send up a plane each day to check on me, and we'd communicate by mirror.'

Constable Frikkie picked up a piece of the glass, studied both sides and shook his head.

Two Miles South of Seal Harbour   1.40 pm

'Number One, launch the rubber dingy and lower both depth charges into her and secure them. Set them to one hundred feet. We'll keep their heads down while you paddle to the submarine. Tie her to the deck gun and then sink the dingy,' Denning ordered.

At that moment the U-boat engines stopped, and a few minutes later something white was waved from the top of the conning tower.

'Fire to keep their heads down,' Denning ordered, and the forward cannon opened up. The flag disappeared.

Denning watched as his two men paddled the loaded dingy the short distance to the U-boat. The sailor clambered on board and tied the dingy rope to the deck gun, and then Lieutenant Ricks slashed the rubber sides with his knife. The two gave a thumbs-up signal and ran around the conning tower to the stern. Helping hands heaved them up onto The Stinker. The dingy had sunk out of sight.

The white flag was waved again, and with no gunfire in response, Kapitänleutnant Sohler appeared, tentatively looking over the rear of the conning tower at the anchor tangled with his submarine.

'Captain, you have deliberately attacked a vessel of the Kriegsmarine,' Sohler said, in a manner of addressing the owner of a dog that just peed on his trousers.

'Without provocation, you opened fire on one of His Majesty's ships,' Denning said.

'Captain, our nations are not at war. We do not want a diplomatic incident,' Sohler said.

'You should have thought about that before you fired on us,' Denning said.

'But Captain, you approached us at full speed, and we were simply defending ourselves. The Führer will not take kindly to such action.'

'Kapitänleutnant, you are a German military vessel, illegally in the Union of South Africa waters. By international law I have the right to board you and take you into custody and if you ignore that order I am at liberty to sink you. You will accompany me to Luderitz, is that clear?'

'Of course, Captain, I understand,' Sohler said, with a lopsided smirk that went unnoticed on The Stinker.

'Kapitänleutnant, you will remain on surface, and not attempt to dive. If you do, I will deploy depth charges. You have been warned.'

Sohler gave a salute and disappeared.

'Cut the anchor away,' Denning shouted.

The capstan whirred and then, with a loud bang and flying rust, the anchor and chain were gone.

'Full astern!' he yelled, and The Stinker screeched and grated off the back of U-46, which immediately started to slide backwards and submerge.

'Forward gunfire on conning tower,' Denning ordered.

The 20 mm cannon opened fire. Sparks flew and the aerial on top of the conning tower collapsed. But still she continued to submerge.

Denning said to his Number One, 'Well, he was warned.'

'Twice, sir, for the record,' the Number One replied.

As the conning tower of U-46 disappeared below the waves, Denning was calculating her rate of dive.

'Full astern. Brace for depth charge in thirty seconds,' Denning shouted through the loudhailer.

At sixty seconds there was a realisation that perhaps the depth charges were dud after all. Then the surface of the sea vibrated, spreading outwards in a huge circle. The shockwave hit The Stinker from below, and every rivet on her vibrated. Then a geyser of water rose up and the air blast hit them, their ribcages vibrating with the power of it. They stared in silence.

'Fuck me. One of them went off,' the Number One said. 'Begging your pardon, sir.'

'That'll teach them to underestimate The Stinker,' Denning said, with a grimace of satisfaction.

Within minutes an oily slick formed on the surface. Denning knew there would be no survivors.

'The good news, Number One, is we'll be a lot faster now. We've shed about ten tons of rust,' Denning said.

'And an anchor, sir.'

'And an anchor, Number One,' Denning said with a chuckle. 'Full ahead both. We'll make for Port Baleen and try and get this radio repaired.'

Leaving Respite Bay   1.45 pm

ST14 departed Respite Bay at full throttle and, based on Tremayne's last sighting of the trawler, they headed west across the top of Possession Island. There was debate as to her destination. It was unlikely the trawler was going to Seal Harbour, because the fastest route would have been down Rip Strait. Could she possibly be going to rendezvous with another ship out a sea? As unlikely as that was, it seemed the only logical answer.

One person on board ST14 was not in the least bit interested in the trawler. Joaba was holding on to the cockpit railing, standing next to Lieutenant Maxwell and enjoying the high-speed bumping and bouncing. She had never had so much fun. When ST14 had picked up Tremayne and Kruger, she had been spotted peering out of the emergency equipment locker on the starboard deck. Crosson had wanted Joaba off the boat, but she kicked and scratched anyone who tried to grab her. Kruger suggested she stay. She was, after all, the only one who could recognise Sidewinder and his accomplice Karl.

They headed due west, leaving Possession Island behind, but soon ran into the fog. The trawler wouldn't be able to make a rendezvous in these conditions. She had to be elsewhere. They turned and headed south down the west coast of the island.

Crosson had kept in radio contact with Luderitz RDF but neither had heard from The Stinker for some time and could not raise her. But he had something more imminent to worry about: Neptune and Sidewinder. As they cleared the southern tip of the island there was still no sign of her.

'Look, if she had engine or steering problems, perhaps she had to go the long way around to Seal Harbour to avoid Rip Strait,' Tremayne suggested.

It didn't seem likely, but the harbour was only a few minutes away and it was worth checking. Maxwell set a course.

Seal Harbour   2.15 pm

Neptune was anchored in the inner waters of Seal Harbour on the south-east corner of Possession Island. The south-west wind was strong and steady and white horses raced out in Rip Strait. In the shelter of the harbour the water was calmer, but Neptune was still bow to the wind, pointing towards land.

On arrival they had uncovered Octopus's name board and hung fishing nets over the side. She looked to the world like a typical Benguela fishing boat, albeit with a more valuable cargo.

A small wooden boat was tied to the stern and men were diving down, trying to disentangle the rope that had snagged the starboard propeller. A man with a rifle stood above them, watching for sharks.

The captain had been right. If they had returned to Port Baleen they would have been able to remove the rope and would now be well on their way to Pomona Island. As it was, the starboard engine had overheated and blown a gasket and the engine room was splattered with oil. The hatch cover had been removed and a thin, hazy smoke drifted out. They had not the slightest inkling that their plight had been deliberately engineered.

The man with the rifle at the stern was the first to raise the alarm. 'Boat approaching from the south!' he yelled.

Nissen looked through his binoculars.

'An MTB. Action stations. Remember our disguise, everyone below deck. Prepare the forward gun.' But as he said it he realised it could not be brought to bear on the approaching boat.

He was about to order the port engine to engage full reverse to bring her around, but then realised the shared fuel line between the port and starboard engines had been disconnected.

∞

As ST14 approached Seal Harbour, Commander Crosson viewed the anchored vessel. She was flying the South African Marine flag and looked like a genuine trawler. She had the name Octopus on her stern.

'Let's not take any chances. Action stations,' Crosson said.

As they cautiously approached the trawler, Tremayne studied her. He saw the name on the stern but couldn't remember seeing that on the boat at Port Baleen. Other than that, she looked identical. There was a small boat tied to the stern with men in the water. Tremayne realised in an instant.

'Commander, that's Neptune!' Tremayne yelled.

In that second there was a shout from the trawler and a hail of fire from rifles and submachineguns. Bullets thudded into ST14 and the forward machine gunner was killed instantly. Then the helmsman on the bridge was hit. He fell beside Joaba, blood gushing from his chest, and she screamed. Falling to the deck, she wriggled away to the safety of the emergency equipment locker. The attack had been carried out with speed and precision. ST14 had been immobilised in less than fifteen seconds. Crosson was angry and in shock. He stood up and raised his hands.

Nissen appeared on the port side of Neptune, joined by other men.

'ST14, who is your senior officer?' Nissen said.

Crosson spoke in a clear, authoritative voice. 'Commander Crosson, Royal Navy. Who am I addressing?'

'My name is not important,' Nissen said.

Tremayne was shaking, not with fear but with rage.

'So how much blood have you spilled this time?' Tremayne shouted, spitting out the words.

'You are my prisoners. I ask the questions,' Nissen said.

Tremayne noticed three men in the small boat rowing towards them.

'I hope you're not still waiting for Moby,' Tremayne said.

Nissen hesitated, and said, 'So, you've broken our code.'

'More than that,' Tremayne said, 'we've broken your network – Neptune, Santa Maria, Scorpion, Cobra and Indigo. And not forgetting Leopold Wenger, alias Moussa.'

At the mention of the last name he saw the man recoil. Indecision was etched on his face. Uncertainty flowed through the other ranks. Even one of the men in the small boat looked back. He'd clearly hit a raw nerve.

'One person has let you down. Let you all down,' Tremayne said, looking around at his captive audience. 'There's one person who has been very careless about his communication, and that's you, Sidewinder.'

Tremayne saw all heads turn to look at Nissen, and he knew it was him.

Nissen snorted, 'No matter. You're all going to die,' and he raised his submachinegun and pulled the trigger.

A loud crack and a whoosh of white sparks shot from ST14 towards Neptune and a bright white cloud exploded from Nissen's chest. The blood-curdling scream he exhaled would have terrified even the demons in Dante's nightmare. The white-hot magnesium flare started to burn at over three thousand degrees centigrade, searing his vital organs. He staggered back like a drunk, smoke shooting from his mouth, like steam does from a train. Everyone who witnessed the scene was transfixed; it was too horrible to watch yet too mesmerising to look away. Nissen, with his embedded pyrotechnic, fell backwards and toppled into the engine room through the open hatch. Smoke billowed, and seconds later an explosion rocked the boat. A mushroom of oily flame boiled up into the sky. Men swarmed onto the deck, like a plague of rats; some were on fire and dived overboard.

Joaba stood there, mouth open, eyes staring, with the signal pistol in her hand still smoking.

Tremayne gently took it from her.

'I got that bastard, didn't I?' she said.

'My God Joaba, you certainly did that,' he said, surveying the scene.

Nearly all the men had now abandoned ship and were swimming to shore and a few towards the MTB.

'Joaba, you got Christo,' Kruger said, putting his hand on her shoulder. 'Are you alright?'

'What?' she said, looking up at him.

'The man with the German codename Sidewinder is Christo, your neighbour at Guano Bay,' Kruger said.

'He not *that* bastard,' Joaba said, shaking her head, eyes blank, staring.

'What do you mean? *That* was Christo,' Kruger said, more as a statement than a question.

'That not Christo. I never seen that bastard before.'

Kruger went white as a sheet at the implication. He shouted to Tremayne, 'Harvey, the man that was shot is not Christo. Joaba's never seen him before.'

'But he acknowledged he was Sidewinder, and our intelligence says that Sidewinder is Christo. Joaba, are you sure that wasn't him?' Tremayne said.

'I told this mister, I never seen him before,' Joaba said. 'I still want to shoot that bastard Christo in the cock.'

'So, where the fuck *is* he?' Tremayne said, looking at the dozens of men, some still swimming, some now climbing out onto the harbour. Two had been pulled on board ST14.

A shout went up from shore as a black dorsal fin cut the surface. Panic swept through those still in the water, like a wildfire through dry brush. Grown men with eyes bulging and mouths open, men who had freely spilled the blood of others for diamonds, were now screaming to their god for help. Those that couldn't swim tried to grab those that could. The huge gliding body swam determinedly towards the splashing and changed from grey to white as it turned on its back to feed, and the water turned red.

Tremayne looked at the scene and then at the two men who had just been pulled on board.

He grabbed the closest one by the throat. 'Where are Christo and Karl?' he spat.

'Karl is dead, killed by the runaway wagon,' he spluttered.

'And Christo?'

The man said nothing, but Tremayne could see in his eyes the crooked flick of deceit.

'Last chance, or you swim with the shark,' Tremayne said.

The man looked nervously to the harbour but turned back to Tremayne, as if he were testing him, daring him. He had no idea who he was dealing with.

Tremayne kneed him in the groin, grabbed him by the shirt and pushed his upper body so it hung over the side.

'Where is Christo?' Tremayne demanded.

There was no response.

'Listen, you're dealing with the Tokolosh. If you cooperate, you might just go to prison, instead of being fed to the sharks or hanged in Pretoria Central Prison with the rest of these fucking lowlifes,' Tremayne spat.

'He's in the s—s—security launch heading for Luderitz, Mr Tremayne,' a voice said, behind him.

Tremayne looked around at the man who'd spoken.

'I know you,' Tremayne said, wracking his brain. 'Your name is Bronkhorst.'

Nico Bronkhorst stared at him, his face as white as a sheet. He was looking at a ghost.

'B—b—but he said, he'd k—k—killed ...' The words froze but his lips kept moving.

'Say that again,' Tremayne said.

Bronkhorst's mind was in a turmoil of loyalties, but above all he wanted to save his own skin.

'What did you just say?' Tremayne shouted.

Tremayne pushed the first man over the side and grabbed Bronkhorst, dragging him to the side of the boat. His comrade was splashing in the water, screaming for help.

'What did you just say, Bronkhorst?' Their noses were nearly touching. 'Fuck you. What did you say?'

Tremayne headbutted him on the bridge of the nose and Bronkhorst's hands went to his face, blood running between his fingers.

'He said he'd k—k—killed you.'

'Who killed me?'

'Scorpion.'

'Who the fuck is Scorpion?' Tremayne yelled, and headbutted him again.

'C—C—Christo Jager is Scorpion.'

Tremayne and Kruger stared at one another.

'And where is this Christo now?'

'He's going to b—b—blow up the MTB base. He has explosives on b—b—board the s—s—security launch,' Bronkhorst stammered.

Crosson felt the blood drain from his face.

'Maxwell, let's go!' he yelled.

Lieutenant Maxwell slammed ST14 into gear and pushed the throttle to maximum. She bucked like a wild horse, knocking nearly everyone on board off their feet, swerved to port in her own length, and sped out of Seal Harbour.

'What sort of head start does he have?' Crosson said.

'At least two hours,' Tremayne said. 'I heard the launch leave when I was sabotaging the trawler. God, that seems an age ago.'

North of Respite Bay 3.35 pm

As ST14 raced north, Tremayne and Crosson scoured the shore for the tiny boat, even though they knew it would be almost impossible to spot against the cliffs. Tremayne guessed that with the bullet holes she'd received at the jetty she would be taking on water; the question was at what rate. Learning that the launch carried explosives brought him out in a cold sweat. If a bullet had hit that when he'd dived into the harbour, he would have been atomised, along with everyone else.

201

'If I were in Christo's predicament, I'd keep close to shore, in case I needed to beach the boat,' Tremayne said.

'There are dozens of small sheltered bays between Respite and Luderitz,' Kruger said.

'I'll bet he had to beach the boat early on. There were several bullet holes in her,' Tremayne said.

'Jackass Cove is the first,' Kruger said.

'That's about ten minutes,' Maxwell said.

As they nudged into the cove, Crosson searched the beach with his binoculars.

'There's something there,' he said, pointing. 'Look to the left. Slow ahead, Captain.'

As they approached, they could see a boat pulled up on the sand, partially camouflaged.

'That can't be the launch. It would take six men to pull it up there,' Tremayne said.

'It needs to be checked out. Cover me,' Kruger said.

He plunged into the water and swam ashore. Pulling back the sail revealed a clinker-built wooden sailing boat with removable mast.

'That the bastard's boat!' Joaba yelled, jumping up and down.

It was empty, and the tide had washed away any evidence of footprints. Kruger searched the rocks at the base of the cliff. Two penguins took fright, scurried across the beach and dived into the water.

'There's no sign that the launch landed here,' Kruger shouted. 'This must be where Christo and Karl landed before the raid.'

'But I want to shoot the bastard,' Joaba said, looking as though she'd missed her turn at the fairground.

At that moment, a plane flew overhead, its red, white and blue decal clearly visible. The radio crackled.

'Come in, ST14. Catalina 12 here. Are you OK, over.'

'ST14 operational, over.'

'We were notified by Cape Town you might be in a spot of bother from a seaborne attack, over.'

'Confirmed. Lewala Mine raided, many dead, stolen diamonds on trawler in Seal Harbour with twenty men at large on Possession Island. Contact Saldanha and Cape Town and request immediate assistance, over.'

'Received, will do. We also have a message from London for Harvey Tremayne, over.'

'Tremayne is listening, over,' said Crosson.

'The message reads: "Sidewinder is Abwehr officer based in Hamburg", over.'

Tremayne and Crosson looked at one another, incredulous.

'Abwehr,' Tremayne said, shaking his head. 'That means Joaba just killed a Nazi officer!'

'Received with thanks, Catalina 12,' Crosson said. 'We are searching for a small launch, believed to be sailing north from Respite Bay to Luderitz. Please locate and report, over.'

'Will do, ST14. Catalina 12 out.'

North to Robert Harbour 3.45 pm

After leaving Respite Bay, the security launch had chugged a steady beat as it sailed north. Jager soon noticed water in the bottom of the boat and worked the handle on the bilge pump, but the level continued to rise. He diverted to a small bay and jumped overboard to check. He discovered four holes in the hull, each the same size. They appeared to be bullet holes. He inserted wads of cloth as best he could, but within half an hour she was leaking again. He was fighting a losing battle, and knew he had to try and plug the leaks properly. The next possible location where he could do this was just north of Great White Point. If he could make it that far. He watched, with consternation, the waves crashing onto the cliffs, the wind whipping the spray and foam high into the air to disappear into the desert.

As the Benguela Current was forced around the point, Jager had no control. The launch went where the sea took it. The eddy carried him just clear of the rocks. He was lucky; had she been sitting higher in the water the wind would have caught her and pushed her to destruction. He looked up to the sky and breathed a huge sigh of relief. And then the engine cut out.

He pressed the starter button again and again, but nothing happened, not even a click. The batteries had shorted. He remembered the two policemen he'd dumped near this very spot and felt a cold hand touch him.

To his right, on the north side of the rocky point was a sheer cliff and to his left the long silver sand beach. With the launch just wallowing in the swell, he contemplated swimming but then thought of the dead-eyed monsters. He had to get closer to shore. He wasn't that far off. Searching in the boxes on either side of the boat, he found two paddles. He grabbed one and started stroking for all he was worth, a few pulls on one side then a few the other side.

It was then that he heard a plane fly overhead.

Within minutes the Catalina reported a small boat in a bay about six miles north. With Kruger back on board, Lieutenant Maxwell gunned the boat out of the cove.

'The next bay is the other side of Great White Point,' Kruger shouted, in Maxwell's ear. 'Keep well seaward of the point because of the rip currents.'

'ST14 to Catalina 12, received with thanks. I have one further request, over,' Crosson said.

'Whatever we can do to help, sir, over.'

'Check out Respite Bay and see if you can find HMSAS Table Bay. She's been out of communication for a couple of hours, over.'

'I can report there is an oil slick south-east of Possession Island. I'll investigate, over and out.'

Crosson's shoulders slumped.

As ST14 turned into the bay, they saw the launch, sitting low in the water, with a tarpaulin draped over the front. She appeared to be abandoned.

Crosson was immediately relieved that she had not made it to her intended destination. Tremayne was dismayed that Jager didn't appear to be on board, and Joaba was disappointed that she wouldn't be able to shoot him.

Under the tarpaulin, lying in the bottom of the boat, Jager eyed ST14 and armed his crossbow. If he could kill one of the men on the bridge, in the ensuing panic he could slip over the side and swim to the beach, no more than a hundred yards away. The trouble was he only had one bolt. The others must have fallen out of his pocket when he was repairing the launch. He waited to get a clear shot but could not get a steady aim. He was shivering as he lay in the icy water.

The first indication of the visitor was a hint, almost a sense. Gulls lifted from the sea in a cacophony of alarm, departing as if all were late for the same appointment. Everyone on ST14 looked around for the cause. The surface between the two boats became glasslike, and it slowly swelled and deformed. A dark grey shiny mass slipped by, and ST14 rocked as the visitor tested the hull. A staring dead eye searched the surface, sucking in information, a dorsal fin followed, black and erect. A lazy swing of the tail propelled the great white between the boats, and it disappeared.

'That a big bastard,' Joaba said, eyes wide.

Kruger's stomach tingled. Only fifteen minutes ago he had been swimming in Jackass Cove.

It happened quickly. The shark came up beneath the launch and bumped it hard. Because it was top-heavy with the explosives, it flipped over, its hull now pointing to the sky.

Jager had been ready to take a shot when the launch jerked, and he was flung backwards into the icy water. He knew what had happened. He swam the few yards back to the launch and held on to the side, keeping out of sight of ST14.

He then thought of his legs beneath the surface, and the cuts from the explosion. As good as an invitation to the unwelcome visitor. He scrambled onto the upturned hull, still clutching the crossbow.

'That the bastard! That Christo!' Joaba shouted, pointing at the man who had just emerged. 'Give me a gun.'

Jager looked around at them, guilt and deceit written across his face in equal measure. Like a dog who's just killed the farmer's chickens.

He had two options: to be captured meant certain death at the end of a rope. Swimming to shore, he had at least a slim chance. But it was his only chance.

'I take it you are Christo Jager?' Tremayne said.

'Who the fuck wants to know?' Jager growled.

'I'm St Peter, deciding if you should go straight to hell now or to Pretoria Central Prison on the way,' Tremayne said.

'Fuck you. You're not my judge.'

'You're wrong there, Christo – or would you prefer Scorpion? Believe me, you are soon to be at the pearly gates, and this is the moment to confess your sins.'

'You can fuck off,' he said.

'Tell me, are you the smuggler of diamonds, killer of Diamond Security Police, murderer of civilians and the rapist of underage girls?'

Jager licked the salt on his cracked lips and glanced at the beach. He could make it. He had to. He eased the crossbow closer and looked to make sure the bolt was still in place.

'You've got it all wrong. I'm a fisherman,' he said.

'I'm not a patient man, Jager. I need the truth.'

He said, 'Who the fuck do you think you are?' and raised the crossbow, snugged it, aimed and fired.

The bolt thudded into the side of the bridge, just below Tremayne.

Tremayne raised his revolver and a shot rang out. Jager yelled, holding his shoulder, nearly slipping from the hull.

'Can I shoot him now?' Joaba said, tugging Tremayne's sleeve.

'Try something stupid like that again and I'll let Joaba here use you for target practice.'

'I want to shoot him in the cock!' Joaba shouted.

'By the way, I wouldn't bleed into the water. Great whites can detect blood for up to half a mile. There must be dozens within that radius.'

Jager looked at the blood trickling down the hull and eased himself a little higher, glancing around nervously.

'Yes, I'd get even higher if I were you. It could easily grab you from there,' Tremayne said.

A large black dorsal fin drifted between the two boats, so large the tip flopped over. Then a huge grey head reared up, its razor-wire tangle of triangular teeth grinning at the world, dead eyes searching.

Tremayne felt a shiver at the size; easily twenty feet long, he estimated. 'You've got a visitor, and he looks hungry.'

Jager looked over his shoulder and stared straight into the open jaws, then turned away in horror, letting out a scream that made the crew on ST14 flinch, just as fingernails scraping on a blackboard do.

'Shoot it, oh my God, for pity's sake shoot it!'

'Not until I get some answers. Why did you shoot the area manager and his wife in March this year?'

'What the fuck has that got to do with you?'

'Oh, that's right, I didn't introduce myself, did I? I'm the one you shot. My name is Harvey Tremayne.'

Jager froze, then turned to look at him. At that moment he knew he was about to die. He was out of lies.

'On the 25th March, in the middle of the night, you entered a hotel room in Luderitz. You must remember.'

'Listen, that wasn't me.'

'You're a liar, Jager. I was shot in the back and left for dead. Eleanor, my wife, was molested and killed. I promised her, on my life, I'd kill the person that did it ... and that person is you.'

The dead-eyed monster reappeared between the two boats, following the scent of fresh blood. It sank almost out of sight and then, with one flick of the tail, its head towered out of the water, mouth open, and slid along the hull of the launch. In horror, Jager rolled away backwards into the water.

With Jager's one-armed manic splashing silhouetted against the bright sky, the shark turned and came up at speed. As it broke surface, Jager was caught in the tangle of teeth, his face wracked with the certainty of death. Then as the jaws snapped shut around his torso, blood gushed from his mouth.

Everyone on board ST14 looked away. It was too terrible to watch. The monster was in a feeding frenzy and the water turned red.

Tremayne felt his head spin and legs go weak, and he grabbed the side of the boat for support. All the vengeance and hatred that had built up, minute by minute, hour by hour, day by day, over the last six months popped like a party balloon. In that instant everything changed. The hatred that had been so tangible, so imperative, had suddenly evaporated.

Eleanor had been a kind, loving, forgiving soul; oh God, would she have wanted such an ending, even for her killer? He now doubted it, doubted himself, and buried his face in his hands. Would she think of him as a deranged killer, someone with no sense of moral boundary, no emotional balance? He had been so wrapped up in his own grief and hatred and rage, he'd convinced himself he was doing it for her.

Joaba watched the torment written all over his face, and with the gruesome death of Sidewinder etched in her mind she grabbed him and buried her face in his chest. And that was it. That was the tipping point. They both broke down, sobbing and hugging one another as they rocked to and fro. Everyone on ST14 looked away. They knew there were some serious demons being exorcised. There was nothing anyone could say or do. It was personal.

Epilogue

Tremayne remained in South West Africa for a further five days while the attack was investigated, and the damage to the mine infrastructure assessed. He had flown to Cape Town that morning, courtesy of the RAF. He was driven to an unassuming, unnamed office on Buitengracht Street near the harbour. It was home to the military intelligence wing of the British Embassy, an MI6 outpost.

He set to work collating a report on the attack for Sir Alistair Wilson in London. Interrogation of the captured men provided a sense of the organisation behind the raid. The main revelation was the identification of the head of Southern Africa Section of Abwehr II, Kapitänleutnant Horst Nissen, as the leader. He had been operating in South West Africa for two years, recruiting and training discontented colonial Germans. Codenamed Sidewinder, he was confirmed as the only German national involved in the raid. The German Embassy in Windhoek categorically denied that any of their nationals were involved.

He had formed six commando units across the country. Three of those, a total of thirty-three men, had been involved in the attack on the mine. Nine had been killed, including two of the ringleaders Christoff Jager and Karl Bosman. A further two were missing, believed to have been killed in the shark attack at Seal Harbour.

Commander Nico Steenkamp had captured six commandos south of Mile 20, and the other ringleader, Siegfried Moritz, was found wounded at Mile 10. The commandos marooned on Possession Island were arrested two days after the attack, all suffering from dehydration and only too eager to surrender.

Captain Denning and the crew of HMSAS Table Bay worked tirelessly to evacuate the wounded from Port Baleen to Luderitz and then supported the blockade of Seal Harbour. No reference was made to U-46 in her ship's log.

The Eureka had sailed up from Cape Town the day after the attack with additional medical staff, emergency supplies and a contingent of South African Infantry to secure the mine and port.

Neptune had been deliberately scuttled by Commander Crosson to deny the marooned commandos any potential access to arms and shelter. And to deter anyone from stealing her cargo. A specialist naval diving team had arrived, and salvage of the diamond drums had commenced.

The failure of the attack was, in part, the result of the sabotage of the starboard engine of Neptune. This had forced her to change the rendezvous with U-46 from Pomona Island to Possession Island. That radio transmission between the two had enabled ST14 to locate her. Tremayne felt relief that his one small act of tying a rope around the propeller shaft had been so decisive.

And Joaba was the unlikely heroine of the day. Without her quick-minded intervention with the signal pistol, the MTB would have been captured and those onboard killed. Everyone on ST14 owed their lives to her. De Beers had relocated her family to Luderitz, and she and her sister were enrolled in school.

The thing that Tremayne had learned on his arrival in Cape Town was the reason for the appearance of the Catalina seaplane at the crucial moment. The alert had originated in Tangier, based upon information given to Captain Mark Timpson by someone in the Port of Tangier Customs Police. His name was not given, but Tremayne guessed it had to be Youssoufi.

Tremayne booked a call to Timpson for 5 pm. He needed to find out what additional information might have been gleaned from him so he could add it to his report.

He called Sir Ernest in the afternoon and they talked through what was needed to get the Lewala Mine back in operation as fast as possible. Tremayne was to personally oversee the work. Churchill had called Sir Ernest when he heard the news of the attack and reiterated the urgent need to recommence production. In his opinion, war in Europe was just days away. Churchill also voiced his personal thanks to Tremayne, and that of His Majesty's Government, for helping thwart the Nazi plot.

A memorial service was scheduled for the following Saturday at the Church on the Rocks in Luderitz. Sir Ernest and General Smuts were going to attend. A plaque was to be unveiled listing the names of the two Navy radio technicians, two crew members of ST14 and the fourteen Diamond Security policemen who had been killed.

When the phone rang, Tremayne checked his watch.

'Hello, is that the British Consulate?' he said.

'Hello Tremayne, it's Timpson. How are you? We heard you were injured.'

'Oh, I'm fine. Healing nicely, thanks. How are you managing without me?'

Timpson chuckled. 'It's much quieter, and the murder rate has dropped dramatically.'

'It sounds as though I should come back, or you'll have nothing to do.'

'Well, Cartwright doesn't want you back,' Timpson said with another chuckle.

'Listen, I take it the person you questioned was Youssoufi?'

'Yes, he's still here with us, enjoying diplomatic protection. He's asked for asylum.'

'So, what exactly was his involvement in the smuggling ring?' Tremayne asked.

'Well, he was accepting money from Moussa in return for information about ship manifestoes from South West Africa. When Tangier customs impounded the Santa Maria, Abwehr thought Moussa must have leaked information about the smuggling ring. Two officers flew in from Hamburg to question Moussa's paid contacts, including Youssoufi. He couldn't tell them anything, but because he knew of Moussa's involvement in the diamond smuggling ring they decided to kill him. They dumped him over a cliff and left him for dead, but I was trailing them and found him, and miraculously he had survived. What got my attention was they asked Youssoufi if Moussa had mentioned Operation Benguela on the twenty-seventh. We put two and two together and Richardson phoned MI6 in London, who phoned Cape Town, who contacted Saldanha Bay.'

'So, I owe you and Richardson a big thank you. The arrival of the Catalina helped bring the attack to a quick and successful end. Can you put me through to her? I'd like to thank her in person.'

'Sorry, Tremayne. She's not here.'

'What time will she be back?'

'She won't be. She's in London, getting ready to transfer to the British Embassy in Washington DC. With the imminent threat of war, there's a move to strengthen ties with the Americans. We'll not win the war without them,' Timpson said.

Tremayne thanked him and put the phone down. He stared out the window across Cape Town harbour, not quite sure how he felt about Charlotte Richardson's departure to the other side of the world. He wondered what now lay in store for his personal life. One thing was for sure: it had been a tough few weeks. He needed a stiff drink.

Other books by Jon Gliddon

Break in Communication

It is December 1941. WW2 has become bloody. The Luftwaffe are bombing English cities and the Nazis are about to launch their super battleship Tirpitz. With the tireless Winston Churchill as his boss, Colonel Julian Bonham-Johns from the Special Operations Executive is under pressure. A ruthless foreign agent is making his way through the south west of England and it becomes clear that a sinister Nazi plot is unfolding. In a bid to stay ahead of the enemy, Bonham-Johns must mastermind a plan with the Allies and catch the agent. It's a race against time to navigate tensions and egos while feeding lies and misinformation to the enemy.

In the beautiful Cornish village of Porthcurno, Home Guard sergeant Bert Chenoweth hoped to live out his days in peace. He never reckoned on having to do battle again, but then he never reckoned on this kind of threat on his doorstep. Will he find it in himself to fight one last time for the things he holds dear?

Mud, Blood and Bayonet; The Story of the 6th Battalion Dorsetshire Regiment, 1918 day by day

This is the story of the last year of WW1 and the daily life and battles of the 6th Battalion Dorsetshire Regiment. They fought numerous and often bloody actions and of the 44 Officers and 757 Other Ranks killed during the entire war, 17 Officers and 359 Other Ranks were killed between January and November 1918.

Their first major action was the German Spring Offensive, which they fought resolutely, against overwhelming numbers of enemy troops and artillery. They consolidated and actively fought skirmishes on the front line culminating in the attack on Y Ravine at Beaumont Hamel in June. In August, the final push saw them attack Thiepval Ridge, Pozieres, Flers, Gauche Wood and on towards Cambrai. The very last fight was in the Mormal Forest near Locquignol on 4th November 1918, the battle in which my Grandfather, 20652 Private Herman Alfred Pike, was seriously wounded.

Whilst the brave men of the 6th Battalion Dorsetshire Regiment are no longer with us, their experiences are captured on the pages of the war diaries, personal diaries and in the orders and operational reports; their hand-written notes still legible on the 'dog-eared' trench maps. This is their story, in their words.

More information on the author and his work can be found on his website: www.jongliddonauthor.com

CPSIA information can be obtained
at www.ICGtesting.com
Printed in the USA
LVHW051051291020
670168LV00001B/146

Managing the world's richest diamond mine in former German South West Africa, Harvey Tremayne clashes with a colonial resistance group, intent on restoring their homeland. They smuggle diamonds destined for the Nazi military rearmament programme. Tremayne got in their way. They killed his wife.

Driven by revenge, he's now hunting for them. His search takes him to places even more dangerous than the terror-filled trenches of his WW1 service. In the process, he is drawn into the shadowy world of British Secret Intelligence. They are hunting the same enemy but for a different reason.

Amid sizzling tensions, days before World War 2 is declared, the web of intrigue and murder he uncovers stretches from Tangier to the diamond-rich Forbidden Zone in the blistering Namib Desert. This land is merciless and treats the hunter and the hunted with equal contempt.

Brought alive by a vibrant backdrop and warts-and-all characters, this fast-paced action thriller delivers from the start until its startling and dramatic finale.

ISBN 978-1-78963-160-9

The Choir Press

£7.99

9 781789 631609